Happy Reading .

N. Dunham

Visionary

Untamed

By

N. Dunham

Visionary
Untamed

N. Dunham

Published in the United States
2014
www.ndunham.com

ISBN-13: 978-1494978341

ISBN-10: 1494978342

∞ CHAPTER 1 ∞

I can't seem to get my hair just right. I should have opted for the salon and got a professional hairstyle. I figured since it was only junior prom that it was no big deal. These oversized curls that keep going astray will just have to do.

As I spray some more god-awful smelly hairspray into my hair, I get a vision of Sebastian knocking on my front door. Shit! He's almost here. My hands start shaking and I continue doubting my hairdo. I haven't seen him since yesterday, but I still feel anxious. I quickly squirt on my favorite fruity perfume, hoping to mask the unfavorable scent from the chemicals in my hair and add a little more gloss to my lips for my final look.

Standing in front of my long mirror behind my bedroom door, I stare at the girl who isn't just a girl anymore. I am different. I am a visionary and my spirit animal is indeed the glorious red-tailed hawk, and I am in awe every time I think about it. I haven't changed into the hawk since a couple of weeks ago when I was taken hostage by Fred and his cronies. That night still gives me chills when I think about it. The fact that Sebastian could have died from severe blood loss bothers me more than the fact that I was left to die in a burning building.

But looking at myself now, I have come to notice a few subtle physical differences. My body appears to be slightly more toned than before and my eyes have a pure golden hue. My heartbeat feels different and I just have this overall feeling that something inside of me has completely changed.

I close my eyes and take a deep breath as I wait for the doorbell to ring. And there it is, the sound that puts my whole body into adrenaline overload.

"Sebastian's here," my mother calls.

I smile giddily, "I'm coming."

Desperately trying not to fall in my gold-colored, sparkled heels, I slowly walk down the stairs. And then I see him, standing there with a bouquet of beautiful flowers in one hand and a corsage in the other. He's smiling too.

"Wait here. I need to grab my camera. You two just look amazing and the tie, oh it matches just perfectly," my mother squeals.

Sebastian waits there wearing a two-button, single-breasted, all-black tuxedo. His golden tie that I had purchased to coordinate with my dress looks flawless on him. Then again, he always looks flawless.

"Hi," I say breathlessly.

"Wow! You look...stunning. These are for you," Sebastian says.

"Thank you. You look very dapper yourself," I say, feeling intrigued by his fetching smile. "I can barely see your scars."

I reach out to take the flowers and he pulls me in close for a quick kiss. He feels amazingly warm and smells so good.

"What scars, dear?" my mother calls out from behind me.

Oops. Stupid me. "Oh, just some scars that-."

Sebastian interrupts me. "Just some bumps and bruises that I got on a hike a week ago." He shares a cunning smile with me. Okay. So his line was much better than what I would have come up with. I was going to say something like he got into a fight with his friend, but that would have sounded ridiculous. Luckily, Sebastian interceded.

My mother frowns. "Well, that happens." She totally bought it.

My bouquet consists of pink and red roses accompanied by white calla lilies, reminiscent of a beautiful floral painting.

"They're beautiful. Thank you. I'll go put these in water," I say feeling the need to excuse myself.

When I return, I find my mother positioning Sebastian against the wall.

"Aislinn. You come right over here," she says while yanking my arm and placing me into Sebastian's hold.

"Wait. I didn't get to put this on you yet," Sebastian says with a grin, holding up the corsage which happens to have gold-colored roses on a small golden pearl bracelet. I couldn't have picked a more perfect arrangement.

"It's perfect," I whisper.

I smile, trying hard to keep from turning red, but I can tell it's not working. I can literally feel the heat radiating off of my face, and only Sebastian can make me feel like this. After what feels like a complete photo session, I politely remind my mother that the prom starts soon. She gives us both a big hug. I still wish that my dad could see me tonight, but he is on a business trip in Philadelphia as usual.

"I can't wait to text these photos of you to your father. He is going to just love them," my mother says.

"Thanks, Mom. I'll see you later," I say as we hug goodbye. She hugs Sebastian too.

We finally get to the car and my nerves begin to spark up again. The thought of going to the prom with Sebastian still feels like a dream. A beautiful dream.

"You should wear that dress more often, it really brings out your eyes," Sebastian remarks.

"Sure, I was thinking maybe tomorrow," I joke. I can always count on Sebastian to lighten up the mood.

As we head over to the luxurious venue that our hardworking prom committee has chosen, I get a vision. It's a vision of Star sitting alone and crying on the side of the prom building. Jason Fiarello stood her up like I knew he would. With all that has happened, I completely forgot about this. I meant to tell Star before, but we've spoken very little since the night of my hawk transformation. She got the awkward texts that I sent her that night and I had to come up with something to explain it. The best I could do was to tell her that I meant to text someone else. Ever since then, we have only exchanged cordial conversation, nothing more than the average hello and goodbye.

We pull into the parking lot and there are cars everywhere, a couple of limos, and one party bus. But nothing compares to the Porsche Panamera. This car holds many memories of Sebastian and me. A sense of relief comforts me whenever I'm in this vehicle. It's like our own little sanctuary.

"Can you wait here a minute for me? There's something I have to take care of," I politely ask Sebastian.

"Of course," Sebastian says. "But not without a kiss."

I give him a sassy look and plant a kiss on his tender lips.

"I'll be right back."

I hurry over to the side of the building where I envisioned Star sitting. Running in heels isn't new to me, but I still need to watch my step. I wouldn't want to fall down in this beautiful dress. I spot Star sitting on the ground with her head in her hands. My sprint slows to an unsure walk and I hesitantly squat down next to Star.

I take a deep breath. "Star, are you okay?"

Looking surprised, Star peeks up from her huddle. She wipes some tears from her face and discreetly rubs her nose.

"Oh, hi," she says unenthusiastically. I sigh. "I don't know. I was supposed to go to the prom with Jason, but he never showed up."

I watch as she sniffs gloomily. "I'm so stupid. I should have known he would do this," she mumbles.

Star's lavender satin dress carelessly graces the dirty ground. We should get up off the ground so not to ruin our prom gowns any further, but Star seems too upset to get up yet.

"You're not stupid. He's the stupid one. In fact, I don't think there's a word that can even describe how stupid he really is."

Star snorts a small laugh while continuing to blankly stare forward. "I can't believe I even drove here. I thought maybe I could come and it would make things better, but then I realized that I came here—alone." She shakes her head and grunts.

"You're not alone. I'm here. And you are going to prom—with me and Sebastian."

With wide eyes, she asks, "Who's Sebastian?"

I knew this was coming. I just didn't know when. I think I'm prepared to answer questions about us. No. I know I'm prepared.

"He's my boyfriend," I say with a confident voice.

Star looks confused. Her squinted eyes and tilted head say it all. I wish I could read her mind. Instead, I try to visualize Shawn Henley. I know for a fact he likes Star. And not only is he a good kid, but he's good-looking too. Maybe if I can distract Star with another date, I can help her feel better and also take the attention away from me and Sebastian. I quickly visualize Shawn inside the prom with a couple of friends. He appears to have gone solo. This couldn't be any better. Thank God my visionary powers worked so quickly.

"Guess we haven't talked in a while," I say.

Star looks down at the ground with a desperate expression and then looks back up at me. "I'm sorry. I shouldn't have ignored you the way I did. I was being childish. I was just so mad."

Damn right you shouldn't have. Feeling relieved that she apologized first, I know it's only fair that I do the same.

"I know. I'm sorry too. I shouldn't have forgotten to meet you for lunch that day."

Feeling my knees start to buckle from squatting for so long in my heels, I stand up and offer my hand to Star. She accepts and I pull her up. Then we both let out an awkward giggle. I go in for the hug that has been long overdue and she squeezes me back.

"I missed you," Star says.

"Me too, chicky, me too," I say.

I take her hand and we walk toward the front entrance where Sebastian is waiting. Seeing Sebastian waiting for me, looking so handsome in his tuxedo, makes me blush. I smile and roll my eyes.

Star stops walking. "Wait. I can't go in there."

"Yes you can. You can't let that idiot Jason ruin prom for you. Besides, I think Shawn Henley came here alone." I shrug my shoulders, hoping this will work.

Star smiles and nods her head. "You're right. I deserve to be here too. Screw Jason and his ugly hair."

"Yes, screw Jason," Sebastian says with a grin. "Whoever that is."

Sebastian's sense of humor couldn't have come at a more perfect time. He winks at me and I send him one right back. I introduce Star and Sebastian to each other and we all walk into prom together.

The place is stunning. Our junior prom committee had selected "A Night in Paris" as its theme. It is tastefully adorned with French décor. The picture area is complete with an Eiffel Tower background and Parisian street lights which carve the path to the dining tables.

"I didn't know that we were visiting France tonight," Sebastian says.

As we walk in further, we see Shawn standing at one of the tables with a couple of his friends. He looks completely dumbfounded the way he stares at Star. His hair is slicked back and he looks fairly dapper in his black tuxedo with a black bow tie.

"Look, Ais, there's Shawn," Star whispers, while nodding her head in his direction. It appears that he has gotten her attention, possibly due to the fact that I planted the seed, but I won't give myself all of the credit.

"I see him," I say, glad to know that she noticed him. "You should go over and say hi."

"You think?" She sounds like a child asking for permission.

I nod my head and smile. She looks over at him again and then makes a beeline in his direction. I guess we weren't going for the subtle approach. Sebastian puts his arm around my waist and escorts me to a nearby table. Then he pulls out a chair for me and says, "Madame."

"Merci beaucoup," I respond.

"So, you do speak a little French?" Sebastian asks.

I chuckle, knowing I don't speak any other language other than English and knowing fully well that he speaks a couple of languages. Yeah, I've taken Spanish in school for three years, but if it's not on a test, I definitely don't know it.

"No, that was about it." I grin.

Star comes back with Shawn and asks if they could sit with us. Of course I oblige. What would prom be like if I didn't sit with Star? She was the one who'd been so excited about it to begin with. I'm happy for her, and I'm relieved to know that things are good between us now. I really missed our friendship.

A few moments later, Jeanette and Ricky join us with their dates. Jeanette looks fabulous in a maroon gown with sparkles on the top. The sparkles make her green eyes shine. Her date, Simon Wells, is wearing a maroon vest to match. Simon is a senior at our school. He's extremely quiet and knows a lot about snakes, and that's an understatement. The fact that he owns eight snakes, is involved with the reptile club at school, and has a picture of a rattlesnake tattooed on the back of his right leg are just a few examples of his passion, I mean obsession, for snakes.

Jeanette looks from me back to Star a few times, and finally figures out that we've made up. She lets out a delighted squeal and comes right over to embrace us both.

"I knew you two couldn't stay mad at each other for long. I'm so excited," Jeanette shrieks.

Ricky eyeballs the situation and smiles at me. Little does he know that I saw him and Star talking about me the day I had forgotten to show up for lunch, but it doesn't matter now.

Ricky wears a thought-provoking white tuxedo with a teal vest and tie. It's pretty bold, but it suits his personality. He has always had a unique and trendy fashion sense. His date, with whom I'm unfamiliar, wears a matching short teal dress and a floral hair accessory on the right side of her head.

Jeanette stands there eyeing Sebastian. I've forgotten that nobody here knows him. Before anyone can ask, I quickly introduce Sebastian to Jeanette and Ricky.

"Jeanette. This is Sebastian." I clear my throat and finish with, "My boyfriend."

"Nice to meet you," Sebastian politely says as he looks at her and then me and smiles. I suppose the word boyfriend may have caught his attention.

"He's just adorable," Jeanette whispers to me.

I smile, knowing that she speaks the truth. He is adorable and he's all mine.

"And Sebastian, this is Ricky. Ricky, Sebastian."

The two shake hands. Ricky turns his attention back to his date and brings her forward.

"Guys, this is Rachel. She goes to Campton High," Ricky says while holding her hand.

I have never known Ricky to date a girl before. The topic of dating has never come up and we've all assumed that he was just too busy for that kind of stuff. But nonetheless, we are all here together and it feels pretty darn good.

After a couple of minutes of awkward conversation, I acquire a vision of Jason Fiarello coming to prom with another girl. That slime ball. I keep my eyes fixed on the entryway, waiting to see him. He finally enters, wearing a stupid grin on his face.

I whisper into Star's ear so that she is aware of his presence. I also provide her with a quick pep talk on what to do. She nods her head and agrees not to cause a scene. I basically explained to her that she shouldn't give him the satisfaction that she even thought twice about the situation. That's what he would have wanted. Jason looks for approval from his peers, but no one seems to care about him. Star continues with her night and doesn't bring his name up again.

During our dinner course, Sebastian pinches me on the leg under the table and I wince loudly. Everyone looks up from the dinner plates and I blush.

"The food, it's hot," I say trying to quickly recover myself.

Sebastian laughs and I laugh too. He handles himself well when asked questions about where he goes to school and where he's from. He tells everyone that he graduated from a school no one has ever heard of. He is very convincing, and I am impressed by his speedy ability to answer questions so effortlessly, knowing that there is so much to hide.

After dinner, people start dancing. Either the DJ is unusually loud or my new profound senses have a decibel cut-off. Most of the people at our table have gotten up to dance except for Star and Shawn. Shawn looks around the table uncomfortably. I wish he would muster up the courage and just ask Star to dance.

"Do you like to dance?" I ask Shawn, hoping to ignite the idea in his head.

"Yeah, it's okay."

"I love to dance," Star says, smiling. If Shawn doesn't get the hint by now, then Star will have to take the lead.

"Aislinn, would you care to dance?" asks Sebastian.

"I would love to." This is the first for us. We have never had the opportunity to dance before and I'm extremely excited. I love going through all of the firsts. First dance, first dinner, first walk.

Sebastian offers me his hand and accompanies me to the dance floor. I look back and see Shawn do the same to Star. She gracefully takes his hand and they join us.

A fast-paced song plays and Sebastian totally lets loose. He's an amazing dancer and I struggle a little to keep up. After a couple of minutes, I ditch the heels so I can be more comfortable. Star bumps into me on purpose and laughs. She looks like she is really enjoying herself too.

Then a slow song starts. Sebastian stares at me and pulls me in close. We have to adjust our body tempos to the rhythm.

"I was waiting for a slow song," he says.

I shudder inside. He stares at me the entire time with those intense eyes of his. His body is warm, and it feels so good next to mine. And I thought the night couldn't get any better. At the end of our dance, I excuse myself to the bathroom and Sebastian heads back toward our table.

As I attempt to enter the bathroom, my arm is suddenly tugged hard and I am pulled into someone's arms. Has Sebastian come to give me a kiss?

I turn around and find my ex-boyfriend, Austin Michaels, holding me tight.

"What are you doing?" I frantically ask. I quickly look around for Sebastian. "Are you crazy? Let go of me!"

"Thought you might want to dance Aislinn. I'm sure your date won't mind."

I try to wriggle out of his tight hold, but he pulls me tighter. The strong smell of liquor lingers on his breath.

"Austin, stop! You're drunk."

"I'm not drunk. I just want to dance with you," Austin says, while he tries to hold me still and dance with me. I make an effort to get out of his grip, but he holds onto me tighter and begins to fondle me. He rubs his hand down the front of my dress and I immediately bite the arm that's holding me.

"You bitch," he grunts as he lifts his hand to slap me.

I close my eyes and wince, preparing for the blow, but to my surprise Austin falls into the wall beside me. It's Sebastian. Thank God! Sebastian picks up Austin and punches him in the face. Austin ducks and tries to wrestle Sebastian, but he is no match for Sebastian's bear-like strength.

"Don't you ever touch her! You hear me?" Sebastian yells. "Do you hear me?" he yells again, only louder when Austin doesn't answer.

"I hear you." Austin grits his teeth and squints his eyes.

Sebastian wraps his arm around me. "Are you all right?"

"Yes," I say. "We should go."

"It's okay. You don't have to leave."

"No. Really. I want to get out of here anyways. I've had enough," I say.

I don't think that I could continue to have a good time knowing that Austin is watching. Luckily, there were no chaperones around to witness the fight. This situation doesn't need to be any worse than it is already is.

We go back to the table to gather my belongings. Apparently, no one at the table witnessed the fight either.

"You're leaving?" asks Star.

"Yeah, well."

"Her boyfriend just beat up Austin Michaels," says Bryan, a fellow classmate, interrupting me. "Way to go dude," he says while trying to give Sebastian a high five. Sebastian doesn't seem enthused as he avoids the high five. Bryan is a spikey haired dude who comes to school when he feels like it. He usually says dude or rad at least five times in one conversation. Star shakes her head and pushes her way in front of Bryan.

"Oh my God," Star says, looking worried. "Is everything okay?"

"Yeah. I'm good. It's just time for me to go."

"You sure?" Star sounds bummed. I nod my head and frown. I really don't want to go, but I think it's for the best.

"Okay. Well, call me tomorrow so we can catch up. Alright?" Star says while giving me a hug.

"Of course."

We say our goodbyes and Sebastian puts his arm around me. While walking toward the exit, I spot Austin up ahead. He's standing outside with a couple of his friends. It doesn't feel like a good situation. I stop and try to vision what's going to happen.

"What's wrong?" Sebastian asks.

"We can't go out that way. Austin's there."

"It's okay, Aislinn. Don't worry."

"No, really. I just saw a vision and they're going to jump you." I abruptly grab his arm and try to pull him in another direction.

"Aislinn, look at me." I look at him. I am worried and panting with fear. He's not listening to me.

"I know what they're planning. And I won't let it happen. Trust me."

I trust him, of course. It's the other guys I don't trust. I don't say anything. Sebastian takes my hand, kisses it, and then holds it tight as we continue to exit the prom.

The minute we walk out the door, Austin and two of his friends start to crowd around us. This can't be good.

"Leaving so soon?" asks Austin with a cruel glare in his eyes.

"Look. We don't want any trouble here. I suggest you and your friends just go back inside," Sebastian recommends firmly.

"We'll go in when we're ready, "says Robbie, one of Sebastian's friends, in a very sarcastic voice.   Austin inches closer to Sebastian while Blake, Austin's third accomplice, grabs both of Sebastian's arms. I try to intercede, but that Robbie kid pulls me back. Austin grabs Sebastian's collar and lunges in with a punch. Sebastian quickly ducks, sending the punch into thin air.

"Big mistake," says Sebastian.

Sebastian rips his arms from Blake's grip and sends him flying with a back kick to the neck. He then takes Austin and flings him effortlessly into the air. Austin smashes into the ground on his back, unable to move. It all happens so quickly. Sebastian turns toward me and looks at Robbie, who is still holding onto my arms. Robbie looks down at his friends and makes the wise decision to let go of me and take off running.

"Oh my God!" I whine, "This is all my fault. I'm so sorry, Sebastian."

"Aislinn. It's okay. It's not your fault."

He takes my hand and we walk past Austin, who is still lying on the ground looking terribly disgruntled and disgraced.

"I told you to go inside. Well, enjoy prom!" Sebastian calls out.

We walk back to Sebastian's car and I keep my head forward, trying desperately not to look back. Sebastian opens the door for me like the gentlemen that he is and I nervously get in.

"Stop worrying," he tells me.

I shake my head, knowing that I can't stop worrying.

"That kid, Austin, he's an ex-boyfriend from last year and-"

Sebastian touches my chin and leans in toward me. He gently places his lips on mine and instantly everything becomes okay again. His soft lips heal my worries and I yearn for more.

In the car, I think about what just happened. Sebastian wasn't concerned at all. He took on three good-sized guys and didn't look the least bit apprehensive. His skills seemed so coordinated and articulate. Could this be related to the grizzly bear gifts? And if so, why can't I kick in my red-tailed hawk gifts when I want to?

"Where are we going?" I ask Sebastian, as we seem to be driving into unknown territory.

"I want to show you something."

What could he want to possibly show me at eleven o'clock at night? He travels up an unpaved road that has a gradual incline. As we get higher in elevation I start to feel relaxed. Heights seem natural to me now. It's probably related to the gifts of the hawk.

Sebastian puts the car in park and gets out of the vehicle. He opens my door and takes my hand. We walk about a quarter of a mile to a spot on a hill that is undeniably breathtaking. Walking in heals has also become more natural to me, although I did insert comfort inserts, just in case.

"I come here a lot, when I need to think or clear my mind," Sebastian says.

"I can see why." I stare at the vast forest, which frames the view of sparkling city lights. It's beautiful. I think this could be the most picturesque setting I've ever seen.

We sit on the ground, despite my beautiful dress and his perfect tux, and unwind. Tonight was definitely entertaining, to say the least. It was all going so well until Austin showed up. I relax and breathe those bad thoughts away.

"I've been thinking about that night," I say to Sebastian.

"That was some night," he says while nodding his head. He knows what I'm referring to. Ever since I learned that I was the red-tailed hawk my mind has been juggling possible explanations, but none seem to make any sense.

"And, I was thinking that I want to know more. I mean, I'm living this life now. This different life, and I just need to know more. Do you know what I mean?"

"I was thinking the same thing," Sebastian says.

"You were?"

"We should go. You and me," he utters.

I am surprised to hear him say this. We have joked about it in the past. But this time he looks serious.

"Where exactly in South America is this visionary guru?" I ask.

"Peru."

"Peru?"

"Yup. It's said to be some biogenetic center of some mystical magnetic power."

"Really!" I say with a wide grin.

"We should go. We should go this June."

"I would love to go, but I don't think my parents will let me," I say remorsefully.

"I'll talk to Jerry and see what we can come up with."

Whatever Jerry comes up with, it better be good. It's not like I'm asking to go Boston. This is Peru. I savor the thought of traveling so far away alone with Sebastian. It would be so much fun! We get up and dust ourselves off. It's time I get home.

When we get to my house, Sebastian walks me to my door. "Thank you for taking me to my prom," I say, still feeling badly about what had happened.

"Thank you for choosing me."

As if I would have chosen anyone else. I blush. Watching his mesmerizing eyes, I decide to be the more aggressive one this time and pull him toward me for a kiss. Instantly, I'm met with his scrumptious lips. I can tell he is surprised, but pleased. He shares a pleased smile. I break away to end our night, and he grabs me back to kiss me once more.

"Okay. You can go now," he says.

I giddily grin. "Goodnight."

"Goodnight, Aislinn."

I walk in and stand against the wall for a moment. I'm on cloud nine, ten, and eleven. Otie starts jumping on me. I pick him up and head upstairs. What a night.

I decide to check my phone, since it has been tucked away in my purse all night. There are a bunch of text messages from Star:

"Glad were friends again, chicky."

"Austin looks like shit-what happened?"

"He's a jerk anyways."

"Let's hang out tomorrow and catch up if u can."

I still can't believe that happened. Now, I'll have to deal with this at school. Luckily, we only have a couple of weeks left. More importantly, how in the world was Sebastian able to defeat three guys? It's completely mind-boggling and impressive at the same time.

I text Star back, "Let's do lunch tomorrow."

"Okay-noon at the Burger Joint. Be there, chicky," she responds.

"Without a doubt, chicky."

This time I will not forget.

∞ CHAPTER 2 ∞

Morning comes too soon. I get a vision of my mother approaching my room. I sit up, rub my tired eyes, and wait for her.

(Two seconds later my mother knocks at the door. "Aislinn, are you up?")

"I'm up. Come in."

"So, how was your night?" she softly asks, sporting a way too excited smile.

"It was perfect."

"You two looked beautiful together."

"Thank you, Mom."

"I have to head over to the office in a few minutes. What are your plans today?"

"So far, I'm meeting Star for lunch."

"Ooh, that sounds like fun. When did you two start talking again?" my mother asks.

"Last night," I reply.

"Well, I'm glad to see you guys have stopped arguing. You two are usually tied at the hip."

She's right. We were tied at the hip. But knowing the truth about people changes things. Star is definitely a good friend, but I know now that she can turn in an instant.

As I'm about to leave to meet Star, I get a vision of Sebastian calling me. Not again. I can't break plans with Star, but I can't wait to talk to Sebastian.

I hold my cell phone and wait for it. It barely rings before I pick it up.

"I knew you were going to call me," I say.

"I knew too," he jokes. I giggle.

"I know you're going to lunch with Star," he says. "I was wondering if you would like to meet up afterwards. There's something I want to talk to you about."

"Last time you said that, you were going to Texas."

"Well, it's not Texas."

"What is it?"

He should know by now that I don't do well with patience. Not yet, anyway.

"Peru," he answers.

My mouth drops. He's serious.

"We'll talk about it when I see you."

"Okay."

"Aislinn," he says with his beautiful voice, "enjoy your lunch."

"Okay, Mr. Mysterious. I can drive to meet you when I'm through, if you want?"

"No. I'll pick you up at your house. It's better if I drive."

Sebastian has this thing about constantly being sure no one is following us to headquarters. A little paranoid, but with good reason. We hang up and butterflies storm my stomach and cloud my head. Hopefully, Sebastian has come up with a plan for me to go with him to Peru. Or is he planning on going solo?

I arrive at the Burger Joint promptly at noon. Star is five minutes late and I anxiously wait for her. When she finally gets here, we hug each other. After placing our orders with the waitress, Star and I begin our catching up.

"I can't believe what happened with Austin and Sebastian!" she says.

"I know, right. It's sad, really, but he had it coming."

"True. Hopefully, he'll leave you alone. He's a loser like Jason. They should start a loser club." I giggle at Star's ranting.

Thinking about school, I pray Austin was too drunk to remember anything. Too bad he had his followers with him to remind him of the sour events. They did make quite a spectacle of themselves. I just want to forget it ever happened.

"So, tell me about Sebastian. Where did you guys meet?" Star questions.

"We met at the Coffee Beanery."

That's not a complete lie. We did first meet at the Coffee Beanery. Only, we didn't exactly speak to one another then. Star and I continue on with innocent conversation for about an hour or so while we enjoy our lunch. It feels like old times again.

I find out that Star and Shawn are officially dating as of last night after prom. I'm glad. He's not a scumbag like Jason. They're actually going out tonight, and if my vision holds true, later they will be sharing their first kiss.

Everything went as well as expected. It felt good to reacquaint ourselves. I missed seeing Star's enthusiastic mannerisms. I will definitely remember to try to make time for our friendship. It's important to hold on to some sort of normalcy in my crazy life.

After lunch, I hurry home excitedly, knowing that Sebastian will be arriving shortly. To my surprise, he is already here waiting for me. I get out of my car and walk over to meet him.

"You're fast," I say.

"You're beautiful."

How can I top that? I throw my arms around him.

"Thank you." I blush.

"How was lunch with Star?"

"It was good. It feels really good to be friends again."

"That's good."

It's a quiet ride, for the most part. I think about Sebastian and Fredrick. I can't help but feel bad for Sebastian. A friend of his actually tried to kill us. It's no wonder that Sebastian doesn't have many friends. As we continue driving toward headquarters, I can't wait to hear about the plan.

"So do you think we can pull off this Peru adventure?" I ask as we approach headquarters, trying to break the silence.

Sebastian's voice sounds excited but cautious at the same time. He doesn't seem as thrilled as I thought he would be. "I think we can. Jerry has come up with a remarkable plan and I think you'll be impressed."

"Is something bothering you?" I ask feeling concerned by the lack of enthusiasm in his voice.

"No. I'm just trying to put everything into perspective. About the trip. It's not exactly in the tourist section."

"What do you mean? Where is it?"

"That's the thing. It's not a definite location. The tribe that the guru belongs to is somewhere in the Amazon Rainforest," he breaths deeply, "and we'll have to try our best to remain safe while trying to find him."

"Remain safe?"

We pull into headquarters and park the car.

"Aislinn, this trip could be dangerous. Very dangerous," he says while looking into my eyes. "Let's go in and talk to Jerry about the details."

Great! Another dangerous adventure. The Amazon can't be too bad. I studied it in school, and there are some really neat animals and exotic birds in the mighty Amazon. I'm sure it will be fun.

Headquarters seems empty today. We go through the dilapidated section and there stands Jerry.

"I've been waiting for you two. How are you, Aislinn?"

I've only been here twice since the tragedy that happened with Fredrick, Sebastian, and myself. I've been busy keeping up with school and trying to act normal. The fact that I changed into a red-tailed hawk is real, amazing, and terrifying all at the same time. And trying to keep that a secret is like not brushing your teeth, which is almost unbearable for me.

"I'm good, Jerry. How are you?"

"Good. Excited is more like it. Come with me. I want to show you two the plans."

Sebastian and I follow Jerry to the office where Jerry spends most of his time. On his desk lay four passports. I wonder who else is coming along on this trip with us.

"These two are your passports," Jerry says while handing them out to us.

"Oh. It's okay. I already have one," I say, feeling proud that I have something to offer. I politely hand back the passport and Sebastian and Jerry both make a small snicker.

"Aislinn. You can't use your real passport. The secret agency will see you taking a trip to Peru and they would be all over you like flies on—"

"What he means is that it would be dangerous for us to use our real identities," Sebastian chimes in, trying to soften Jerry's bluntness.

"Oh, I see," I say feeling like this trip might not be as fun as I had originally planned. "Who are the other two passports for?"

"It would be unsafe for you and Sebastian to travel alone, so Caleb and Mya volunteered to go with you," Jerry answers while gathering some of his things together.

"What?" Did I just say that out loud? Sebastian and Jerry both look at me. Yeah, I did. *Quick, Aislinn, make a recovery statement.* "I mean, what's so dangerous about this trip?"

Sebastian smirks. He knows me too well now. I can't concentrate now that I know Mya is going. This sucks! Since when did she become a big part of all this? I thought this was going to be a trip for me and Sebastian only, not a whole big visionary affair. Jerry clears his throat.

"Well, there are particular terrorist groups which are still known to be active, and typical tourist crime that can happen anywhere including the U.S., and the secret agency of course," Jerry informs.

"But more importantly, there is an unrelenting guerrilla group always waiting for an opportunity to strike at visionaries," Sebastian explains in a very solemn voice.

"Of course we don't know much about them, that's why it's best to play it safe," Jerry intercedes.

"Sounds like more people that don't like us," I say.

"Pretty much," Sebastian agrees while putting a hand around my shoulders.

"What about my parents? What do I say to them?"

Sebastian laughs. "This is the more interesting part. Meet Mr. Johnson, your new High School Abroad Liaison, and you're going to Brazil to see if you are interested in their academic and cultural immersion program," he clears his throat, "and the trip is scheduled for June when school is over. You game?" Sebastian spits out, sounding casually professional while wearing an endearing smile.

Sebastian speaks so eloquently that he must have practiced this speech before. What a perfectly constructed plan. This will work! It sounds so academically enriching that my parents will be thrilled. All they will hear is the sound of an enhanced resume builder for Harvard. They can't say no.

"It's perfect." I say. Jerry and Sebastian smile, knowing that it is.

"Why not just say Peru?" I ask.

"Well, I think it would be best to keep your actual location confidential. And Brazil tends to be more believable," Jerry answers. I shrug my shoulders and agree. I just hope I don't mix up the two.

We continue to go over the plans and important travel information. Everything about this trip sounds exciting except for the fact that Mya is joining us. She just rubs me the wrong way and I don't care for her much.

After about an hour of information gathering and plan reviewing, Sebastian and I break away and head outside. The weather is beautiful. It is a cloudless blue sky and the air feels warm and fresh. This is my kind of weather.

"It's beautiful outside," says Sebastian.

"My thoughts exactly."

Sebastian looks as handsome as ever in his spring apparel. He's sporting a tight white polo shirt, blue jeans that perfectly accentuate his strong physique, and his adorable boat shoes.

We grasp hands and head toward the path. It's been a while since the last time we took a stroll through these woods.

"So, you ready for this trip?" asks Sebastian.

"I'm excited, a little nervous, and a tad worried."

"It's definitely going to be huge," Sebastian chuckles.

"No, it's going to be epic," I chime in.

"Definitely epic! At least were not going alone. It's better to be in a group. You know?"

I guess he's right about being in a group. Strength in numbers right? I was just hoping that the numbers wouldn't include a massage therapist who practices on fellow male visionaries, like Sebastian.

"True," I simply state.

When I get home, I dash through the house looking for my mom. During the car ride home, I got a vision of her being home, so I figured I would plant the seed of the whole trip idea in her head now so it has time to grow and flourish.

"Mom," I call out anxiously.

"In the office, dear," she yells back.

I walk in and find my mom with a pile of papers stacked high on the desk.

"It's organization time, Aislinn. What can I do for you?"

I discreetly suck in a scoopful of air and pray for the courage to deliver my lines just right. I can't screw this up. There's no way I would be able to live knowing that

Sebastian had to go to Peru without me because my parents didn't agree.

"Well, there's this school trip I've been thinking about. The new school Cultural Abroad Liaison organized a trip to Brazil for students to check out the new academic and cultural program. I guess it's really academically enriching or something."

My mother looks at me inquisitively. She's probably wondering where I'm going with all of this. I wait a second to let the idea rattle her brain, and then I go in for the kill.

"But I don't know. It might be too difficult for me." I just gave my mom a message of hope and then squashed it with uncertainty. My eyes look down for a minute, giving her ample time to reflect on what I just said. Wait for it. Wait for it.

"Aislinn, I think that sounds great!" my mother shouts with pure joy. "It wouldn't be too difficult for you. If anything, it would be a wonderful experience, and God, Harvard would find that educationally inspiring."

Mission accomplished. I look at her and solemnly say, "I don't know. I guess I'll think about it."

"Aislinn, you should do this, honey!"

And just like that, the plan worked. I feel a sense of pride and yet a tiny bit of guilt seems to take that all away. But I had to do it. This is about me and my future. If I don't do this, then I'll never know what my point of existence is. It's one thing to be a visionary, but the red-tailed hawk is something I never expected and I need to know more.

I leave the paperwork with the contact information and parent permission slip on the desk for my mother to review. This was way too easy.

A few minutes later, I get a text message from Sebastian. It reads, "Nice work, Aislinn! Talk to you tomorrow. Get some rest, beautiful."

I respond: "Thank you. You too!"

It's funny how a simple text message can give me instant butterflies. As I head to the kitchen in search of a banana, my mother calls me back to her office. There's no way she could have changed her mind. She must have a question about the trip. I need to stay cool.

"You called," I say.

"I just got off the phone with your father, and he is just tickled pink about this. I wish you'd told us about this sooner. It seems so soon."

"I know. I just wasn't sure how I felt about it."

"Well, it's a good decision. Your father and I would like to meet with Mr. Johnson to go over the details.

Maybe I'll stop by your school tomorrow to meet with him."

Did she just say that? Now what do I do? I can't stop her from coming to my school. My brain freezes and a dumbfounded smile is plastered on my face. Then my phone beeps and I quickly look down to check my text. It's from Sebastian. It reads, "Tell her that Mr. Johnson will come to your house."

I look up at my mother and hastily spit out, "Mr. Johnson will come to your house." My mother purses her lips and squints. "I mean, Mr. Johnson could probably make a home visit. Why not just call him?"

"That would be better for your father and me. I think I'll do that."

I stand there frozen while she reaches for her cell phone to call Mr. Johnson, aka Jerry. My heart is pounding with anticipation and fear.

"Mr. Johnson? Hi. This is Mrs. Murphy, Aislinn Murphy's mother. How are you?" I watch my mother converse with Jerry. They banter back and forth with casual conversation. I can't believe this is working. She closes the conversation with a meeting scheduled for tomorrow night. It's really rather odd watching my mother talk on the phone with Jerry. I feel like I'm watching someone else's life and I am just a bystander.

She finally hangs up and says to me, "That was easy."

"Yeah," I say. My thoughts exactly. I excuse myself and go back to the kitchen in search of that banana. My nerves are awakened and I need to do something to relax them. Eating sounds like a good remedy.

After feeding my nerves a hard, unripe, green banana I decide to text Sebastian back.

I text, "You're good! How did you know?"

Sebastian replies, "I was thinking about you."

I text, "I see."

"Do you?"

I text back, "You'll never know."

Sebastian texts back, "I always know."

I reply, "You wish! Goodnight."

Sebastian ends our text conversation with, "You're right. Good night, beautiful."

No matter how many times he says that, it never gets old.

∞ CHAPTER 3 ∞

My whole day today is spent concentrating on tonight. I try to vision how it might go. The only vision that comes to me is of my mom and dad shaking Jerry's hand and smiling. By the looks of it, they appear to be pleased, which is a good sign.

Luckily, my conversation with Sebastian earlier still plays in my head. He basically talked to me about what will transpire tonight and how saying less will work best for me. Sometimes less is best. He tells me that Jerry has everything in control and not to worry. I try to take him up on his suggestion, but having a fellow visionary come to my home and pretend to be my teacher makes me a little apprehensive and that's a complete understatement. Thankfully, we make plans to see each other tomorrow and that makes me feel a little better.

About two minutes before Jerry is supposed to arrive, I begin to pace in my room: back and forth, back and forth. The tension is unbearable. Luckily, the doorbell rings and stops me from my compulsive behavior. I remind myself that everything will turn out all right. I take three long, deep breaths and head toward the door. Otie barks tirelessly until my mom gets there. She beats me to it. Then my dad comes out of the office. This is going to be quite the family event. Usually my parents are both busy, but because this little trip might boost my resume, both of them have made exceptions to be here.

Jerry walks in and I barely recognize him. He wears a plain, white collared shirt, khaki pants, and an interesting hat resembling a beret with a modern twist. He looks like an explorer out of a storybook. I suppose he is playing the part of an expert-traveler-slash-teacher. He shakes both of my parents' hands with a huge grin. I inhale deeply and let it out. This should be interesting.

"Aislinn, good to see you," Mr. Johnson, aka Jerry, says.

"Nice to see you too, Mr. Johnson." I blush.

We all take a seat in the living room. A suitable meeting place, which is less formal than the kitchen. My heart is working overtime along with my mind, and I can't wipe this stupid grin off my face. As soon as we become comfortable, my mother starts with the questions. They're mostly about the academic enrichment program. I sit quietly while Mr. Johnson explains it all in great detail. He's so convincing that I start to believe him myself and almost forget that this is all a complete lie. He actually hands out pamphlets of the hotel, school classes, you name it. He came with one purpose and he delivered it. My parents bought every word.

The end finally comes and I barely speak. Just as planned. Then my dad offers Mr. Johnson a drink, but he politely refuses and tells my parents that he has to go to another student's home after ours. They shake hands again. It's a done deal. I'm going to Peru! I'm so excited I could almost scream.

"Yes!" I quietly squeal to myself. My mother looks my way.

"Brazil, here I come," I say to my mother. She shoots me a proud smile.

As my parents continue their own conversation, I quickly sneak away and run upstairs to call Sebastian, but my phone is already vibrating. It's him!

"So, you excited?" he asks.

"Oh my God! So excited! Everything went as planned. It was perfect."

"I knew Jerry could do it. He lives for that kind of stuff," says Sebastian.

"I could tell. The way he answered every question with such certainty, it was like...so realistic, I believed him myself. He did an amazing job. I'm psyched!"

"Good. I'm glad it's finalized, "Sebastian says.

"Do you want to go out and celebrate?" I playfully ask.

"I thought you'd never ask. Are you ready?"

"Are you here?"

"Yup."

"I'll be right out," I say and hang up. Oh my God, Sebastian is here! I quickly change my clothes and dab on some pink lip gloss. One quick look in the mirror and I fly out of my house. My parents are in their office going over their work now. They can't ever stay away from it too long. It's like they belong to some magnetic force that makes them work all the time as if they were robots. I yell to them that I'm going out and that I'll be home soon, but they seem to be distracted by whatever it is they are doing. I give Otie a kiss and head out.

As I step outside, I notice Sebastian standing by the car holding the door open. I smile.

"Hi," I say, while going in for a hug.

"Hi."

We hop in the car and head off. He's still driving around in the Panamera. I don't think he'll ever give this car up. He loves it too much.

"So where should we go?" I ask.

"What do you feel like doing?"

"I don't know. Something fun!" I say.

Sebastian continues driving and smiles.

"Okay. I have an idea," he says with a cunning grin.

"What is it?"

"It's a surprise."

"You know I don't do well with surprises. Come on. Tell me."

"Nope," he laughs.

I grunt with frustration and then surrender. We change subjects and talk about Jerry. I can't help but laugh. Jerry really is quite the actor. I think he missed his calling in life. He was so serious and charming at the same time when he spoke to my parents. It was just so bizarre to watch.

We finally pull into our destination. Sebastian has taken us to a place called Game Town. It's a facility that boasts fun games, great food, and good music. I couldn't have picked a better option myself.

"Nice choice," I say.

"You like?"

"I like."

We play an array of different games from glow-in-the-dark golf to various arcade games to bowling. We eat cheese fries, nachos with cheese, cheese sticks, and pretty much everything else that has cheese on it. The rock-climbing race was the best of all. I was positive that Sebastian was going to beat me, so I flirtatiously shoved him and made him lose his balance, causing him to fall.

The end of our night comes, and I can't seem to rid my face of this stupid smile. It's practically glued on. This was the most fun I've had in a while.

"Did you have a nice time?" Sebastian asks.

"The best," I say, and I pull him in close for a kiss. He deserves it. He was a complete gentleman, even when I made him lose his balance on the rock climb.

"This is my favorite part," he whispers.

"Mine too."

Coming home from such an exciting night out makes it difficult for me to fall asleep. I toss and turn all night. Too many things to think about. Eventually, I succumb to the white noise of my TV and drift off.

The last few days of the school year seem to glide by super quickly. Luckily, Austin has suffered from such embarrassment that he has avoided me entirely. Thank God! I don't think I could stand much more of his erratic behavior. Star, Jeanette, Ricky, and I are back to how we used to be. A sense of regularity has cleared the air and I couldn't feel any more content. I continue with my yoga classes, and that has aided in my need to unwind. I'm actually becoming quite good. My visions are frequent but only of minor matters. They have become a part of my daily routine as if they were always there. And my disturbing dreams of something calling me have suddenly altered. My dreams now are more like peace and serenity and happy thoughts.

∞ CHAPTER 4 ∞

It's finally the last day of school, and I couldn't be any happier. I'm finally getting closer to the date of our trip to Peru and excitement lingers in my veins just waiting to pop open. It's also my last time in this wretched math class, and knowing that I won't ever have Mr. Grant as a teacher again makes me as ecstatic as a million-dollar lottery winner.

"So chicky, wanna head over to the Coffee Beanery after school?" Star asks.

Of course I can only think of Sebastian and wanting to see him, but I also want to maintain my friendship with my friends, so I must learn to juggle both.

"Of course, chicky."

"Great. 'Cause there's something I want to tell you and Jeanette and Ricky."

More surprises. Great! I smile politely and try to vision what Star is going to share with us. The only thing that pops into my head is the five of us eating in the corner table at the Coffee Beanery. Five of us?

"Shawn's coming?" I ask.

"Not that I know of. He has a summer job interview at the Dairy Mart."

By the looks of my vision, the interview didn't go as planned, and Shawn ends up meeting us at the Coffee Beanery. But it's best that I keep my mouth shut. These visions are subject to change based on human interference.

At the end of the day, we follow one another in our cars to the Coffee Beanery. Ricky is well dressed as usual, Jeannette is sporting a way-too-short summer dress, and Star and I are wearing the same matching jean skirt. We use to purposely match all the time and now it just happens accidentally.

It takes all my will not to ask Star what she wants to share with us. I want to be fair and let her share it with the group, but for some strange reason I think she's going tell us that she is moving with her parents, due to her father's job offer. I remember that being an issue a couple of months back, and maybe the topic has resurfaced again.

"So, are you going to tell us your news, or are you going to make us wait till we're seniors?" I ask when everyone is there.

Star nervously smiles as she bites her lip. "Well, it's not major news or anything, but my parents are moving to Florida for my dad's job."

All of our faces drop while Star continues to rock a smile. I knew it, and there was no current vision of this. How is she smiling right now?

"What?" the three of us say simultaneously.

Star's eyes widen, and her smile widens from ear to ear as if she's enjoying the suspense. Finally, she blurts out, "But my parents both agreed to let me live with my Aunt Maggie as long as I keep up my grades—so I can stay!" she squeals.

"That's great, Star!" I cheerfully say as the others agree. And here I thought I was losing my best friend again. As we begin rejoicing from the good news, Shawn casually walks in. What a surprise.

"Hey guys," Shawn says. He quickly hugs Star and gives her a quick peck on the lips. It's funny to see them together.

"Hi, babe. Aislinn knew you were coming. Weird. She must be psychic," Star jokes. He picks her up and swirls her around. I'm so glad that she decided to date him. She finally realized that someone likes her for her and not whoever she was posing to be.

"Yeah, I'm real psychic. Let me guess—you, ah, didn't get the job," I tease back.

Shawn stares at me with a baffled look on his face. *Shit, Aislinn! You and your big mouth. What was I thinking?*

"Wow! You are a psychic," Shawn says eerily, staring at me while pursing his lips tight. Everyone stops what they're doing and suddenly becomes quiet. I don't know what to say. Without looking, I can feel all eight eyes gawking at me.

"Gottcha," Shawn teases as he busts out laughing.

Thank God. I thought I just put my foot in my mouth or rather my whole leg, but luckily Shawn was just making a funny. He did get the job after all. I guess visions aren't always what they seem.

Later, Star shares the details of her living arrangements with her aunt. It sounds like she has everything all figured out. Since I am going away to Peru on a supposed school trip, Sebastian and I thought it would be a good idea to let my friends know just in case they run into my parents.

"So what are your plans for this summer, Ais?" Star asks.

"Funny you should ask. I'm going to Peru, I mean Brazil, in two days," I say with a quick recovery.

"Brazil? Like the country?" Star asks, looking surprised.

"Yeah. Like the country."

"Oh my God! Who are you going with?"

"Well, it's not as exciting as it seems. I'm going to check out this academic enrichment program thing that my parents want me to do."

"Okay. That just went from totally exciting to desperately boring," Star says while playing with Shawn's hair.

"Pretty much."

"Okay, so how long will you be gone? I mean, we have beaches to go to and shopping to catch up on," Star asks.

"About a week. So, it's not too bad."

"I can deal with that."

Thankfully, Star doesn't pay that much attention to my trip after she realizes it's an academic adventure. She also has a male distraction here, which helps.

After a harmless night of fun with my friends, I give a heartfelt goodbye, knowing that I will be traveling to Peru in two days to decipher my future. Having this night of normalcy was important. I needed to feel the same as I did before I received my gift. I needed to feel that I was still human.

When I get home, I search the house for my parents. I don't go through the garage to see whose car is here since that takes too long. Instead, I scamper through the living room looking for any sign of life. I would like to spend as much time with them as I can before I leave. I suppose I'm feeling a little anxious about the trip, not that I think anything bad is going to happen. I just feel like things might be different after I find out about my gift. Luckily, my father is home. I hear him on the phone in his office. I patiently wait by the door and watch him pace the room as he consults with a new client. At last he hangs up. He finally looks up and sees me.

"Hi honey. How was your last day of school?"

"It was good."

He walks over to me while stuffing his cell phone into his pocket.

"Did you eat? There's nothing good here. Mom's working late."

"Yeah. I'm good. I ate at the Coffee Beanery."

"Okay. Well, you could always order pizza if you get hungry."

"Dad?"

"Yes," he answers.

"Were you ever nervous to go on a trip before?" My nerves are starting to get the best of me and who else to look for comfort in, other than your own parents.

"No. Why? Are you nervous, dear?"

"A little, it's in two days," I lie. I'm a whole lot nervous. I have no idea what I'm getting myself into.

"It's normal. You're traveling out of the country without your parents. But your teacher seems logical and caring. You'll be in safe hands."

I smile, thinking about Jerry playing the role as my school liaison.

"I know."

"You're going to have a great time. You'll meet new friends and learn new things. It'll be great," he says with a hopeful smile.

My dad's cell phone rings before I can say anything. I give him the look to answer it and he complies. We give each other a wink and I head toward my room with Otie. I know I'll be safe with Sebastian by my side. I don't know why I'm worrying so much. Maybe because the day is almost here, and it's starting to actually feel real now.

The next day comes early and I feel extremely refreshed and wide awake. The air is beautifully warm and sweet. I've been sleeping with my window open lately because the fragrant smells of summer help me sleep more soundly. I figure that it has something to do with me being part red-tailed hawk. I think about my plans for the day and prioritize.

1) Pack bags

2) Check bags

3) Check bags again

I begin my duties and pack my luggage. When I finally feel comfortable that I have everything I need, I get a surprise phone call from Sebastian.

"Good morning, early riser," I greet him.

"Good morning, over packer."

"Excuse me?" I ask.

"I meant beautiful first," he jokes.

"That's better." I blush.

"Wait a minute. Did you see me pack? How come I never get visions of you? Lately, I seem to only vision the mailman coming, my dog barking, and other nonsense matters," I say, feeling jealous.

"Yes. I saw you packing. Then I saw you pack some more. You did look very beautiful packing though."

"Oh. Thank you."

"Aislinn, I'm sorry to disappoint you, but you can only bring what you can carry."

"You're joking!" He has to be joking.

"I wish I was. But we aren't going to be staying in an actual hotel."

"Where are we staying?"

"I'm not sure yet. We just can't be too tied down. We'll be doing a lot of travel by foot."

"But, but, ugh." I am at a loss for words. What can I say to that? "Okay. So I pack what I need in a backpack. But won't my parents find it odd that I'm not bringing any luggage?"

"You can still pack your luggage, but Jerry will hold on to it at headquarters."

"That works, I guess. So, you excited?" I ask, hoping to take the attention away from my ridiculous over-packing. I had three suitcases packed to the point of borderline explosion.

"Yeah. I can't believe we're really going to Peru...together. What about you? How are you feeling about it?"

"Me? I'm excited. And a little worried. I mean it's coming so fast. It's basically here already!"

"Well, don't worry about anything. Leave that to me. Just get plenty of rest and take it easy today, because you have to be ready to leave at five a.m."

"That's not too bad. But why five, I thought our plane left at ten of eight out of Boston?"

"It does. I just wanted to have breakfast with you first."

I blush. "I would love that."

Now that I have spoken to Sebastian, I feel a little less stressed and a little more enthusiastic. He brings out a sense of calmness that I keep hidden under my many layers of emotions. And right when I slip into my dreamy state of thinking about Sebastian, the unsettling thought of Mya pops into my brain and kills my fantasy like a squashed bug.

∞ CHAPTER 5 ∞

The obnoxious sound of my alarm clock goes off and I instantly jump out of bed. No pushing the snooze button today. I speed-wash through my shower and get ready as fast as possible. I look through my backpack, which barely has any contents. It's as if I'm going to live off the earth itself. I packed only the necessities. Lip gloss, fruity body spray, deodorant, floss, toothpaste, toothbrush, hairbrush, make-up, underwear, bras, two shorts, two shirts, one pair of socks, a bathing suit (just in case), and sandals. I'm wearing my tight black jogging pants, hot-pink tank top and coordinating sneakers. I grab a sweatshirt, sling my backpack over my shoulders, and head down the stairs.

"Where's the rest of your luggage, honey?" my mother questions as she notices me.

"Oh right. It's upstairs. I'll get it."

She makes her way up toward my bedroom with me, "Let me help you."

I help my mom with the other two pieces of luggage. We barely make it down the stairs without tripping. My dad would have normally helped with this sort of stuff, but he had to go to New York City last night for an early conference this morning.

"God, Aislinn! This stuff weighs as much as a ton of bricks. What did you pack in here?" my mother questions as she catches her breath.

"Everything and anything I thought I would need," I say sadly while thinking about all the items I'm actually not taking with me.

Just then, the doorbell rings. I giddily open it, expecting to see Sebastian's warm and gorgeous face.

"Jerry," I say, confused. He looks at me oddly, and then I remember that he is not Jerry today.

"I mean, Mr. Johnson," I correct myself. Luckily, my mother didn't notice my blunder.

"Good morning, Aislinn." Jerry grabbed the luggage and carried it to the van.

"Thank you," my mother says. "What a nice teacher you got there, Aislinn."

My mom gives me a tight squeeze and a kiss on the cheek.

"Bye, Mom."

"Goodbye, Aislinn. Call me when you get there. And be careful," she says, sounding tearful.

"I will. Mom," I say with a big sigh. "I love you."

"I love you too, sweetie. Okay, now have fun, would you already. You're going to Brazil!"

Jerry closes the last gaps with my mother by handing her another form with all of the contact information on it. Jerry and Schooner have arranged all the details. They were somehow able to connect the school's phone lines to theirs and alter email addresses. They pretty much covered the whole gamut. They are technological geniuses!

"Sorry about that back there," I say to Jerry apologizing for my slip-up.

"Don't worry about it. It's just traveler's jitters or disappointment that it wasn't someone else at the door." He laughs. I smile, knowing he's right.

"We are headed to the airport, and Sebastian will be there waiting for you," Jerry informs me. He answers my question without me even having to ask it.

"What about Mya and Caleb?"

"They should be there soon. They are traveling together." My face drops.

I'm still sour about the whole thing; perhaps I'm not giving her a fair shot. I don't even know her. Maybe she'll surprise me and turn out to be the most genuine person, but most likely not. I'm usually able to pin down peoples' personalities rather quickly, and Mya's has bad, bad, bad written all over hers.

When we get to the airport, Jerry gives me a heartfelt hug. I can see worry etched on his face by the way his wrinkles gather around his eyes and the way his mouth seems to stay flat-lined.

"Be careful out there. It's a jungle," he says. I chuckle and nod my head. I look over at the entrance to our airline and notice Sebastian walking toward the van. I run over to meet him.

"Well, you look as beautiful as ever. I'll have to keep a close eye on you," he says, sounding extremely charming. I smile.

"Yeah, right. I'm sure you say that to all the pretty ladies," I joke.

"Only mine," he says while taking my backpack from me. I quiver from his words. Sebastian and Jerry say their goodbyes and we head into the airport. We check in together. Sebastian whips out our passports, and I glance at them to see what my name is. I am Rose James and he is Michael Miller.

When we clear the check-in and head toward the security line, I question Sebastian.

"Rose James?"

"And you're saying your name because why?"

Oh I get it. We're in character mode. I play along.

"I don't know, Michael. I just felt like trying it out a little." He grins and taps my nose.

"You are like a rose."

"And how is that exactly?"

He leans in and whispers, "You continue to grow more beautiful each day and you come off looking delicate and sweet, but you have hidden thorns that make you more powerful than you realize."

My eyes watch him with wonder. How can this man be so poetic and handsome at the same time? "How can I argue with that?" I whisper while reaching upward for a kiss.

We pass security and head toward our breakfast destination. Sebastian finds us a cozy little restaurant not far from our terminal. We enjoy a breakfast of pancakes and eggs and share a couple of laughs.

Then, as I take a sip of my orange juice, a familiar male voice sounds. "Here you two are."

I look up and find Mya and Caleb standing over us. Great!

"We were looking everywhere for you guys," Mya declares, sounding frustrated. I can already tell that this is going to be fun, not!

"Good morning to you too," Sebastian says.

I smile, sensing his underlying sarcasm.

"Hey, are you going to eat the rest of your toast, blondie?" Caleb asks while picking it up.

"Well, not now," I joke.

"What? There's no food on airlines anymore," he clarifies.

"Aislinn, you remember Mya," Sebastian reintroduces.

"Yeah, how you doing?" I ask, trying to sound polite, knowing that my voice really exemplifies scorn and mockery.

"Good. Yourself?" Mya questions back. I can tell that she doesn't care for me, and the feeling is one hundred percent mutual. It's going to be all peaches and giggles. That's something Star and I used to say whenever we ran into a difficult person.

After Sebastian grabs the bill, the four of us head over to wait by the gate. Sebastian pulls me close so that I am basically on his lap and I curl up into his embrace.

Caleb takes out some information on Peru and goes over it with us as if he were a geography teacher. Mya nods her head continuously and pretends to know everything Caleb is talking about.

"So, since Peru's dominant language is Spanish, it would probably be a good idea if we all used this Spanish-English translation dictionary or the new app on my iPhone, if we get service down there that is," Caleb says.

"Well, no worries on the Spanish part because I speak Spanish. It's the tribal languages that worry me," Sebastian says.

"Right, where can I find an app for that?" Caleb asks.

Mya interjects, "Your phone is not going to work in Peru. We're going to be in the jungle."

Sebastian and I give each other a look as Mya and Caleb continue to disagree about the informal name of jungle. They are rather amusing. Their petty disagreement seems like something an old couple would argue about.

Our flight is finally called and I jump up with excitement despite my sleepy right foot. I hate it when that happens. I shake it out as we walk through the gate to our plane. Sebastian looks at me.

"Foot fell asleep?"

"Obvious?"

"It was either that or you were doing some sort of 'here I come' airplane dance."

"Haha." I smirk.

Luckily, Sebastian and I are seated next to one another, and Mya and Caleb are a few rows behind us.

"How come they're so far back?" I ask.

"Jerry booked everything. Maybe he sensed that we would need some quiet time." I grin, knowing that Jerry is the master of all plans, and he most definitely planned this accordingly. He probably was able to sense that I wasn't exactly fond of the idea about Mya tagging along. Thank you, Jerry. Thank you!

"So how long exactly is this flight?" I ask Sebastian while making myself comfortable.

"Like three and half hours."

"Really? 'Cause I thought it was much longer. This must be one of those fast jets," I say.

He chuckles. "Well, three and half hours to Miami and then about another six hours on our transfer plane to Peru."

"Ahhh. I should have known."

He grabs my hand and tangles it into his. His hands are strong and soft. They are much bigger than my tiny hands. Just as I was admiring the beauty of his hands, I get a vision. I see a man touching my face. Not in a sexual way but in a way that is unusual. It's as if he never touched a face before. This vision is very strange compared to the ones I've been getting lately. I lean over and whisper it to Sebastian.

"That's strange," he says while attempting to access a vision. I can tell by the way he concentrates his eyes. It isn't noticeable to others, but I have become accustomed to his mannerisms.

"Anything?" I ask.

"No. Don't worry about it. I'm sure it's nothing."

I forget about the vision and take out a notepad and pen. Sebastian looks over and watches me and then quickly smiles when he sees that I have made a tic-tac-toe game. We play games and share sweet nothings until we arrive in Miami. Three and a half hours go by like nothing.

"I wish we could stay here for a few days first before we enter the jungle. I need to work on my tan," Mya says as we exit the plane. Caleb rolls his eyes.

The next flight boards very quickly. We basically just make it. We take our seats and luckily Jerry has maintained continuity by placing us apart on the aircraft again. Now that we have been traveling for a little while, I begin to feel sleepy and ask Sebastian if I can lean on him. He gives me a look as if to say, *of course*. His strong arms provide a safe place for my worries and I fall fast asleep. I drift off to dreamland for almost half of the flight. Slight turbulence wakes me and I find Sebastian sleeping like a baby. I stare at his face and admire his beauty on the inside and out.

Suddenly, he opens one eye and says, "I'm not sleeping. Just resting."

"That's what my grandfather used to say."

"I couldn't sleep because someone was making loud breathing noises."

"What? Are you implying that I snore?" I question. "I don't snore. Maybe you snore, but I don't." He smiles and plants a kiss on my lips. "It's okay if you snore. I like it."

I stop kissing him, realizing what he just said. "Um, I don't snore. You're confused." He laughs and I purse my lips trying hard to hold in a smile. It's impossible to be mad at Sebastian. It would be like being mad at ice cream for tasting so damn good, wouldn't happen.

"Guys, I was wondering if we could all have a drink together? To celebrate our time of, whatever time it is," Caleb mumbles while crouched down in the aisle next to us.

"What?" I ask, confused by his question and slurred speech.

"According to my and Mya's passports, and I'm assuming yours, we are all twenty-one. I thought that maybe we should kick off this trip with a small shot or two, maybe just three, of something."

"Have you gone mad?" I ask Caleb.

Sebastian cuts in. "It's not a good idea, bro. We don't know what's in store for us when we get down there, and I need you to be as focused as me. We'll have a drink on the return flight, okay buddy?"

"You're right. It's not a good idea. It's not a good idea at all," Caleb says while laughing. This isn't the Caleb that I thought I knew. He's acting bizarre. Sebastian looks at me and tells me that he'll be right back. He walks behind Caleb, following him to his seat. I tilt my neck and strain my ears, but I can't hear a thing since the plane is so loud. I turn around again and spot Sebastian heading back toward our seats. As Sebastian takes a seat he smiles cunningly and snickers. Curious, I turn around and find Mya and Caleb sleeping.

"What happened? Did you drug them?"

"They'll be okay. It seems that Miss Mya and Caleb already had a drink or two or three."

"Okay. But why are they sleeping all of a sudden?"

"I gave them something that will hopefully eliminate the effects of alcohol in their systems. When they wake up, they should be as good as new." Since when did Sebastian become a pharmacist? I'm impressed. I peek back at them one last time and see both of them passed out, Mya drooling while resting her head on top of Caleb's. I laugh.

"This is going to be an interesting trip," I murmur.

"Yup. Interesting."

Finally, we arrive at our final destination. I stand up and stretch my body, as it feels cramped from sitting for so long. Sebastian rubs my neck for a few moments, which helps to relieve my soreness.

"Hey, I never did get to do any of that training you promised me," I tell him.

"When we get back, you'll start as soon as possible. I promise."

"Good."

A few weeks ago, Sebastian had told me that it would be a good idea to start training soon. Being in top shape mentally and physically would provide me with more in-tuned visions and better self-protection. It could be the difference between life and death when you're a visionary.

We exit the plane, each of us wearing our one and only backpacks. We must look rather strange, being in a foreign country and only having one backpack each.

"How you guys feeling?" Sebastian asks Mya and Caleb.

"I feel amazing!" Mya answers.

"Me too. Surprisingly," Caleb shares. Sebastian and I both smile at one another.

"I'm so happy to be off the plane," I tell Sebastian. I need to walk around. My legs have been so restricted.

"Don't get too happy yet. We'll be on another plane soon."

"What?" Caleb, Mya, and I say in unison.

"Did I forget to tell you guys about that part? We have to take a local flight to get to where we are going. It's the only way."

"So which group of indigenous people are we looking for exactly?" Caleb asks.

"We are looking for a group that has been hidden from civilization and other native groups since the beginning of time. There is no official name that I know of, but hopefully with the information Jerry has given us, we'll be able to locate them and find the guru," Sebastian answers.

"So it's going to be like looking for a needle in a haystack," Mya exclaims.

"Pretty much," Sebastian says.

"Sounds like my kind of adventure," Caleb says excitedly. "I can't wait to see the pink dolphins and electric eels. It's going to be great!"

And I thought I was excited. Our next flight should only be about two hours. I suppose if I was able to deal with our last two flights, I can certainly deal with another.

"I don't know about great," says Sebastian, in response to Caleb's eagerness.

"I just want to learn how to focus my energy so that I can see my visions more clearly," Mya says sounding self-assured, "I have visions, but they aren't that clear."

"When was the last time you actually had one?" Sebastian questions.

"Um, I can't remember. Not too long ago."

I bet she hasn't had any in a long time. I still don't know why she's even on this trip, but I continue to keep a phony smile on to keep the peace.

After our next flight, I start to feel jet lagged. I know I shouldn't be worn out just yet, but I can't help it. I'm tired. Really tired. I mean, we spent the whole day flying.

"Here, take this," Sebastian says, handing me a large green pill of some sort.

"No thanks. I'm good."

He chuckles. "It's not drugs, Ais. It's made out of tree bark, roots of grass, and other things from nature. Jerry makes them."

Skeptically, I grab the pill and look it over.

"You don't have to. It just wakes up your inner energy and clears your chakras." Seeing as I trust Sebastian to the fullest, I take one last look at the large green pill and decide to swallow it. It can't be that bad. A few minutes later I burp up a disgusting burp that tastes of tree and grass. Yuck! But, remarkably I do feel more energized and less drained. I guess it works.

"Thank you."

"Of course," Sebastian says.

As we walk through the bustling city of Iquitos, I notice the beautiful, historic buildings and stunning city life. It doesn't seem that bad here. People appear to be going about their everyday business. It looks like a really fascinating place.

"Can we stay here while we search for the Guru?" I ask.

"I wish," Sebastian says.

"Did you guys know this place serves as a popular starting point for many excursions into the rainforest?" Caleb offers.

"I didn't," I say.

"Yeah, it's the world's largest city that can't be reached by road," Sebastian adds.

"This place rocks," Mya declares.

"Too bad we can't stay long. We have to find a guy named Apumayta. He's supposed to help us get to the guru," Sebastian interjects.

"Apumayta, Apumayta, Apumayta. Fun name to pronounce," Caleb says with an accent.

∞ CHAPTER 6 ∞

During our walk through the lovely Iquitos, Mya stops suddenly and blurts out, "Wait. I'm not going any further until we eat something from this place. I don't know what the Amazon River holds for us, and I'd like to eat a real meal, just in case."

"Way to go for positive thinking," I mumble.

Mya looks at me with squinted eyes. "You're not hungry?"

"I'm hungry. It's the *just in case part* I'm not feeling," I say. I mean, really. We're entering an unknown world, and you start it off with negative thoughts. Not good.

"Okay, ladies. Let's find something quick. It's getting pretty late and we still have to find Apumayta," Sebastian states.

"How about that place over there?" Caleb suggests with a friendly smile. He points to a restaurant that boasts beautiful vibrant colors on the outside. It looks very inviting. The four of us agree and quickly head over there.

Upon entering, we are immediately greeted with the friendly personality of a young, beautiful Peruvian woman. She happily seats us and hands us the menus.

"My recommendation is the Juane. Very good here. Everything good here," she says with a charming accent.

The four of us cheer our non-alcoholic drinks and wish each other good luck on our upcoming adventure.

After much debate with the authentic menu, I finally make a selection and order her suggestion along with potatoes on the side. Sebastian orders the same.

When our meals arrive, I am hesitant to try my meal because it is wrapped in large, green leaves. I open it up as if opening up a Christmas present, half excited and half unsure of its contents, but to my surprise, the mixture looks and smells delightful.

Sebastian speaks to the waitress in Spanish and mentions Apumayta's name. She shakes her head and displays a curious grin. She then begins to point toward the door while using various hand gestures as she speaks. It appears that she is telling Sebastian how to find Apumatya. And then her small grin fades as she appears to say something in Spanish that sounds disconcerting.

When the waitress leaves, I whisper to Sebastian, "What did she say to you?" Caleb and Mya pay us no attention as they eat their food and share a flirtatious conversation.

"She knows who Apumayta is and where we can find him."

"And?" I probe, knowing that she must have said more.

"And she told us to be careful, that where we're going, no one goes. Guess she thought we were here for Inti Raymi. "

"Inti?"

"Inti Raymi, festival of the sun. It's celebrated on the twenty-fourth of this month in Cuzco."

"Festival of the sun? I like the sound of that, but I don't like the sound of her warning. It's disturbing," I say, feeling worried.

Caleb and Mya stop talking and look at Sebastian. Apparently that got their attention. None of us say anything, as we all anticipated that this trip might be dangerous. The real question is, how dangerous is it?

Before we continue on our journey, I break away to call my parents. Jerry took my cell phone before we left for the trip and added a small silver attachment to it. It will help him locate us if he needs to as well as provide my phone with a strong signal. Luckily, it works. I reach my mom and tell her all about my flight—the modified version, of course. Hearing her voice warms my heart. When we hang up, a few small tears escape from my eyes, and I quickly wipe them away so as not to look weak.

We hurriedly head out toward Apumayta's location. It's very dark and warm out. It feels strange romping around a foreign country with fellow visionaries. I've never been out of the country without my family before and here I am backpacking it with fellow visionaries in unfamiliar territory.

Finally, we reach an area where the city meets the Amazon River. Walking down the embankment, I notice a timeworn shack along the bank of the river. The river reflects the moonlight in such a way that I feel awe-struck. It is pretty unbelievable. Even at night, the sight is amazing. The four of us are breathless at the sight of the Amazon River and the four Amazon River boats that stand before us. Sebastian holds out a small jar containing a green, jelly-like substance. "We need to put this on before we head out there."

"What is that exactly?" Mya questions, making a skeptical face.

"Jerry's special anti-malaria cream," Sebastian says, sporting a cute smile. Mya crinkles her brow.

"Mosquito repellent. One application should give us protection up to twenty-four hours." We all take turns spreading on the homemade mosquito-repellent serum, which smells horrific. There's no way I want to catch malaria.

Suddenly, a voice calls out to us, "Hola!"

"It's Apumayta," Sebastian says, and waves him over. He makes his way toward us with another man. Sebastian takes the liberty of introducing all of us. Apumayta introduces himself and his friend, Cayo.

"I like your name and yours too," Caleb says, pointing at Apumayta and Cayo. I can't help but laugh when hearing this. Sometimes Caleb sounds so juvenile it cracks me up.

Apumayta and Cayo smile and shake their heads hesitatingly. Sebastian rolls his eyes and I try to muffle my laugh. Apumayta's English is very good and Cayo's not so much.

"We can get on the boat now," Apumayta instructs.

"In the dark?" Mya questions. My thoughts exactly. I was hoping to stay the night in a hotel in Iquitos and leave in the morning. But, Sebastian thought it was best for us to find Sir Mateo right away.

"Yes," Apumayta answers.

Sebastian helps me and Mya board one of the Amazon River boats.

"It doesn't feel too stable," I share.

"It'll be okay," says Sebastian.

"What happens if we fall in the river?" Mya dares to ask. What kind of question is that? Duh. You would climb back on board.

"No fall. Piranha and snakes. No good," Apumayta answers.

"What!" Mya screams.

"Shhh, you don't want to cause any attention. Who knows who's out there," Sebastian warns.

"I'm not a big fan of flesh-eating fish either," I say softly to Sebastian. He puts his arm around me.

"I think it's just a myth," Caleb says. His warm smile attempts to reassure me.

"No fall, no fish," Apumayta says. Apparently, he heard me.

Apumayta is a strong, young man with petite facial features. He has long, black hair tied back and arm muscles as big as my thighs times two. His friend, Cayo, has a much smaller build and curly dark hair.

The small boat is big enough to fit all of us, but not big enough for comfort. I feel claustrophobic not being able to move around freely.

"We will find Sir Mateo early tomorrow, get rest," Apumayta calls out. Sebastian gives him a nod of approval.

"What does that mean?" Caleb asks.

"It means we'll be on this boat for the night so cuddle up," says Sebastian.

"Who's Mateo?" Mya asks, while placing her hand on Sebastian's leg. I can't help but glare down at it.

"Sir Mateo is the guru's name. Or that's what the locals know him as," Sebastian responds.

After Sebastian answers the question, Mya slowly releases her hand from his leg and offers Caleb a neck massage. Here we go again. Caleb happily accepts the invitation and groans with relief as they head to one of the hammocks on the boat.

After a while, the lights from the city are no longer visible. And there is nothing to talk about while Apumayta and Cayo man the boat, so the only logical thing to do is to rest. I make myself comfortable in Sebastian's embrace. The motion of the boat, on the less than rocky water, lulls me to sleep.

My dreams are even more vivid than usual. Bright colors and massive animals make up the whole spectrum. Animals are everywhere and pandemonium sets the theme. There is fighting between animals and humans and animals against monsters. No rationale for the irate behavior, just pure mayhem everywhere.

Suddenly, I awake to real life commotion. My eyes attempt to adjust to the bright light shining in my direction. Is it morning already? No, it's the light from a boat lodged next to us. People seem to be boarding our boat and Apumayta and Cayo have panic painted all over their faces.

∞ CHAPTER 7 ∞

I tug at Sebastian's arm. "What's going on?"

"I don't know. I just woke up myself. But it looks like trouble."

Caleb and Mya start to wake up and notice the troublesome situation.

"Um, there better be a good reason why someone woke me up," Mya shouts. Great! We have a superficial drama queen here to make matters worse.

"Shhhhh," Sebastian hisses quietly. Mya eyes widen as she looks around and realizes that there is something strange happening.

Sebastian and I intently watch the two men who boarded our boat. They appear to be arguing with

Apumayta. They seem hostile by the way they shout and push Cayo out of the way.

"They have nothing," Apumayta yells.

Sebastian looks forward without blinking. He is attempting to access his visions. Although I can access my visions that way too, I close my eyes in an attempt to speed up the process. In a matter of seconds a vision kicks in. I see the men taking us to an undisclosed location. They go through our things and ransack the boat. I also get a vision of them doing this again to others. Immediately, I figure out who they are.

"Pirates," I whisper to Sebastian as he says the exact same thing. Caleb looks at us with concern and Mya stands, shaking her head nervously. Not so tough now, is she?

"We'll be good as dead if they take us or the boat," Sebastian whispers to Caleb. Caleb nods his head. Suddenly, I get a flashback of that day in the woods where Sebastian and Caleb both understood each other without saying a word. They seem to work well together.

The two pirates, who stand there arguing, are wearing ragged clothing and are carrying large sticks. They look like dangerous characters. As they stagger toward us, Apumayta and Cayo try to stop them. One of the pirates yells at Apumayto and Cayo. That pirate then pulls Cayo by the shirt and punches him fiercely in the face while the other pirate continues toward us.

Cayo falls to the ground and huddles in the fetal position, holding his head. Apumayta tackles the pirate, knocking him down.

Sebastian and Caleb attack the other pirate instantaneously. The small boat rocks from the commotion. Mya and I carefully back up toward the edge of the boat while the men continue to fight. I scan the boat for a weapon, but I see nothing that could be of use.

Just then, a third man boards our boat and begins heading toward Mya and me.

"Aislinn, what do we do?" Mya screams.

Honestly, I didn't expect a third man to come out of nowhere.

"I don't know."

"You're the hawk girl. Do something," she yells.

She is right. I have the red-tailed hawk as my spirit animal. Why not try to access it? I desperately try to contact my spirit animal even though I know it's virtually impossible. I haven't felt or seen any signs of the red-tailed hawk since that night I transformed into it. I don't know how I did it before, but it doesn't seem to be working now.

The third pirate quickly reaches us and seizes Mya by the arms. He attempts to drag her with him back to their boat. Without hesitation, I lunge at him. I grasp at his long, dark hair from behind and punch him in the back of the head repeatedly with as much force as I can muster. But he doesn't flinch a bit. I've only managed to anger him. He lets go of Mya and grabs my hair instead. I notice his arm in front of my face is covered with tattoos. Words written in another language wrap around his large forearms. He angrily grumbles something to me. Why did I have to grab his hair? It only gave him the inclination to do the same to me. It hurts! Mya does nothing to help me. She stands there useless, stricken with fear. The pirate prepares to throw a fist at me. I close my eyes and prepare for the blow, but to my surprise it doesn't happen. Sebastian tackles the pirate first.

While Sebastian and this raging pirate battle it out, I scurry over to the pirates' boat and yell for Mya to follow me. She grudgingly follows.

"Stay here and make sure the boats don't disconnect. Got it?" I shout.

"Okay. I got it. Don't get killed," Mya says. She sounds frightened, but not without an added edge of sarcasm. That's probably the thing she wants most so that she can have Sebastian all to herself. Fat chance, girlfriend. *Focus, Aislinn.*

As I board the pirates' small ship, I anxiously look around for an idea on how to sink it. Suddenly, I notice the boat's engine. *That's it!* Mya watches me as I run over to the other end of their boat.

"Um, what are you doing?" she asks. Her tone mocking.

"Trying to find something strong. I'm going to break their engine so they can't follow us."

Mya turns away and looks back at the chaos on the boat. Luckily, she finds one of the large sticks that the pirates had carried on. She runs between the fighting and grabs it.

"Try this." She throws it to me. It's pretty heavy. It feels more like a baseball bat. I quickly begin smashing the engine. I don't know what I'm doing exactly; I just go with my gut. I smash the engine over and over again.

I stop decimating the engine after a moment of rage and then hear a loud splash. Someone must have fallen into the river. I worriedly look over to find Sebastian or Caleb, but luckily it's one of the pirates who have fallen in. He is thrashing around and desperately screaming for help. Can't he swim?

The other two pirates stop fighting and try to save their accomplice. Sebastian, Caleb, Apumayta, and Cayo also stop and stare at the unusual circumstance. The two pirates lean over with their sticks while yelling at their friend to grab a hold of them. Shouldn't they just jump in to save their friend?

Apumayta and Cayo share words and Cayo shakes his head. What's going on? The rest of us stand there frozen and watch. It's like I'm watching a movie. First these guys board our boat and try to attack us and now they're trying to save their friend but won't go in the water. This is very peculiar.

The pirate that has fallen begins to scream louder and becomes more panicked. His arms thrash in the water and his head starts to bobble in and out restlessly. He's screaming so loud.

"He's drowning," I shriek. I'm surprised at myself for feeling emotion for a man who was just attacking us.

Sebastian grabs hold of me and whispers, "No, it's the piranhas."

"What? Oh my God! I can't watch this," I bury my head into Sebastian's chest. He holds me there. The screaming is absolutely heart wrenching. I cover my ears to block out the horrifying sounds. Soon the screaming and thrashing come to a stop and the pirate is no longer visible; only a pool of red remains in the dark water.

Apumayta and Cayo say something in Spanish to the two remaining pirates. They nod their heads and immediately abort our boat.

"What just happened?" Mya asks.

"It looks like Captain Sparrow and his pathetic friend decided to leave," Caleb answers.

"Why did they leave so willingly?" I ask.

"Apumayta and Cayo told them if they come near us again, they'll feed both of them to the piranhas limb by limb," Sebastian translates.

"But, I thought it was just a myth about piranhas eating people?" Caleb questions.

"These are blood death piranhas. Very rare to see here. These fish come from our River Gods when they are angry," Apumayta shares.

I look at Sebastian with wide eyes. "It must be some sort of mythological creature," Sebastian explains.

Either way, the thought of a fish eating you alive is unsettling no matter what it is. The pirates board their boat and yell when they see that their engine has been ruined. Apumayta quickly steers the boat away from them and continues on our path.

"What happened to their engine, Aislinn?" Caleb asks, sporting a playful grin.

"She beat it to a pulp. Must be all that hawk rage inside of her," Mya cunningly responds. I ignore her and turn my attention toward Sebastian.

"Good thinking. Now they can't follow us," Sebastian states.

As Sebastian pulls me toward the warmth of his body, my mind spins at the thoughts of piranhas and all of the other dangerous species that possibly lurk out here. The sounds of that pirate screaming for his life while being chewed to a million pieces remains in my ears. I try to think of a song to wash out his screams.

"Where are we exactly?" I ask Sebastian.

"We are headed to one of the hidden tributaries off of the Amazon River. Hopefully it won't be much longer."

"Oh," I say, as I continue to hum the lyrics of a song to myself.

An hour passes and my mind is still unable to rest. I'm wide awake with anxiousness and uncertainty. Apumayta and Cayo appear to be in deep conversation and Mya and Caleb are joking around as usual. Sebastian's arms are wrapped tightly around me like a warm blanket, but I still feel apprehensive. How can I not? I'm traveling through a remote location on a dangerous river with all sorts of unknowns.

Cayo takes over the boat and Apumayta walks back to Sebastian and me. Apumayta speaks to Sebastian in Spanish. Desperately, I try to make out what they're saying.

Just then, an unusual cold breeze comes by and takes me by surprise. I glance up and find that everyone else looks taken back by it too. It wasn't the typical warm breeze that occasionally blew by. It was oddly cold and uninviting. The boat's engine stops and everyone becomes quiet. Even though we are all submerged in complete darkness, I can see a grim mist hovering above the boat. It's like a dense fog, but in long, thick strips all around the boat.

"We're here," Mya says eerily, as if in a horror movie. As she speaks she begins to resemble a tarantula. It's as if a strobe light is shining on her and she keeps switching back and forth from human to tarantula. I blink and try to register a vision, but I'm unable to see anything except for what I see in front of me. I stop staring at Mya and turn my attention over to Caleb, whose image starts to reflect that of an African elephant. This is no surprise, because I had seen him change briefly a while back at the secret agency's campsite. Then I look over at Sebastian and find that my grizzly bear is staring directly into my eyes.

"Do you see what I see?" I ask him.

He nods and reaches out his hand. I take his hand and ask, "What's happening?"

"I don't know. I can't access my visions so stay close to me."

∞ CHAPTER 8 ∞

Everyone looks around at each other stupefied. Then, a harsh jolt from the boat sends us all falling to the boat's wooden floor boards. Eerily, the boat has docked on its own!

"We cannot take you any further," Apumayta says to Sebastian. He sounds concerned and frightened.

"Is this the right place?" Caleb asks.

"I think so," Sebastian answers.

"How do we get a hold of you when we're ready to leave?" Sebastian asks Apumayta.

"We will know." Apumayta gestures for us to leave the boat.

"I guess this is where we get off," Sebastian tells us. We grab our backpacks and hesitantly depart.

"Thank you," I say to Apumayta and Cayo as I get off the boat. The two of them gaze at me as if they saw a ghost and say nothing in return.

"Did I say something wrong?" I whisper to Sebastian.

"No. They can see you now. The real you."

This is strange. They can see me as a hawk, yet I don't feel like I transformed into a hawk at all.

"But how? I didn't feel like I altered one bit."

"It seems like only images are flashing. Like a mirror image or something," Sebastian whispers.

Without saying goodbye, Apumayta and Cayo head off and the four of us venture into the world of the unknown.

"Bye," Mya calls out sarcastically.

Two steps into the jungle and the four of us stop walking simultaneously. We have been instantly stunned by some sort of invisible force.

"Did you guys feel that?" I ask.

"Um, yeah. What was that?" Caleb questions, looking at Sebastian for answers.

Sebastian turns back toward the river and slowly raises his right arm. He grazes the invisible force with his fingertips and says, "We can't walk back that way. Not now anyways."

"Hopefully, we can get out of here when we need to," Caleb says doubtfully, "or this is going to be one long trip."

Sebastian tells us, "We walked through an invisible shield of some kind. But, it doesn't let us pass back. There must be a way around it."

"There better be a way around it," says Mya. Caleb rolls his eyes.

I try to put my hand through it and I can't. I can still see the river, but it's as if I'm looking through a kaleidoscope or a foggy glass. The colors seem mismatched and the landscape seems choppy.

"We're trapped," I bellow.

"It's okay. I think that's a good thing. We must be getting closer to the guru. Jerry told me that unusual things like this happen in these jungles. He just didn't say what exactly," Sebastian says.

Sebastian takes my hand and we continue through the magical rainforest. Caleb and Mya follow.

A loud screeching stops us dead in our tracks again. "Relax. It's just a monkey," Caleb says, sounding confident.

"And how do you know that?" Mya asks.

"Because I can see it up there. Look for yourself."

The four of us try to find it, but it is clearly out of our view.

"You're lying," Mya says with squinted eyes.

"No, I can see it. It's all the way up there to the right. You can't see that?"

Then I remember some of the gifts from Caleb's spirit animal. Among his many talents, he is able to see things from far away.

"He can see it. It's a gift from his spirit animal, the African elephant," I blurt out.

Sebastian looks at me with a peculiar stare. Mya starts to laugh. "Elephants can't see far. They have terrible eyesight. You're wrong."

"True, but elephants are supposed to have good perception, they pick up on things, and that's probably where he gets his exceptional eyesight from," I quickly say.

"Well, don't we sound like we know it all." Mya's eyes scream sarcasm as they glare at me. I start to feel furious at her negative demeanor, but I know I must not let her get the best of me.

"Obviously I don't know it all. None of us do," I answer back.

"Okay, so let's keep walking, shall we," Caleb says, looking surprised by our not-so-friendly tones.

"Jerry said that once we get off the boat, it shouldn't be much further until the guru or his tribe finds us," Sebastian interjects. As Sebastian speaks, I stare at his handsome jawline trickled with warm sweat, which makes his facial features seem that much more attractive. How he takes my breath away is still a mystery to me. I find myself engulfed by his every word.

"We're going to need sticks to get through this," Sebastian says, pointing to the dense rainforest that lies ahead.

"You're right. It looks pretty thick," Caleb agrees.

I stand back and watch as both men pull on a low-hanging, flexible branch. Sebastian takes out a thin gray plastic case from his pants and reveals a good-sized pocket knife.

"Do I want to know how you got that past airport security?" I ask.

"Yes, how did you pull that off, Sebastian?" Mya asks with a flirtatious grin.

"Jerry," he answers in short breaths as he and Caleb continue cutting down the branches, "created this plastic lining out of a special material that is virtually invisible," he grunts while cutting, "to all scanners." What hasn't Jerry come up with?

Sebastian and Caleb grab the two large branches that they cut.

"These will also help to ward off any lurking cats or caimans," Caleb jokes while swinging around the makeshift swords.

"Are you serious? Cats?" Mya questions snidely.

"Not domestic cats, jaguar and ocelot, I believe," Caleb corrects. He's right. I studied this in school, and Sebastian and Jerry went over some of the possible dangers with me before we left for the trip.

Without further ado, we continue on our journey into the tropical rainforest. Sebastian and Caleb lead the way with their sticks as they open up space for us to walk through. Caleb sports a large grin while whipping the stick around.

Bright green trees hover above us like a huge umbrella, blocking the sun at times. Sounds of various animals fill my ears and astounding sights of colorful birds and butterflies delight the eyes. A few vibrant, large birds, most likely Macaws of some kind, fly above us. The air is pure and dense at the same time, making it slightly uncomfortable to breathe thoroughly. But, the jungle is so breathtaking that describing it doesn't do it any justice. The way it looks, feels, even smells is awe-inspiring. My senses have been awakened. Maybe I don't get out much, but this is probably the most beautiful place I have ever seen.

After some light travel, we decide to take a water break. Luckily, we packed several bottles of water in our backpacks when we stopped to eat in Iquitos. The weather is hot and humid, but not as unbearable as I thought it would be.

As I enjoy my lukewarm water, my senses urgently tell me to look over at Mya. She is leaning against a tree with a peculiar olive-brown and black spotted branch near her torso. Looking closer, I see that it is not a branch at all. It's a snake. An enormously large snake.

"What are you looking at?" Mya snidely remarks.

My eyes open wide! I have never seen a snake quite that large in size before. My heart pounds. While continuing to stare at the snake, I grab Sebastian's arm and nervously whisper, "Snake."

"What was that?" Mya asks, still glaring at me.

I hold on to Sebastian's arm firmly without taking my eyes off of the snake. I point at the snake, which is now starting to slowly coil around Mya's ankles.

"Anaconda," Sebastian says.

Mya looks down and becomes terrified. Her face drops. "What do I do?"

The snake appears to be preparing to suffocate her with its muscular body as it moves up her legs. I have no idea what to do. I stand there frozen. Sebastian and Caleb quickly run over to Mya. They tell her not to panic as they try to pry the large snake off her body. As they struggle to remove the snake, it seems to restructure itself and squeeze her even tighter. If only Simon Wells, the snake expert from my school, were here. He would definitely know what to do.

"Oh my God! Get this thing off me," Mya shouts as tears begin to stream down her face.

So much for the not panicking part. I close my eyes and try to think of what I learned about anacondas in school. When we studied the Earth's biomes, I paid close attention to the tropical rainforest biomes because I found them to be the most intriguing. I remember being terrified of the anaconda, especially because around that time, reports started coming out about people spotting anacondas and pythons in Florida. I can recall what people had reportedly done to rescue their loved ones from the constricting snakes.

"Start at the tail," I yell to Sebastian and Caleb. They look at me and back at the snake. "Just do it!"

They start to uncoil the tail and, incredibly, it begins to unravel. It's working.

"Sebastian, do you have any rubbing alcohol or something stinky in your bag?"

"Yes, look in the first pocket and you'll find packets that look like hand wipes."

I rummage through his bag and pull out the wipes. I open one of the packets. The smell is extremely putrid. I gasp for air. "This will work."

"What is that? What are you doing?" Mya frantically asks, fearing for her life as I near her with the packet. I smirk, knowing that she doesn't trust me. I dangle the packet in front of the huge anaconda's face and let it inhale the scent of the stench from the wipes.

It seems to paralyze the snake, and it quickly releases its tight grip. I sigh with relief as it slithers back into the dense jungle.

"What was in that thing?" Caleb asks Sebastian.

"You don't want to know. Jerry made it."

"You're right. I don't want to know. Get it away from me. It stinks," Caleb jokes.

Mya regains her composure and looks at me as she wipes away her tears. Her pretty face seems full of questions, yet she can say nothing.

"Nice work, Aislinn," Caleb announces as he gathers up his belongings.

I humbly smile. He stares at me longer than usual.

Sebastian takes my hand and pulls me close to him. Apparently, he's not afraid to show his affection in front of Caleb or Mya. This pleases me.

He leans into my neck, toward my ear, and softly whispers, "You continue to amaze me at every turn."

Completely speechless, I move in closer and kiss him gently on his soft, full lips. His kiss brings a radiant sense of enthrallment to me that I have missed since we've been on this trip. We pull away slowly and notice our audience.

"You guys ready to head out or should we take a seat somewhere?" Caleb says, chuckling. Mya rolls her eyes.

"We're ready, let's get out of here," Sebastian confirms.

We continue on our journey through the thick forest. I stay near Sebastian, and Mya trails behind close to Caleb. After a few moments of quiet, Mya makes her way up next to me. I notice her but keep walking.

∞ CHAPTER 9 ∞

"I didn't get a chance to say thank you," Mya starts to say. Um, she had plenty of chances, but okay. "So, thank you for helping me out back there."

"No problem. You would have done the same for me."

She smiles at me and says nothing else as we keep up with Sebastian's pace. The more I think about it, she probably wouldn't have done the same for me. But, whatever. I'm not sure what her deal is. I know she doesn't like me, and I'm not particularly fond of her either.

Caleb pushes up forward with Sebastian, leaving Mya and me behind. We both choose not to converse. We simply walk in silence while Sebastian and Caleb talk about the anaconda and other dangerous animals that might show their presence while we're in their territory. I don't know what I would have done, if the anaconda was slithering around me. I probably would have passed out for sure.

Sebastian and Caleb stop suddenly, and Mya and I barely stop ourselves from plowing straight into them.

"What is it?" I ask, alarmed.

"Shhh," Sebastian whispers with his finger to his lip. This brings back memories. I look around trying to see what it is they see or hear.

"Someone is nearby," Caleb whispers into my ear while staring into my eyes again longer than usual. I nod my head, feeling a little uncomfortable. I can hear a light rustling in the woods. Maybe it's an animal.

To my dismay, a tribe of natives come out of the brush and circles us in a threatening manner holding up their bows and arrows.

"Sebastian!" I call out, reaching for his hand. I don't know why any of us haven't had any visions lately. It's like being near the secret agency's blockers all over again.

The men circling us wear very little clothing and brown beaded jewelry. They remind me of real Native Americans that I have read about in textbooks. They look so authentic it's scary. The four of us start to huddle together as the men close in on us.

"We are not here to harm you. We come in peace," Caleb says. The tremor in his voice shows his uneasiness.

Sebastian reiterates in Spanish. I hope they understand. The men stop circling us, but continue to stare at us. One man, who is wearing a large beaded necklace, comes closer to us. He nods his head and stands there, as if waiting for us to say more.

"We have come to see Sir Mateo," Sebastian says kindly to the intimidating man standing in front of us. The man stands there in silence. He gives us a once-over and mutters something to the others. They begin to back away and the man holds out his hand and says, "Juleayo."

I let out a deep sigh of relief knowing that we are okay. Introductions are usually a sign of respect. Each one of us takes a turn holding out our hands and telling Juleayo our names. He signals for us to follow him and mentions Sir Mateo's name.

"This is it, guys. We're finally going to meet the visionary guru," Sebastian says with excitement. We follow Juleayo, and the rest of his tribe trail behind us.

"Yeah, finally," Mya mutters.

After a couple of minutes, we exit the density of the rainforest and enter a small village. I've never seen anything like it before. There are small, man-made huts sporadically placed throughout the village. Some of the huts are built into the trees, resembling simple tree houses. Others stand alone. Women and children wander around the village dressed in similar attire to the men. The women stop what they're doing and watch us enter their territory. The children hurriedly come near us and circle us with amusement. One little girl tugs at my shirt, and I bend down to greet her. She tugs gently at my hair and calls out to some of the other children. They quickly run to my side and start fondling my hair.

"Guess they've never seen tangled hair like that before," Mya comments under her breath. What is she talking about? Just because her hair is short and isn't easily tangled doesn't mean mine is. I roll my eyes.

Caleb laughs at this, and just then two little boys start tugging at his backpack. "Easy guys," he jokes as he circles with them. The children hastily leave us when one of the women starts shouting at them.

Juleayo brings us to one of the huts made of cane and palm leaves and gestures for us to wait. The four of us eagerly await our first meeting with the legendary visionary guru. Each minute seems like an eternity. The overwhelming feelings of excitement and anticipation are simply unbearable. What if the guru tells me that I am immortal? What if he says that Sebastian is immortal?

Finally, Juleayo comes back out of the hut to escort us in. Sebastian reaches out his hand to hold mine. I grab it and hold it tight. He looks at me and smiles. He must be able to tell that I'm anxious. I catch Mya out of the corner of my eye. Her eyes glued on Sebastian. Great.

Juleayo announces us in their language to the visionary guru and then looks to us and bows.

Sir Mateo stands there dressed in much more elaborate clothing than the other members of the tribe. Beautiful feathers are positioned in various places of his garment and several large necklaces made out of beads wrap tightly around his neck. It's hard to determine his age due to the beauty of his bronze-colored skin.

Sir Mateo slowly sits down on the ground and gestures for us to sit with him. Juleayo bows to Sir Mateo and leaves the hut. Not quite knowing what to do, the four of us take a seat on the ground and patiently wait for Sir Mateo to speak. He looks around at each of us and nods his head. The silence is killing me.

I let out a deep breath of exasperation, not realizing how loud I was. Everyone looks my way including Sir Mateo. He unexpectedly stands up and walks toward me.

As he walks my way, my eyes meet with his and I start to feel like I'm in a trance. I quickly rise to my feet without even thinking about it. Our eyes stay locked on one another's. He stops in front of me and hums. I continue to stare back into his eyes and then I start to see things. Real things. I can see chaos and fighting everywhere. It's terribly petrifying. People are dying and animals too. It's like his eyes are a gateway to visions. Then something touches me and breaks me away from the vision. It's Sir Mateo. He is gently caressing my face as he looks at me in awe. This is the vision that I had yesterday.

"It's you," Sir Mateo says in English, "You have come." He speaks English?

"I'm sorry," I say feeling confused by his statement.

Sebastian, Caleb, and Mya continue sitting quietly on the ground with their eyes fixed on us. A nervous feeling comes over me and I begin to fear that he is referring to something much greater than I can comprehend.

"You are the red-tailed hawk," he says. "You have come to help us, yes?"

"No, I mean, I don't know. We thought maybe you could help us," I say.

Sir Mateo steps back and smiles. He takes my hand and escorts me back to the floor to sit with the others.

"Sit," he says. He smiles and looks at Sebastian.

"Sir Mateo, I am Sebastian and this is Caleb and Mya. You've already met Aislinn," Sebastian says while pointing at me. "We have come a long way to find you, and we were hoping that you might be of some help to us."

"Of course I can help you. What is it that you need?"

"A lot of information," I spit out. Sir Mateo grins.

"Come with me. I want to show you all something first," Sir Mateo says.

Hesitantly, we follow Sir Mateo away from the village. He turns around to see if were following.

"Come," Sir Mateo says. "Come now."

"Where is he taking us?" I whisper to Sebastian.

"I'm not sure," Sebastian says.

Sir Mateo takes us through a tight trail, causing us to walk single file. I make wide eyes at Sebastian and he politely shrugs his shoulders.

Suddenly a particular noise, besides the whimsical sounds of the rainforest, catches my attention. It's a gigantic waterfall! Its beauty is overwhelming. I've never seen a real waterfall before. Endless amounts of water magically cascading down a giant drop are utterly soothing to my tired eyes and the residue of fresh spring water smells so delicious.

"This is Agua Magia," Sir Mateo says.

"Wow!" says Caleb.

"It's beautiful," I say.

"If you touch it, you will be forever enhanced with clarity. If you swim in it, you will be forever blessed with healing powers, and if you drink it, you will be forever immortal."

I almost choke at his words. Did he just say immortal? "Let's be sure to stick with our water bottles, guys," I remind the others. Mya gazes at the waterfall as if she is actually considering drinking the water.

"Immortal, huh? So, I'd live forever with just one small sip?" Mya snidely asks.

"Yes," Sir Mateo says.

"Don't be stupid," Caleb remarks. My thoughts exactly. Who would want to be immortal? That's so science fiction. I can't imagine living forever alone. I would be petrified.

"We didn't come here to make hasty decisions," Sebastian adds.

"If one's spirit animal agrees," Sir Mateo says in a serious tone of voice. "I brought you here not because of the temptation of the waterfall, but because I want to see you change into your spirit animals in a safe place. A sacred place."

"But that's just it," Sebastian says. "We don't know how to control it."

"You know more than you think you do. Trust yourselves more and it will trust you," Sir Mateo advises. He sounds like Sebastian.

"You want us to just change into our spirit animals? Right here? Right now?" Mya asks.

Sir Mateo nods his head and smiles sincerely.

The four of us look around at each other. Sebastian looks at the waterfall and then back at me again. He shoots me a small nod telling me to loosen up and believe. I take a deep breath and close my eyes. I try to relax my brain and continue taking small breaths. I picture the red-tailed hawk and appreciate its magnificence.

Suddenly, my feet begin to elevate off the ground and my body starts to tighten. My muscles squeeze and I feel myself transforming into my spirit animal, the red-tailed hawk. I open my eyes and find that my human body has changed. I look at my elongated wings and admire the beautiful colors of white and gold and deep hues of red. I glance over and see that Sebastian has also changed into the almighty grizzly bear and Caleb into the African elephant. They are large and their features are exaggerated, but I am larger. I look over at Mya. She has not transformed into anything. However, I distinctly remember seeing her transform into the tarantula back on the boat.

Mya looks at all of us and her jaw drops. She shakes her head. "I can't do this. This is stupid."

I attempt to speak to her and then remember that I am a hawk right now and all I can do is screech. She looks at me and mumbles something under her breath.

"It's okay. You can change. You are a visionary—have no more doubts," Sir Mateo confirms as he holds Mya's hands in his. Mya takes one last, long look at Sir Mateo and closes her eyes. Finally, she starts to transform into the eight-legged tarantula. Yuck! I'm so glad that I'm not a spider. I am extremely petrified of spiders.

Mya starts to creepily move around with her eight creepy legs. She looks over her body with astonishment. It's the first time she has ever transformed into her spirit animal. I stand back and clumsily bump into Sebastian.

Sebastian nuzzles his big long grizzly nose into my wing and I tap him gently with my beak. It's absolutely amazing to be able to be one with our spirit animals. It feels just like before, only it was much easier to transform this time. Caleb makes an extremely loud trumpet. Sebastian and I watch him romp around in his new formation. This is a first for all of them and twice for me now. They have never seen themselves transform. Being connected to your spirit animal is unlike anything I have ever experienced. It's an amazing feeling that brings a feeling of pure bliss.

After a few minutes, Sir Mateo gathers us around to speak with us. "Now friends, you must get used to your spirit animals because they will be with you always. They will teach you new things. They will show you a new life and they will protect you. Remember, you have not chosen them, they have chosen you."

Sebastian lets out this incredibly loud grizzly roar and then Sir Mateo nods his head yes. I wonder what Sebastian has asked Sir Mateo?

Listening to Sir Mateo speak has awakened all of my senses. They are super keen right now and I can smell everyone and everything around me. I can feel every organ in my body, even the blood flowing through it. And I can hear even the smallest of sounds in the rainforest. A small animal in the far distance catches my eye and I watch it walk away.

"You must all be hungry. Let us go and eat. My people have prepared a celebration dinner for you. Come," Sir Mateo says while turning away from the waterfall to head back to the village.

The four of us begin to follow him and one by one, we transform back into our human bodies fully clothed.

"It's amazing how our clothes magically appear back on our bodies when we change back," I whisper to Sebastian.

"I never gave it that much thought, but you're right." Sebastian looks down at his body and clothes.

Mya turns back around and eyes the waterfall once more. She must be thinking about what Sir Mateo said about becoming immortal. Of course she would consider it. She would love to feel more powerful than the rest of us.

Thinking about what Sir Mateo has said, I realize that he hasn't told us everything we need to know. I hastily grab Sebastian's hand and whisper into his ear. "That can't be it. He hasn't told me or any one of us anything about our spirit animals. I mean, there has to be more information, right?"

"Yeah. There is definitely more, but I think he just wants to celebrate right now."

"And what was it that you said to Sir Mateo back there?" I eagerly ask Sebastian, knowing fully well that he did indeed ask Sir Mateo something of importance.

"You caught onto that, huh?"

I nod my head and smile.

"Well, I asked him what his spirit animal was," Sebastian answers.

"And?"

"And, he doesn't have one."

"So, he's not a visionary?"

"He was the son of a very spiritual man. He's also what some consider a divine shaman."

"A shaman?" I ask.

"He's more than that though. He can see things too. He's just on a different level. His life purpose is to help others heal earth and to spread peace," Sebastian says as he reaches for my hand.

Listening to this makes me realize that there is so much more to life than what meets the eye. We are in another country where there are people trying hard to heal the world. It's incredible and I'm so happy to know that I am part of all this. When I first received my gift, I was hesitant. I didn't understand it. I constantly went back and forth from accepting it to finding it a burden. Not that I'm starting to understand it a little more now, somehow I have grown. As teenagers, we're allowed to change our minds and be indecisive. It may make us seem flaky, but I don't think anyone at our age is completely confident of the decisions one might have to make. We learn to try on different hats, so to speak, to figure out who we really are and who we want to be. That's what growing up is all about. Now that I have become a visionary, I know that I have another purpose in life; I just have to figure out what that is exactly.

When we get back to the village we find a roaring fire and children running around freely. The women have all gathered near one of the huts, attending the food. One of the tribal women comes over to me and Mya and escorts us with her. My fingers reluctantly let go of Sebastian's hand and I follow her.

She brings us inside another hut and sits us down. Although I do not understand her, I can read her mannerisms. It appears that she wants to give us something. She gracefully bends over and rummages through a large clay pot. She pulls out two beautifully beaded necklaces, kisses them, and gently places them around our necks.

"Okay" Mya snidely says. I roll my eyes with disgust for Mya's inconsideration. This woman took us into her hut and basically blessed us. The woman doesn't notice Mya's rude remark and continues to take out another clay bowl. A creamy mud mixture appears to be inside. She dips two fingers into the bowl. Then she comes over to me, murmurs something softly into my ear, and gently rubs a mark on my forehead and chin.

"Thank you," I say. The woman proceeds to do the same to Mya.

"No thanks," Mya says while shaking her head no. The woman's face drops and she looks rather surprised by Mya's refusal.

"Just let her do it," I whisper. Of all the times to offend a tribal member. How does she not get it?

"Okay, well just a little," Mya says as she unwillingly accepts her gift. While the woman rubs the mud concoction onto Mya's face, the woman mumbles something under her breath and shakes her head. Perhaps it's just me, but I don't think the woman appreciated the lack of courtesy displayed by Mya.

I gently stroke my face to feel the wet mud concoction. It feels like a mask that I would normally apply to myself back home. I smell my fingers and smell the sweet aroma of earth.

"Thank you," I tell her as she gently smiles and proceeds to clean up.

Mya and I exit the hut and find Sebastian and Caleb sitting around the fire with other tribal members. As I make my way toward Sebastian, a small boy comes up to me and smiles. Mya continues toward Sebastian and Caleb as I kneel down to greet the young boy. He giggles a little and runs off.

The fragrance of the smoke fills my senses and the abundance of warmth emitted from the fire surrounds me like my down comforter at home. It brings a great feeling of security and peace. It makes sense that many cultures worship the sun. The sun provides you with warmth, light, and growth. The fire reminds me of the sun in that they are both very powerful.

I make my way over just as Mya takes a seat next to Sebastian.

"Like it? It's edible. Go on, see for yourself," Mya flirtatiously says as she pushes her face in front of Sebastian.

∞ CHAPTER 10 ∞

I stand there infuriated. I try to hide my face with a phony smile, but it doesn't work. I can feel my eyes about to bulge out of their sockets.

"Um, no thanks," Sebastian says in a matter-of-fact tone. Sebastian turns my way and gestures for me to sit by him.

"Nice mask." Sebastian laughs.

"I think it's for good luck," I tell him. Sebastian lifts his hand and swipes a little for his face too. I look at him strangely.

"Just borrowing a little luck if that's okay?"

"Of course."

At that moment, several men come out from a couple of the huts and begin chanting simultaneously. I turn my head toward the men to get a better view. This must be the entertainment. The men are dressed alike in brown leather coverings and large feathered headdresses. They are not superficial looking. They look authentic as can be and almost animal-like. The chanting becomes louder and louder as they circle the fire in quick, sharp movements. It is unlike anything I have ever seen before. My head begins to bob to the sound of their voices. The tempo is fast and appealing. Their movements begin to flow into one another and I become lost in it. Suddenly the men stop. They look down at the ground and say something that sounds meaningful, and then they walk back to the huts that they came from.

I clap with excitement for their stellar performance. It was definitely an amazing show, and I feel blessed to have witnessed it. Sebastian, Caleb, and Mya all clap too. Then Sir Mateo stands before us and raises both of his arms.

"Sitting here before you are the future saviors of our world, takers of the enemy, and lifters of the spirit, but more importantly they are our friends. Please welcome Aislinn, Mya, Sebastian, and Caleb," Sir Mateo announces to his people, quickly reciting it back in their language as well.

Sebastian stands up and says something in Spanish. It sounded something like a thank you. Even though the tribal members don't speak Spanish, it was probably a closer match to their language than English would have been.

"Now we must eat," Sir Mateo exclaims, putting out his hand for me to take. Hesitantly, I take his hand and he escorts me. Sebastian, Caleb, and Mya follow behind. The tribe has prepared a beautiful array of food. I recognize many of the fruits on the table. Avocados, coconuts, bananas, guava, mango, and pineapple beautifully line the handmade wooden table. And a plentiful selection of fish is brought to the fire. Some of the tribal people eat it raw. Since we are in a foreign country and far removed from a nearby hospital, I think I'll have my fish cooked and lessen the risk of any foodborne pathogens.

Dinner is amazing. The coconut juice is unlike any coconut juice I've had from home. It isn't in a plastic container or glass jar sitting on a shelf forever. It was handpicked and pried open for me to drink. The fruit is sweet and satisfying and the fish is amazing! It's better than a five-star restaurant. Priceless. Sebastian looks pleased as well. We have eaten out a lot together, but this is the most I've ever seen him eat in one sitting.

After dinner, Sir Mateo gathers everyone around the fire again. He shares a story with all of us, switching back and forth from English to his native language. He tells us about a little boy who endured a terrible war. This little boy was forced to survive on his own. He learned valuable lessons and one day he received the gift to see things. He was deeply connected to the rainforest, earth, nature, and animals. And the spirits of his ancestors would talk to him. The spirits showed him the way and taught him many things. One vital lesson was the importance of togetherness, meaning how to see earth and all of its organisms as one. The end of the story was that the little boy grows up and continually tries to salvage the turmoil of the earth, but that non-believers continue to shadow his teachings and wreak havoc on those who follow. This story sounds oddly familiar.

"He must be talking about himself," I whisper into Sebastian's ear.

"My thoughts exactly."

I glance over at Mya and find her rubbing Caleb's shoulders. Although he appears to be enjoying it, his body language also shows some slight discomfort. Perhaps he's worried about what the tribal people will think of this public display of affection.

I look at Sebastian and admire his humbleness and charismatic ways and I feel thankful to be here with him. He catches me staring at him and flirtatiously taps my nose.

We look back at Sir Mateo as he suddenly alters the sound of his voice. He is about to begin another story, only this time his eyes darken and his voice sounds somber.

"While visionaries have trouble with modern-day warfare, we continue to have trouble with the Líderes Rebeldes," Sir Mateo pauses and repeats himself in English. "Rebel Leaders. These Rebel Leaders are non-believers. They believe that those who speak about unity and peace are wrong and should be persecuted. They teach others this belief, and what's worse is that they teach it to their young. Their own children are learning at an early age to disregard the earth and all of its natural elements."

Watching Sir Mateo speak brings a sudden sense of sadness to me. I feel his pain, his concern, and his fear for his people. The Rebel Leaders sound a lot like the secret agency, only less sophisticated. The secret agency wants to harm us without even getting to know us. They seem to value the same things as the Rebel Leaders.

"The Rebel Leaders are always watching. They feel no compassion for the earth or its people. They are so far removed from the spiritual realm that they can't even comprehend what it means," Sir Mateo finishes.

After listening to his speech in two languages and listening to a few of the other tribal members speak out against the Rebel Leaders, my eyes start to tear. Sebastian gives me a look of concern. I shake my head and share a soft smile. "I'm just tired."

"We should get some rest," Sebastian says to the three of us.

"Sounds good. This was fun and all but maybe tomorrow we can go zip lining," Caleb jokes.

"Can I ride with you?" Mya flirts.

"If you can keep up," Caleb retorts.

"Well, I'm ready for bed," I say, hoping to change the subject. I don't know why it irritates me when they flirt with one another in front of me. I don't care for Caleb in that way. I suppose it's because Sebastian and I don't act like that in public. We have a more important agenda ahead of us.

Sebastian nods over at Sir Mateo to get his attention and he comes over to us. He can tell by our tired faces that we need to rest. He accompanies us to a hut on the outskirts of the village. It's large enough for all of us to sleep comfortably together. Safety in numbers, I console myself, when I start to regret the fact that Mya will be sleeping so close.

In the hut I find a bowl of water. The water appears clean and available for us to use. "If no one needs this water, I'm going to use a little to clean my face." No one seems to jump at the offer, so I begin to cleanse my face from the mud mask that was applied earlier.

"Save some of that water for me. I can't wait to get this crap off my face," Mya says. She hurries over and begins to wipe her face.

"Here, guys." Sebastian holds out his small jar of special mosquito repellent. "Reapply time." It's crazy to think that one bite from an infected mosquito could give us yellow fever or malaria. I rub it on lavishly. Sebastian takes a little and rubs more on my cheeks and chin.

"It's a good look for you," he says.

"You think?" I say batting my eye lashes.

The manmade hut reminds me of an exhibit at a museum. It's so surreal that I am here in Peru right now about to be sleeping in this hut, with tribal people and the visionary guru. Is this a dream? Sebastian and I comfortably settle down next to one another and take solace in each other's embrace.

"Well, guys. This has been one hell of a day!" Caleb says while cozying up next to Mya.

"Hopefully we'll learn more tomorrow," Sebastian utters, sounding somewhat drowsy.

The grotesque sound of knuckles cracking sends a shudder down my spine. I look over and find Mya stretching out her hands.

"A little neck rub will help you relax," she whispers to Caleb.

"Yeah, I read that once," says Caleb.

Sebastian and I laugh.

Just then, my eyes flutter and all is black. A vision appears to be desperately trying to come through. But it feels blocked by something. I try to attune my mind and body. I can make out quick scenes with little detail. The image makes no sense. I see Caleb and me running about. Our feet pound the lush Amazon ground. Rain pours, making the run more difficult. Then small visions of trees and smoke flash in my mind.

"What is it? What's wrong?" Sebastian whispers while holding on to me.

"I had a vision. Well, part of a vision. It was images of me running in the rain and there was smoke everywhere."

Sebastian closes his eyes while continuing to hold me.

Then his eyes finally pop open and he shares, "The only thing I got was a picture of us talking to Sir Mateo. I didn't see anything alarming."

"Maybe it's nothing. None of us have had any of our typical visions since being here. I'm sure it's my mind being scatterbrained or something."

Sebastian plants a small, gentle kiss on my lips. I clutch his hand and hold it tight.

"Get some rest. You're going to need it," he tells me. Sebastian's warm embrace puts my mind well at ease. I close my eyes and allow myself to sleep deeply.

In the middle of the night I wake suddenly from an intense dream about fire. I start to panic, but luckily I find myself safely nestled in Sebastian's arms. Sometimes I can't tell the difference between my dreams and visions. And since being here, I can definitely tell that things have changed. I breathe deeply to relax myself. *It was just a dream*. I take one final look at Sebastian's sleeping face and drift back to sleep.

The sound of children playing awakes me early in the morning. I sit up and notice that Caleb has already left the hut and Mya is still peacefully sleeping. She actually seems pleasant while she's asleep. Suddenly she wakes up and I quickly turn away.

"Good morning," Mya says as she stretches and glances around the hut, presumably looking for Caleb.

"Morning," I say, trying to sound cordial.

"Any more visions?" Sebastian questions while rising to his feet.

"No, strange. It seemed so out of place. Like that one I had at the secret agency campsite where I saw the female agent. Except this one was way choppier. I hope it's not a warning."

"Warning for what?" Mya nosily chimes in.

"Nothing. It's nothing really," I say.

"She had a brief vision, that's all," Sebastian answers.

"Well, it's probably nothing. None of us can access our visions," Mya says, trying to sound like she knows what she's talking about, when really she doesn't.

The three of us leave the hut and venture into the warm Amazonian air. One deep breath feeds my body with relaxation. It is so fresh and real here. We head over toward Caleb and Sir Mateo, who are standing next to one another.

"Good morning. Sleep well?" Sir Mateo asks.

"Yes, thank you," I reply.

"You must eat and then we will go to the sacred grounds. There you will learn more about yourselves," Sir Mateo says reassuringly. Finally, some good news.

Sir Mateo leads us to where four women have arranged a table for us. The women hold out wooden bowls for us, encouraging us to take some food. I graciously take the bowl and load it up. I select a white, grainy mixture, which resembles risotto. I top it off with what appears to be some sort of meat.

"You are a very brave girl, Aislinn," Caleb says while eating some fruit.

"Why do you say that?"

"Well, that meat that you have right there was hanging from the trees earlier."

"What do you mean?"

"Hanging from trees," he says expressively while jumping in the air.

I squint at Caleb's weird behavior while slowly munching on my breakfast. Caleb chuckles and decides to give in, since apparently I'm unable to connect the dots to his unusual performance. "It's monkey meat!" he shouts.

I spit out the meat faster than the speed of light.

"Oh my God!" I almost vomit at the thought. "I ate monkey meat."

Sebastian turns around to see what all the commotion is about and Caleb practically laughs himself to death. Mya takes a seat next to us and rolls her eyes, as if I can't see her.

"I'm glad you're amused," I say to Caleb. "Now I've probably offended everyone here." Nervously, I look around and find only a few of the women staring at me.

"Relax. You're fine. Besides, now you're able to say that you tried monkey meat," he chides while still laughing.

"That's great," I say sarcastically. Caleb winks at me and smiles.

Sebastian sits next to me and offers me some of his fruit.

"No thanks, I'm not hungry anymore."

I'm usually always hungry. But I can't bear the fact that a cute little monkey was sacrificed for this meal. I sip on my water and try not to think about it.

"It's not like they kill the animals for sport. I hear that it's actually a very sacred matter. They show gratitude for the animals they sacrifice," Caleb shares, trying to make me feel better. I casually smile, but I'm still not eating it.

As the others finish their meals, I notice the children of the village running around carefree. They seem so at ease and happy here. They don't see us as strangers anymore. The women move about their regular routines and some of the men have gone off for the day.

Sir Mateo gracefully walks over to us and asks us to take a small journey with him today. Today is the day we visit the sacred grounds.

"Should we grab out backpacks?" I ask Sebastian.

"You guys can leave your backpacks here if you want. They should be safe. I'll bring mine in case we need anything," Sebastian answers.

"Less baggage. Works for me," Caleb shrugs.

"Me too. My shoulders are killing me," Mya agrees as she reaches for her own shoulder and rubs it. However, I beg to disagree. It's going to take a lot more than leaving her backpack behind to eliminate the baggage she comes with. I smirk.

The four of us follow Sir Mateo out of the village and three men follow behind us. Periodically, I turn to peek at them. It's slightly uncomfortable knowing that there are people trailing behind you. I smile respectfully at them, but none of them smile back. Perhaps I'm paranoid because of the secret agency.

Our journey takes us well into an hour through the thick tropical rainforest floor. We are greeted by several monkeys and beautiful exotic birds. The sounds of the rainforest are delightfully intoxicating. Every bird call, every monkey noise, every mammal is telling their story as we navigate through their home. None of us talk during our hike. It's too remarkable to interrupt these sounds with our insignificant words.

Even though it's early in the day, it's rather difficult to tell. The warm sun skillfully hides behind the enormously tall trees, making it appear much darker than it really is.

"I thought it was supposed to rain a lot in the rainforest," Mya asks, breaking the silence.

"I think it's the dry season right now," Sebastian answers.

"This year the rain has not been enough. It shows. The circle of life has become affected by this. Very sad," Sir Mateo chimes in.

Finally, Sir Mateo stops walking and pulls aside some smaller trees so we can escape the crowded forest floor and enter into a lush, open field filled with large, unusual stones.

"How did these stones get here?" I ask.

"No one knows how. But they are here for a reason. These stones hold the forces of nature. They are very imperative to your past," Sir Mateo says solemnly.

The four stones are huge. They are each about the size of a school bus. They seem so out of place out here. It's like they fell from the sky and landed in perfect order.

"Wow, it's like visiting the Stonehenge in England. Only without the ring," Caleb says.

"Almost," says Sebastian.

"Come," Sir Mateo calls as he walks closer to the stones. "Mya, touch this stone."

Mya looks around and says, "Sure, ladies first, right?"

The sound of her voice continues to irk me for reasons unbeknownst. Mya lifts her right hand and places it on the first stone to our left where Sir Mateo directed.

"Now, close your eyes," Sir Mateo instructs.

Mya closes her eyes and the rest of us stare at her, not knowing what to expect. Mya's body jolts back as her hand remains on the rock. Her eyelids flutter in different directions. I grab Sebastian's hand as I watch her body move spasmodically. It resembles an out of body experience.

"Wow!" Mya shrieks. "That was insane!"

"What happened? What did you see?" Caleb questions.

"I saw myself before I was born. It was strange, like I was in another world as another form and I was told that I would be a visionary. Then I saw my mother give birth to me. I was stuck in her birth canal. Finally, I came into this world and I was terrified. And the most amazing part," Mya says while taking a deep breath, "was that I got to see how I received my gift. I got it when I was only two years old. I hit my head on the corner of a wall in my house. Right after that, I started having visions. I can't believe it! I never knew how it happened until now."

The three of us stare at Mya with disbelief. If that stone really can see the past, then it's a miracle.

"What about your future? Does it tell you what your destiny will be?" Caleb asks.

"No. It cannot see more than the past. It is here to help you remember things you may have forgotten," Sir Mateo says while signaling for Caleb to go next.

"Why don't you go and see for yourself."

Caleb quickly runs up and heads over to the second rock. He kisses his hand and places it on the rock. His body does the same awkward movements as Mya's had done and his eyelids flutter wildly.

"Hope I didn't look like that," Mya mumbles.

Suddenly, he opens his eyes and says, "Incredible!" He paces back and forth to gather his thoughts.

"I saw everything in a matter of seconds. Like a DVD on fast forward," Caleb says while catching his breath. "It's the craziest thing I've ever seen in my entire life. I saw how my mother contracted her illness. I saw how I got hit with the baseball and I saw my brain light up, like a lightning bolt. Oh my God. I want to do it again!"

"That sounds too good to be true," Sebastian says. His voice sounds skeptical.

"Ah, but it is. You're next," Sir Mateo says to Sebastian.

Sebastian lets go of my hand and walks up to the stone. He gracefully places his strong fingers over the third stone and closes his eyes. His body jolts, but his eyes do not flutter. Watching Sebastian makes me feel uneasy.

"You're right," Sebastian says while glancing at Caleb and Mya. "It's incredible. It's like everything that ever happened to you is being showcased all over again. I saw my parents the day of the accident. I saw their souls leave their bodies."

Then Sebastian looks over at me. "I saw myself as another being. But the stranger part is that I saw you." He continues to stare at me. "Images of you at different times of your life flashed through my brain as if I were there the whole time. No real story line, just you." He swallows. "It was unexplainable."

My eyes are fixated on Sebastian's. Could this be real? What does this mean? Sir Mateo signals for me to step up to the fourth stone. I slowly head to the stone, taking deep breaths as I walk. My hands are trembling and my heart is beating loudly.

I take in a deep breath and close my eyes. Everything happens so fast. I feel like my brain can't keep up with the images. There is too much going on to focus on just one thing.

And just when I think that I cannot take a second more, my eyes shoot open and I see everyone staring at me. Uncomfortable silence fills the warm air and now it's my turn to share my experience. A part of me wants to stay silent and mull things over a bit, but I know that it wouldn't be fair. Mya clears her throat as they stand there patiently waiting for me to divulge. I ignore her and look at Sebastian who smiles at me.

"I saw everything." I close my eyes tight, trying to see it all again. "I saw my transformation into the hawk. I saw its insides as if it were my own body. I saw myself living a life, but it wasn't with my parents. I was living with very different people, as if they were from a different era. The way they dressed seemed so old-fashioned. I was still a visionary but it was different. Maybe it was my future? I don't know."

I stop talking because I don't know how to further describe what I saw. How can I explain this vision if I don't even understand it myself? I look to Sir Mateo for guidance.

Everyone continues to stare at me silently. Sir Mateo takes my hand and closes his eyes. I stand there motionless and watch him.

He opens his eyes and says, "The stone showed you your past. You had a different family long ago. You were a visionary then and you're a visionary now and you've come back to this time to finish what was started."

"What?" I ask, alarmed.

"Aislinn, don't be scared. It will all come back to you. You have to trust yourself, and then you will know the truth. Believe."

"I don't understand."

Sir Mateo's eyes soften as he puts his hand on my shoulder.

"You were a visionary in a past life and you were brought back here to finish the war. You will remember soon what it is you need to accomplish."

"But, I fell in the school cafeteria. It was an accident!" I exclaim.

I can feel two small tears stream down my face and drop below my jawbone. I wipe the wet from my face.

"There are no accidents," Sir Mateo says in a serious voice. "Only purpose."

Sebastian comes near me and puts his arm around me. "It's okay, Aislinn. You're not alone."

"Thank you," I say, feeling more lost than I have ever felt before.

Knowing that I am supposed to fight some war that I can't even remember brings about a sudden feeling of urgency. I need to know more now!

"Sir Mateo," I call out just as he starts walking away. "I can do this, I just, I need to know more."

Sir Mateo stands still and nods his head. "My dear, I only know what you see. You have to reach deep inside your heart and pull out your memories. It is within those memories that you will find the truth. Do not be afraid. With time you will see."

I'm fixated upon Sir Mateo's dark brown eyes. This is the most information I've heard in a while and I wish I could understand it better.

"Come now, we are not done yet," Sir Mateo tells us.

Without another word, we continue on toward our next stop. Sebastian holds my hand and I squeeze his hand tight. He is the only thing that makes sense right now.

Faint whispers of Mya and Caleb joking around buzz through my ears. But I block them out, trying to concentrate on what I just saw. It was amazing to say the least. I was able to see things from my past. Apparently, it was my very early past. I thought that it was crazy seeing the visions that I get now that I'm a visionary, but this certainly tops the cake.

"What do you think all that meant back there," I whisper to Sebastian, hoping that no one can hear me.

"I don't know. This is more than I expected. But I do know one thing."

"Oh yeah, what's that?"

"That we're more connected than I thought."

∞ CHAPTER 11 ∞

After a vigorous thirty minutes of walking through dense terrain, Sir Mateo announces something to the men who have been accompanying us. They stand back and position themselves to be on guard duty. The rest of us follow Sir Mateo to another section of the rainforest that has been cleared out. Only this clearing is more intriguing than the last. Ancient ruins surround the open region.

"I don't remember learning about this being part of the Amazon Rainforest," I share.

"That's because this place is unknown to man, well, most men that is," Sir Mateo confirms. "Five hundred years ago, this ancient land belonged to our ancestors. It was home to visionaries and many different healers. It was a very sacred place. A wonderful place."

"What happened?" Caleb asks.

"A war! A terrible war," Sir Mateo solemnly says while taking a seat on a large stone. "This place was a great empire filled with spiritual beings. This is where it all began. Close your eyes and picture the Amazonian people moving about with their everyday business. They were busy teaching each other about the power of connection to the earth. Many different rituals were held here celebrating the purity of Mother Nature. Our people had a special way with nature. They could make things grow with the touch of a finger. They could heal with a simple blessing. They could entice animals to come near with the beauty of their voice and more importantly, they could transform evil to good. But, they were being watched by terrible people who wanted them to pay for their advances in life. These people were evil. They wanted the power for themselves. They did not care about the earth or its magical forces. They were ruthless and lacked compassion."

"Líderes Rebeldes," Sebastian mutters.

"Yes," Sir Mateo confirms.

With inquiring eyes, the four of us stare at Sir Mateo.

Sir Mateo sighs. "So a war broke out. More like a malicious attack on innocent people. They raided the empire. They burned down their homes and killed everyone. Well, almost everyone."

"Except you?" Sebastian asks.

My, he's quick. That took me a minute or two to figure out.

Sir Mateo closes his eyes and nods his head. "They missed a scared little boy hiding in the brush. A little boy who would never forget what they have done."

This is the same story that Sir Mateo told last night around the fire.

"But this was so long ago. How is this possible?" Mya asks.

"You're immortal!" I say with such astonishment that I barely get the words out straight.

Sir Mateo smiles at me and answers, "That I am."

I've never met anyone immortal before. How could this be real? But what I'm witnessing is very real. This is a sacred man with a deep compassion for the earth. He's a survivor and a living hero.

Mya's eyes expand with bewilderment. "What's it like? I mean, it must be amazing to be able to live forever," she asks, sounding mesmerized.

"What's it like, you ask? There are no words that can describe it." He looks around the ancient ruins and then attempts to answer Mya's question again.

"As a little boy I used to wander all around. I had so much energy. I wanted to play in the rainforest and act like a wild animal. It was who I was, inside. My mother would tell me to stay close and to never play in the Agua Magia. But my curious nature led me there. It was so beautiful; I simply could not resist it. It called to me and I answered it by carelessly jumping in. I was hot and tired from playing all day. It was the dry season. So I did what any thirsty young boy would do."

"You drank it," Caleb says intently.

"So it's true then?" I ask.

"I don't know for sure. That is what I've been told. But, here I am and here you are today."

What an incredible story. One I will never forget.

"This place was my home and the home of my family. Look around if you like. It's quite beautiful."

The ruins are an intricate maze of stones and paths. It's breathtaking. We meander around aimlessly, mystified by what we see.

"Look over here, guys," Caleb calls.

Sebastian and I make our way over to Caleb and find him standing on some sort of throne. There are rocks strategically stacked high in perfect order. It is a seat fit for a king.

"It suits you," I joke.

"It would suit you better," Caleb says flirtatiously. I look away.

"Check this out," Sebastian says. Sebastian points to a large wall covered with ancient markings. Beautifully sketched animal pictures embellish the stone. The detail is impeccable. Excitedly, we scan wall after wall.

"Where's Mya?" Caleb suddenly asks. The three of us look around and realize that Mya is not with us.

"Mya!" Sebastian calls out. No response.

"Mya!" Caleb calls. Still no response.

"She couldn't have gone too far," Sebastian says.

The three of us frantically start searching all around the ancient ruins while calling out her name.

"I think Mya may have had other plans," Sir Mateo says. His voice sounds sarcastic mixed with doubt.

"The Agua Magia!" I call out.

"We've got to stop her before it's too late," Sebastian says with great alarm.

If we don't stop her, she might drink the water and become immortal. Making a decision like that, should take time and thought. I wouldn't drink it. We don't even know what the consequences are yet.

"I'll go," Caleb says. "How do I get there?"

"Forget it. I'll go. I remember how to get there. Stay here and keep Aislinn safe!" Sebastian yells to Caleb.

"Of course," Caleb assures Sebastian.

"I'll be back," Sebastian says. He quickly plants a kiss on my lips and takes off before I can tell him not to.

"I can't believe Mya would do this," I say, feeling pissed off since it interferes with our exploration and my time with Sebastian.

"I can. It's all she's talked about since she found out about it," Caleb says.

"That's crazy. I would never even consider it, no offense, Sir Mateo. It just scares me."

"It's okay. I understand. It's a tempting force. But, one should consider it very carefully before deciding, because there are no returns," Sir Mateo says.

"So you wouldn't consider it? Like at all?" Caleb questions me.

"No. Not at all. It's too much to even think about. I can't imagine living alone forever without my family. That's just nuts."

"I don't know. I mean I wouldn't do it, but I would think about it," Caleb admits.

"It's going to take them some time to get back. We can head back to the village if you like," Sir Mateo offers.

"No, I would rather wait here. What if they come back? They won't know where we went," I answer.

"You can go back if you need to. We will wait here," Caleb tells Sir Mateo.

"I will stay. I would not want you to get lost. It's a jungle out there," Sir Mateo jokes.

Caleb and I laugh.

"Do you mind if I look around here some more? It is so amazing," I ask.

"Please. Look around. I will wait over there," Sir Mateo says while pointing to the other men who have been standing on guard.

"Do you mind if I accompany you? I was told to keep you safe," Caleb asks. Here is the playful Caleb. I haven't seen this side of him since the last time we went to the Coffee Beanery together.

"Are you sure I'm not the one keeping you safe?"

"Funny," Caleb snorts.

We walk back toward the animal sketchings.

"Remarkable, aren't they?" I say amazed. My mouth remains open as I stare at these ancient drawings. It's like being on an archaeological find.

"They are," Caleb says while tracing the indent in the stone with his finger. "I can't believe that Sir Mateo has been here for over five hundred years."

"I know. It's crazy," I begin to say until my eyes freeze. I start to have a vision.

"What is it? What did you see?" Caleb questions.

"That obvious huh?" I know I need to control my eyes when I get a vision. I hate it when I forget to do that.

Caleb shrugs his shoulders and smiles while looking into my eyes.

"The details aren't really clear. But, I keep seeing fire and people yelling. It's starting to creep me out."

"What do you mean you keep seeing this? Have you had this same vision before?"

"Yes," I admit. "Once."

"We should go get Sir Mateo and find Sebastian and Mya. Maybe it's something important."

"Yeah, you're probably r-" My words are interrupted by the sudden sound of men screaming.

∞ CHAPTER 12 ∞

"Oh my God! It's happening!" I shriek.

"Come on," Caleb grabs my hand and pulls me along with him. We run to the other side of the ancient ruins to get a better view as opposed to running right into whatever it is that's happening. It's difficult to see through the dilapidated ruins and the outskirt of the forest. Strange men are fighting with Sir Mateo's men. Perhaps it's the Rebel Leaders. The invading men hold torches and continue to yell viciously. Sir Mateo's men fight back. Sounds of pain and agony echo in the dense rainforest.

It's terribly frightening to think that we are being attacked by these people and it's even more frightening knowing that Sebastian isn't nearby. I shudder at the thought of losing Sebastian. Within seconds the screaming stops and Sir Mateo and his men succumb to the unknown invaders. A few bodies lay still on the forest floor.

"Let's get out of here," Caleb whispers. Caleb has fear painted on his face.

The two of us turn around simultaneously and start running. We head into the surrounding thick rainforest. Not only do we have to be extremely careful not to make a sound, and potentially run the risk of announcing our presence to the enemy, but now we must travel through the rainforest with no guide, no protection, and worst of all, no Sebastian. This can't be happening. How are we going to get out of here? How will Sebastian find us?

"We need to find Sebastian and Mya. I think I remember the way back to the Agua Magia, I'm just not a hundred percent positive," Caleb says. His voice is stern. I can tell he's nervous.

"Between the two of us, we got a pretty good shot," I remind him. "How hard can it be?"

Caleb looks at me with quizzical eyes. I suppose he doubts my confidence. I like to think positive in situations like this, although I'm starting to become a tad doubtful as well.

I follow Caleb through the forest. We are fairly far from the assailants now. In fact, we are very far from everything and my rapid breathing is the only thing I can hear.

"Are you sure you know where you're going? Because I could have sworn I've seen that tree before."

"All the trees look the same, Aislinn. How can you tell you've seen that particular tree before?"

"By its markings, look," I protest.

Caleb goes up to the tree and stares at it.

"Okay. So maybe we went in one big circle. Do you have a better plan?"

I stare at him and think about our dilemma. I really don't have a better plan. I expected him to come up with one. And then it dawns on me; we need to access our powers. Since we're out of the ancient ruins, maybe our visions will work better.

"Our powers!"

"What?" Caleb asks. His eyebrows are raised and his eyes are wide. He looks confused.

"We need to access our powers, our visions; anything that we can do to help connect to our visions would be helpful right about now. Just concentrate and see what happens," I say hastily.

Caleb smiles and turns around. He probably can't concentrate while facing me and I don't blame him. I feel a little awkward myself when I do this. I close my eyes and hope for the best. My mind and body are in a relaxed state and I start to center my thoughts on our current situation.

"Did it work for you?" Caleb asks.

I ignore him and continue trying. I block out all sounds except the sound of my controlled breath. And nothing happens.

"No. I got nothing."

"I don't get this place," Caleb says, sounding frustrated. "When we entered the rainforest, an invisible force surrounded our entry. When we headed out near the Agua Magia, our powers heightened and we transformed into our spirit animals and now nothing."

"It's like there's another force interfering with our ability to access our visions. Not the secret agency, but something else. Maybe that group of men that attacked Sir Mateo's people are somehow blocking our visions," I say.

Caleb angrily grunts, "This is crazy!"

It's getting late and we've made little progress. Knowing that the rainforest is home to the anaconda, jaguar, poison dart frog, and many other dangerous species, I begin to worry.

"If only I could change into the red-tailed hawk. Then I could fly up high and find a way out of here."

"Did you try?" Caleb asks.

I nod my head. I tried when I was concentrating on accessing a vision, but sadly I didn't sense or feel any connection to my spirit animal.

"Or maybe we could climb to the top of these trees and get a better view of the area. We'd be able to see Sebastian and Mya," I say hopefully while gazing up at the infinite sight of trees.

"Good luck. These trees reach heights of two hundred feet and higher. One wrong move and you're history."

He's right, again. I just wish there was a faster way to find them. We could travel through this endless forest for weeks and still make no progress. And what's worse, there's always the possibility that Sebastian and Mya are looking for us and we might actually be getting farther apart than when we originally started.

"Look, it's getting late and I think we should plan on making some kind of shelter that we can spend the night in," Caleb suggests.

"No, not yet. It's still daylight. We should keep looking," I insist. I need to find Sebastian.

"But, what happens when it gets dark? How are we going to see what we're doing?"

I realize Caleb has a good point. But the thought of spending the night in the wild rainforest without Sebastian is excruciating and most of all, terrifying.

"Good point. How about we search just a little while longer and if we don't find them, then we can prepare for the night?"

"Okay, Captain Hawk," Caleb says with an edge of sarcasm. I glare at him and move on. We need to keep trying to find Sebastian and Mya.

∞ CHAPTER 13 ∞

Sebastian & Mya

Sebastian runs through the rainforest as if he were on a clear running track. He moves under and over brush with little effort. He remembers the way to the Agua Magia with no problem. In less than a half hour, he arrives at the beautiful infamous waters. Only he doesn't see Mya anywhere. Frantically, he looks all around, and then the faint sound of a low whimper leads him toward her.

Mya is sitting on the forest floor on the opposite side of Agua Magia. She's bent over with her face in her hands, sobbing. Sebastian notices her wet clothes and soaking wet hair.

"Mya, what the hell are you thinking?" Sebastian yells, sounding rather irritated and downright pissed off.

Mya looks up, surprised to see Sebastian.

"I wasn't. I wasn't thinking at all."

By the looks of her red face and swollen eyes, Sebastian can tell that she has been crying for some time.

"I didn't mean to yell. You just worried us."

"I worried you and your sweet little girlfriend? I hardly think so." Mya sounds more like her sassy self.

Sebastian stands there impatiently waiting to find out if Mya took a sip from the water or not.

Mya lifts her head up and looks into Sebastian's eyes. "You want to know if I drank it, don't you?"

"Did you?"

"Well, I surely took a dip in it, that's for sure."

"So you didn't drink it?"

"What do you think?"

Sebastian could tell that the conversation was becoming a game. A game that wasn't worth playing. If Mya did indeed drink from the Agua Magia, then that was her business.

"Come on. I don't have time for this. We need to get back," Sebastian stresses.

Mya reluctantly stands up and wrings out her short, dark hair. "Fine with me. I'm done here anyway."

Sebastian leads the way through the dense rainforest. He enjoys the smell of the earth and the vibrant colors of the forest, despite having to accompany Mya back to the group.

Suddenly, the noise of crackling leaves and an uneasy feeling stops Sebastian dead in his tracks.

"What? What is it?" Mya asks. She seems alarmed as she frantically looks all around.

Sebastian turns and gives Mya a threatening look to "shut up." Mya shoots Sebastian big eyes in return. He scans the environment slowly so as not to miss anything, but seeing anything further than thirty feet ahead is wishful thinking. The wet forest floor is smothered with exotic plants and extremely large tree roots. The lack of sunlight due to the overlarge canopy trees impairs their view drastically.

Mya begins to anxiously stomp her leg.

"Shhh," Sebastian replies. He continues to scan the woods.

But Mya continues to jump around making even more noise. She shakes her leg and hits her pants.

Sebastian quickly determines the cause of her erratic behavior. Ants. Fire ants!

Sebastian runs over to Mya to help her, but she won't stand still. She is all over the place screaming in agony and running in circles while pulling off her pants and shoes. Sebastian tries not to laugh, but it is almost impossible.

Finally, Mya rids herself of the fire ants and heads toward Sebastian who is beside himself.

After regaining his composure, Sebastian wipes the smile off his face and takes a quick glance at Mya's leg, "Luckily, you only have a couple of bites."

"First a giant anaconda, now this. What's next?" Mya exclaims while gazing into Sebastian's eyes. "Well, as long as you're here to save me, I guess I'll be all right. Can you help me? Please."

Sebastian chuckles at Mya's flirtatious statement. She has that way about her when it comes to men. Sebastian has no choice but to help rectify the situation and ease her pain from the bites. He grabs a small jar from his cargo pants and spreads a small amount of the cream onto Mya's leg.

"That feels so much better. What is that stuff?"

"Special stuff for all kinds of stuff."

"I see."

Mya's eyes stay locked on Sebastian's as she reaches for her pants and puts herself back together. Sebastian uncomfortably looks away.

"Maybe since I took a dip in that magic water my bites will heal faster or maybe it's just a bunch of hocus pocus," Mya grunts. "I don't feel any different. Not yet anyways."

"Shhh."

Sebastian hears the same noises as earlier, only this time they sound closer.

"We need to get out of here, fast," He grabs her arm and they hurriedly run through the thick rainforest.

"Did you get a vision?" Mya asks while panting from running.

"No, I heard something. Just keep going."

"It was probably," Mya pauses to catch her breath, "just an animal or something."

"No. It's not an animal. It was human. A few humans."

Finally, Sebastian and Mya stop running as they reach a small, dark river. Sebastian looks back and closes his eyes. "Come on!" He scowls not understanding why he is unable to access his visions. Sebastian begins to feel as if the Amazon Rainforest decides who and when visionaries can access their visions.

"Agh," Sebastian grunts in disgust. "What about you, Miss Immortal? Are you getting any visions?"

"Just the one of you becoming pissy."

"Haha," laughs a sarcastic Sebastian.

"No, really. What has gotten into you? Ever since you started seeing Aislinn, you've been different, on edge even."

"Let's see. Secret Agents. Crazy Amazon Rainforest, a ton of unknown answers about being a visionary and, oh yeah, being stuck with someone who takes off trying to become immortal. I'd say that would be more than enough reasons for anyone to become edgy," Sebastian answers while quoting the word, edgy, with his fingers.

"I don't know. I'd say she's got you wrapped around her tiny little finger."

"Now's not the time to have this conversation, Mya. Probably never is a better time."

"It's okay, Sebastian. I'm here if you want to talk," Mya says in an alluring voice while trailing Sebastian's upper arm with her fingers. Sebastian looks down at Mya's hand.

"Could you stop? Please."

"Sorry. I was just reminiscing about that time we had together."

"Mya, that was a long time ago and nothing ever happened."

"Um, I beg to differ," Mya answers back sarcastically.

"You were drunk. I brought you home. End of story."

"Except for a couple of small details. Like the part where you tucked me in and gave me a goodnight kiss."

Sebastian shakes his head. "I brought you into your home and left you on your couch. You were plastered. I did what any Good Samaritan would do."

"And you kissed me!"

"In your dreams. I never kissed you. You grabbed my head and tried to kiss me. But, I never kissed you. Get it through your thick head!" Sebastian's face is becoming red with rage.

Mya mischievously grins and says, "If that's how you choose to remember it."

"It's not how I remember it. It's the truth! Now are you done? Because we need to keep going. We have to find the others."

"I hear she's a great singer. But you probably already know that," Mya continues with her outlandish statements.

"Who's a great singer?" Sebastian asks sounding confused.

"Now that I think of it, Aislinn might have a little thing for Caleb. He's a good singer too."

"Look, Mya. Whatever game you're playing, you're playing alone. I've got things to do and this isn't one of them."

"Oh, I'm not playing any games. Well, actually I think Aislinn is the one doing all the playing."

Sebastian ignores Mya and continues walking alongside the dark river, being careful not to trip over any of the large tree roots. The conversation is clearly a waste of his time and energy.

"You know Aislinn went out with Caleb, don't you?" says Mya in a cunning voice.

Sebastian slows his fast-paced stride and stops walking, but doesn't turn around. Mya smiles mischievously as she watches him.

"Oh, you didn't know? Aislinn went to the Coffee Beanery with Caleb. I thought she would have told you. I believe it was on karaoke night, and I heard they had a pretty amazing time together. It's cute isn't it? Two visionaries falling in love with one another." Mya inches closer to Sebastian.

Sebastian furiously turns around to face Mya. He comes in so close that their faces are about two inches from one another. Mya begins to pucker her lips and close her eyes.

Instead of kissing Mya, Sebastian whispers into her ear, "Let me tell you something. If you do anything, and I mean anything to hinder my relationship with Aislinn-"

Mya interrupts, "What are you going to do? Hurt me?"

"Let's just say you better watch yourself, before I leave your ass in this jungle to survive on your own."

Mya scowls and says nothing as she slowly backs away from Sebastian.

"Now, let's go!" he yells.

∞ CHAPTER 14 ∞

Aislinn & Caleb

After walking aimlessly for an unknown amount of time, we come across a small stream.

"Yes, water," I cry as I race to quench my thirst and wet my sweaty face. I never realized how important water really is.

"Wait," Caleb calls. "Wait," he hollers again while trying to catch up to me.

"What is it?"

"You shouldn't just drink that."

"Why not?"

"It could have parasites in it that can make you sick. We should boil it first."

"What? It's probably the cleanest water on the earth. Look at it."

"I didn't say chemicals or pollution. I said parasites. Look, it's probably fine, but just to be safe we should make a fire and boil it. I wish we had the iodine tincture, but Sebastian has it."

"You're right. We should sterilize it." I frown with disappointment that I can't just drink it. "Let's boil it then," I say, hoping this won't take too long.

Caleb looks around for materials and begins gathering some branches.

"How about these?" I offer while picking up some wood nearby.

"Too damp. We need dry wood," he proclaims.

Caleb pulls down some low hanging branches. The wood he found on the forest floor was too damp to use. He carefully places the branches against one another, making a pyramid shape.

"And how are you going to light this, Ranger Caleb?"

"Five years in scouts didn't go to waste. Watch and learn." Caleb winks at me. At least he's showing humor during a time like this. I suppose I should lighten up a little and give him a break. Besides, if we do get this fire burning, perhaps it will signal Sebastian as to our location.

Caleb finagles with the sticks in hopes of lighting a fire. I look around in search of anything that might be useful. I find nothing and head back to Caleb.

Caleb looks at my face. "Of course this would be a whole lot easier if I had my backpack, but who doesn't welcome a challenge." I smile.

Caleb continues to try and light a fire with a few grunts of frustration. Luckily, a small flame finally sparks and he arranges a small fire.

"Okay. I need to learn that," I say, impressed.

Caleb smiles. "I'll show you sometime.

The fire gives me instant relief and renewed strength. We both stand there for a minute admiring the miracle of fire.

"Aislinn, we don't have anything to put the water in though. Guess I didn't think about that."

"Let's look around for something that we can use," I say.

The two of us scour the area endlessly. We find absolutely nothing that would suffice as an adequate container for boiling water.

"Should we just take our chances and drink from the stream?" I ask.

"I don't know," Caleb admits.

Caleb and I follow the stream a short way and find that it connects to a pool of water. "I would love to take a dip in that right now," I say, admiring the beauty of the glistening water.

"Want to?"

"It's probably not a good idea. We don't have anything to change into."

And without even answering me, Caleb whips off his shirt, pants, and shoes, leaving only his boxer briefs to cover his essentials. His huge biceps are barely noticeable compared to his six-pack abs.

"Are you crazy? What are you doing?" I fret as Caleb jumps in.

"What does it look like I'm doing? I'm taking a quick dip to cool off. Come on in. It's amazing."

"I probably shouldn't. I'll live vicariously through you."

"Come on. Are you worried about what Sebastian would think?" Caleb says with a flirtatious voice. He smiles and points to the water.

Well actually, I am worried about what Sebastian would think, but I'm not about to let him know that.

"No. Of course not."

"Do you think that if Sebastian ran into a pool of water in this hot and humid rainforest that he wouldn't jump in right now?"

He has a point. Standing there dripping in sweat and parched as ever, I decide to stop over-thinking everything and just do it.

"Okay. I'm coming in. Just, turn around would you?"

"Of course." Caleb turns around with a mischievous grin.

Without further ado, I take off my shirt since I have a cami on underneath. I quickly pull off my pants and place them near Caleb's. I nervously take one deep breath and jump in before he can see anything.

"Oh my god. It is amazing."

The water is perfect and it feels exceptionally refreshing. I sip mouthfuls of water to satisfy my extreme thirst. It's so fresh and clean. It's unlike any other body of water that I've been in. No pool, lake, or stream back home could compare.

"Told you," Caleb says while diving underneath the water. Anxiously, I look around and find him swimming directly toward me.

"Don't do that."

"Don't do what? Go under the water?" He laughs.

"You know what I mean." I swim to the other end of the glistening pool of crystal clear water and try my best to wrap my hair in a bun without any hair accessories. I never cared for hair all over my face while swimming. It just gets in the way.

"So, do you miss him?" Caleb asks while swimming toward me once again.

"What are you talking about?" I decide to play dumb to Caleb's questions. I need a minute to gather my thoughts. Why is he asking me this? Caleb swims even closer to me, causing me to back up to the embankment. Water drips down his face and onto his lips. He doesn't answer me. Instead, he just stares at me, waiting for a response.

"Sebastian? Of course I miss him," I say. "Why? Do you miss Mya?"

Caleb laughs. "Mya? Hardly. No, it's not like that."

"What is it like then?"

"Mya is just a friend. She's too crazy for me."

"So crazy is bad?"

"No. Not all crazy. Just Mya crazy."

Caleb is now just a couple of inches from me. Since I only have on my underwear and cami, I become uneasy and move back a little. Caleb looks at me and says, "What? Do I smell?"

"No, it's just-" Water suddenly splashes in my face interrupting me. I wipe my eyes and soon realize that Caleb just splashed me in the face.

"Did you just splash me?"

"Nope," Caleb says as he flirtatiously splashes me again.

"You so just splashed me."

"Uh-uh," he murmurs as he does it again. I splash him back continuously and we have an all-out splash war. His splashes are much harder, so I stop splashing and curl my head into my hands and play victim. I figure it's my only chance for survival.

"What's wrong? Are you all right?" Caleb asks as he stops splashing to see if I'm okay.

I snidely lift my head and yell, "Gotcha" while splashing him wildly in the face.

"You better run," he says.

"You mean swim," I correct as I hurriedly try to get away, but he catches me.

"Where are you going?" he asks while holding on to me and tickling me. I turn around and beg him to stop. I was never much for tickling. Also, I think he's getting a little too touchy.

Caleb stops tickling me and looks deeply into my eyes and for just a second, I forget where I am. I stare back at him and everything stops. My throat swallows water left from the splashing. And just as he is about to presumably kiss me, thunder rumbles in the sky. A sign from above has clearly spoken saying that this play was way too much, and I couldn't agree more. What am I doing?

"I think we should get out of here," I say.

"Yeah, you're right."

We hastily get out of the water and put on our clothes. I almost fall over trying to put on my pants and Caleb catches my elbow. It reminds me of Sebastian when he does that. My sweet Sebastian. Oh, how I miss him. It's funny that Caleb only acts like this with me when Sebastian isn't around. I feel guilty now for having gone in the water in the first place. I don't feel anything for Caleb and hopefully he doesn't have any feelings for me either.

The mud on my feet makes my shoes feel squishy and gross. I push them onto my feet and try to ignore the wet, slimy feeling inside of them. We hurry back to the fire and find that it has nearly died out.

"Guess it won't last anyways with the storm coming and all," I say, trying to break the tension.

"True. But there is one thing we need."

"What's that?" I ask.

"Shelter," Caleb replies. "We need shelter from the storm."

"Well, we don't have enough time to make a shelter. Look," I point up toward the canopy where a small opening of the sky is visible. The blue sky has rapidly become dark and a cool breeze has started to pick up.

"Come on, we need to find shelter now!" Caleb shouts while holding out his hand for me to climb up over a large tree limb.

"Thanks."

The two of us hurriedly dash through the thick forest in search of a safe resting spot for shelter. Rain starts to fall from the sky more rapidly. It has changed from a slow drip to a hard downfall. Now I really feel the rain, as the canopy trees can't protect us any longer. Sudden bursts of thunder make me jump. Eventually, the rain starts to feel like small pellets of rock on my tender skin.

Finally, we stumble upon a series of caves. I walk behind Caleb as we cautiously enter into one of the caves.

"We should probably stay near the opening," I say. "You never know what's living in there."

"I agree. At least we're safe from the storm."

"You didn't happen to pack a flashlight in your pocket, did you?"

Caleb shakes his head.

"I didn't think so."

The cave is extremely dark and it appears to go much deeper. The thought of something dashing out at us terrifies me.

We look around a little. There isn't much to see since it has become so dark outside and we don't have the luxury of a flashlight or any of the necessities that we originally packed in our backpacks, because we left them at Sir Mateo's village. Only Sebastian has his. I remember he was wearing it when we left the village early this morning.

I wonder what Sebastian is up to this very moment. Then I sadly remember that he is most likely with Mya, which makes me wonder what the two of them are doing. Of all people, he had to end up with Mya, the massage therapist.

"So what do you think about Mya?" I ask Caleb. "Besides the crazy part." The question just spills out of my mouth like a bag of marbles. Caleb's eyebrows furrow and he looks at me strangely.

"I don't think much of Mya. Why do you ask?"

"No reason. Just curious."

"You're wondering if she's hitting on Sebastian right now? Come on. Tell me. That's why you asked, right?"

"That's absurd. I'm not worried about Sebastian. I know he would never do anything to hurt me." I bite my lip for having started this useless conversation. Where did I think this would end up, anyway? Stupid me.

"Maybe so. But do you trust Mya knowing that she has the hots for him?"

My mouth flies open with shock. I can't believe he just said that. Is he telling the truth? *Careful, Aislinn, you're swimming in dangerous waters,* I think while mentally kicking myself for having opened a large can of worms.

"And how do you know that?"

"It doesn't take a genius or a visionary to see it. You can just tell by the ways she flaunts herself in

front of him. I mean, she's a pretty girl and sometimes she's fun to be with, but don't get me wrong.

I would never date her. She has way too much baggage. And she's not- never mind."

I think about what Caleb has said and now I feel even worse. My mood saddens and what was turning out to be a remarkable trip is getting worse by the minute. Sir Mateo's men have been attacked, I've been separated from Sebastian, and he's alone with someone who has the hots for him. Great! This is what I get for lying to my parents.

"Don't worry about it," Caleb says.

I look up at Caleb, trying to figure out what he's talking about. I was so busy feeling sorry for myself that I was only able to make out the last two words he said. Plus, the unexpected noisy sound of the rainforest animals at night also contributed to my lack of focus.

"Huh?"

"I said, don't worry about it. If he really cares about you, then you have nothing to worry about."

I nod my head and pretend not to be worried, but really I feel nauseated just thinking about the two of them being alone in this magical forest together. She's probably loving every minute of it. *Stop it, Aislinn*!

∞ CHAPTER 15 ∞

Sebastian & Mya

Sebastian and Mya have been walking for a while in the hot rainforest. Sebastian sensed that someone was near, and he wanted to lose them. Along the way, he made false tracks to throw off whoever was following them.

"Can we stop walking now, my feet hurt?" Mya asks.

"No."

"Do you know where you're going?"

"Yes."

"Do you mind telling me where? We should have been back at the remains over an hour ago." Mya whines.

"Somebody was trailing us. We needed to detour."

"It could have been Sir Mateo."

"It wasn't."

"So what? Now we're lost?"

"I wouldn't say lost. Just way out of the way from where we need to be."

"Just admit it. We're lost in the Amazon."

Sebastian glares at Mya. "We're not lost, just far from where we need to be."

"I know you're pissed at me," Mya states.

"Congratulations."

"I'm sorry, okay," Mya says in a pleading voice.

"Okay," Sebastian replies, not fazed by Mya's antics.

"Can you stop please?" Mya begs.

"Stop what?"

"Your non-emotional answers, just stop!"

"Sure. Whatever."

Mya rolls her eyes. "Look, my feet are tired and I'm hungry and thirsty. Can we please stop?"

Sebastian stops walking.

"Finally," Mya says. A look of relief is painted on her face as she sighs.

"I stopped because of the stream, it's getting smaller."

"I don't care why you stopped. I'm just glad."

Sebastian heads over to the stream and takes a small, empty container from his backpack. He fills the container with water and carefully carries it back to an area near a fallen tree. Then Sebastian takes out another container and adds some elements into the water.

"What is that? A science experiment," Mya says. Her eyebrows arched.

"It's called survival. Ever hear of it?"

Mya makes a sarcastic facial expression while Sebastian continues to sterilize the water.

"Here, drink."

"Is it safe? I thought iodine is supposed to sit for much longer," Mya says. Sebastian shakes his head while taking back the container and drinking it to prove it's safe.

"A simple yes or no would have worked," Mya says mockingly. When Sebastian holds out the water for her, she hastily snatches it from his hands and tastes it.

"Yuck. What, are you trying to poison me?"

"No, not yet." Mya rolls her eyes. "Thank Jerry. It's his concoction."

"So it's not iodine?" Mya asks.

"I don't know what it is. I only know it works," Sebastian replies.

Sebastian and Mya take turns drinking the water. Sebastian tries to avoid any further conversation. He knows how Aislinn feels about her, and based on how Mya is behaving, Sebastian is starting to feel the same way.

While Mya checks out the ant bites on her legs, Sebastian sets off to find something for them to eat. He comes across a tree with a suitable trunk that would make for a safe meal, but now he needs to figure out a way to chop it down. He takes out his small knife from the gray plastic case. As he attempts to chop down the nearby small tree with the edible root, he thinks about what Mya had told him earlier about Aislinn. Did Aislinn go to the Coffee Beanery with Caleb and if so, why did she neglect to tell him about it?

It takes Sebastian a while to get through the tree with such a small knife, but with some patience, effort, and a little luck, he manages to chop enough to access the good part of the root.

"I'm not eating that. Can't you find us some nice fish and grill it?"

"Let me think about that. No."

Sebastian wasn't particularly fond of being ill-mannered. Very few people in his life have managed to upset him. But when Mya began to mess around with the one thing he cares about the most, Aislinn, he became instantly intolerant of Mya's antics and didn't want anything to do with her. Anyone who could potentially bring Aislinn any harm lit a fire in his belly, and he would do anything to protect her.

"You need to eat to keep your strength up. Eat!" Sebastian demands.

Mya reluctantly obeys. Although she thought it was virtually tasteless, it filled the empty void in her stomach.

"It's so dark out for daytime," Mya remarks.

"I was afraid of that," Sebastian sighs. "We're going to have to find somewhere to sleep."

"No way! We have to make it back to the village," Mya pleads.

"We can't go running around the rainforest in the dark. You think it's dark now, just wait. It looks like a storm is rolling in."

Mya looks around.

"If you didn't take off in the first place, we wouldn't be in this mess," Sebastian adds.

"Great! Blame it on me."

Sebastian shrugs his shoulders and finishes eating the root. "All right. Time to go. Ready?"

"Ready for what?"

"We have to find a safe place to sleep so we don't get eaten during the middle of the night."

"Eaten? I can't believe we have to do this," Mya remarks while grudgingly following Sebastian.

"We need to work quickly. Sleeping on the forest floor is not an option." Sebastian thinks of all the animals that could attack them in the middle of the night and decides it would be best if he didn't share those thoughts with Mya.

Sebastian and Mya travel through the rainforest in search of an adequate place to rest their heads for the night.

"I don't see any place that looks safe enough to sleep," Mya says woefully.

"I know. I think we're going to have to make something," Sebastian informs Mya as he feels the first raindrop of the day. Then another and another.

"Work fast. We're in for a rain storm."

"This is crazy. It's starting to rain harder and harder. I can't work under these conditions."

"Well, you better try."

"But I can't sleep out in the open."

"Okay, so don't," Sebastian nonchalantly replies.

"I'm serious, Sebastian! I need a roof over my head. You would think that these trees would cover us, but they don't!"

Sebastian takes his small knife and begins to feverishly cut down sapling branches. Mya stops complaining and grudgingly helps out by bundling up the branches and aligning them in a row. She also gathers various ferns from the forest floor and adds them to the makeshift bed.

"This is nuts. I just can't believe we have to sleep out here in the rain. I just can't believe it!"

"Believe it," Sebastian says angrily. "We don't have any other options at this point. Now keep building! The bigger the better and the more distance between us and the forest floor, the better."

∞ CHAPTER 16 ∞

Aislinn & Caleb

Night begins to fall, and I start to feel chilly. The temperature has dropped significantly, but luckily my clothes are almost dry from the torrential rain.

"You can wear my shirt if you're cold," Caleb offers. Although I can't stop shaking and his offer sounds amazing, I think it would be best if I separate myself from him. Our earlier encounter in the water was uncomfortable enough, and I don't think that Caleb taking off his shirt would make matters any better.

"No thanks. I'm good."

"You're lying. If it weren't for your teeth chattering and constant shaking, I might actually believe you.

Here," Caleb says while taking off his T-shirt and throwing it to me.

I catch it mid-air and immediately throw it back. "No. Really. It's not that cold. I need to tough it out, and if I wear your shirt, then what kind of visionary would I be?" I don't know where that stupid statement came from, but it was all I could think of. Caleb's eyes crinkle as he smirks.

"Well, if you change your mind, just ask." Caleb takes his shirt and rolls it up as a pillow and places it underneath his head.

"Thank you."

"No problem."

The rain seems to stop as quickly as it had begun. Seeing on how it is too late to venture into the rainforest, we both agree that it would be in our best interest to stay here for the night and continue our journey in the morning. Some of the jungle's fiercest predators, including our new enemies, are most likely lurking around in the night, and I sure as hell do not want to become their prey.

After my body adjusts to the cold night air, I start to relax and unwind. Caleb and I are close to one another, so we can share body heat. Although, I am careful not to get too close. I don't want him to get the wrong idea or any ideas at all for that matter. I close my eyes and try to sleep, but I can still feel Caleb staring at me. My eyes want to peek at him to see if I'm right, but my subconscious tells me to keep my eyes shut and go to sleep. I listen for once, and fall asleep.

Morning finally comes and the early sounds of exotic birds and other various animals wake me up slowly. For a moment, I feel like I'm at some sort of day spa listening to relaxing nature music, and then reality sets in and I realize that I'm actually in nature, only it's not relaxing. The thought of being hunted by an unknown group of men isn't particularly soothing.

"Good morning," Caleb says while stretching his large arm muscles.

"Morning. How was your sleep on your comfortable rock floor?" I joke.

"Let's just say, we're not sleeping here tonight. My body is definitely aching. I could use one of Mya's back massages right about now," Caleb replies while rubbing his shoulders and stretching. I almost vomit in response to his comment.

"Right, well we should get going and try to find them," I suggest, while peering out the opening of the cave.

"I'm ready. Let's get out of here."

Caleb and I venture out and decide to drink from the same pool that we drank from yesterday. Seeing that we both appear to be in good health, we figure that it would be safe to drink from it again.

As we head back to the pool of water, my stomach lets out an angry growl. I squeeze it in tight hoping to hide the noise. But it growls again even louder.

"Is that you or is some hungry, wild animal approaching us?"

"Haha."

"I'm hungry too," Caleb confesses.

"Well, I don't know what we're going to eat. I'm certainly not killing anything. Well, not yet anyways."

"I don't think we'll need to do that just yet," Caleb says while observing some shrubbery where a gap in the canopy above has allowed them to grow. Because the forest floor receives such little light, it's rather difficult for any shrubs to grow here. Caleb strolls over and begins to fiddle with the shrubs.

"What are you doing? You should be using a long stick. There are venomous snakes pretty much everywhere here."

"I'm looking for something to eat. What about these?" Caleb says, holding out some berries that he picked from a smaller bush.

"I don't think so. It's too risky. We don't know if they're poisonous or not."

Since the pickings are slim, I hurriedly try to muster up possible solutions to rectify our starvation.

"How about this plant? It looks like something I saw on the food table the other day back in the village."

"Are you sure?" Caleb questions. He makes an awkward smile suggesting doubt. A shrug of my shoulders doesn't provide Caleb with enough confidence to try it.

"How about we just start with water and then go from there? Maybe we'll run into some fruit trees that are recognizable," Caleb suggests, trying to sound diplomatic.

The taste of the water is delightfully satisfying. It definitely beats the taste of water from plastic bottles.

"Good, huh?" Caleb says between taking large sips of water from the palms of his hands.

"Too good!" I agree. He watches me drink water and shyly smiles as he quickly turns away.

Unexpectedly, I get the urge to stand up and scan my surroundings. Something inside of me nudged me to become alert. I survey the area while Caleb continues to satisfy his quench. After looking around the shaded forest, I finally locate my disturbance.

"Um, Caleb, we have company," I whisper, feeling an elevated level of concern. "Don't move."

"What is it? Another snake? Because I really don't care for those things too much and-"

"Shhh. It's not a snake. It's a cat. A large one."

Caleb turns his head and looks around. "Where?"

"This way, two o'clock," I proudly say. I instantly think of Sebastian. He's the one that had originally used that phrase with me at the special agency's campsite, only I didn't get it then. Caleb finally spots the jaguar and quietly picks up a nearby fallen branch. Although the branch is on the small side, I suppose it's better than nothing.

The jaguar stands still and watches us. It is quite large, probably weighing at least two hundred pounds or more and measuring about eight feet in length. Caleb and I stand there frozen by the water's edge. Suddenly, the jaguar sprints right toward us! Caleb holds out his stick, as if that will hold off this wild beast.

Each millisecond feels like an eternity as we stand in horror at the events that are about to unfold. If only we could access our visions or our spirit animals. I close my eyes in one last, desperate attempt to access the red-tailed hawk, but nothing happens. The jaguar gains speed and ejects itself into the air in one giant leap; only the predator doesn't land on us. Instead, it lands about five feet behind us in the shallow water, pouncing on an innocent turtle. Its powerful jaw tears through the shell with little effort. Caleb and I look at one another, stunned.

"Oh my God!" I mutter in shock.

"Holy shit! I thought we were dead," Caleb cries.

"Oh my god!"

"Shit!" Caleb shudders.

"Let's get out of here. It might still be hungry after it devours that poor little turtle," I say. Caleb and I quickly leave the area and head out toward the unknown.

As soon as we're far out of sight from the jaguar, I start to ponder protection. We have absolutely nothing to use to protect ourselves. We're like sitting ducks.

"This is crazy. We came here with high tech weapons that Sebastian packed, only we have no access to any of them," I say. "We need to make some weapons, like right now."

Caleb stares at me earnestly and says, "Okay. Let's make us some weapons."

The two of us look for broken down trees and gather some wood remnants. We work feverishly at the branches, using sharp stone to carefully chip them into pointed daggers. We speak very little and concentrate on the task at hand.

While admiring the handiwork of my completed wooden dagger, I hear a small rustling in the woods. This place is full of danger, but at least we have some sort of protection now. Caleb looks at me and notices my concern. We both stand up and prepare for the unknown.

Suddenly, the sly jaguar appears again out of nowhere. Caleb positions himself with his makeshift dagger and I watch as the slowly approaching animal gradually makes its way toward us.

∞ CHAPTER 17 ∞

Sebastian & Mya

After much hard work, Sebastian and Mya climb up onto their homemade bed and pull large leaf branches over themselves. The bed stands approximately two feet off of the forest floor and stretches about six feet wide. They picked a place that hosts many trees, which serve as protection from the harsh rain.

"I still don't feel comfortable with this. There's like zero protection out here. Zero!" Mya complains.

"Look, we're hidden behind these large trees and we're as high as we can get. I think we're doing all right."

"Well, what about the rain. We're going to get soaked."

"I think we'll live. Think of it as warm shower."

"Think what you want. But you're not the one that had an anaconda wrapped around your body or crazy fire ants biting the crap out of you. And I don't about you, but I'm cold."

Sebastian continues to get comfortable and ignores Mya's ranting. He rolls over and tries to sleep.

"You're just going to go to sleep, just like that? In the rain?"

Sebastian opens his eyes and looks at Mya. "Yes. Just like that."

"And with all of these animals making peculiar noises? It's as if they're discussing who's going to eat us first. How can you sleep like this?"

"It's magic."

"Well fine then, don't come running to me when you're being eaten by a lion."

"Mya."

"What, Sebastian?" Mya replies sarcastically.

"There are no lions in the Amazon."

"You know what I mean," Mya says.

After a few more protests followed by some pitiful sighs, Mya finally falls asleep, leaving Sebastian to doze off peacefully. The temperature dips, leaving Mya shivering. She inches closer to Sebastian in hopes of utilizing his body heat to stay warm while enjoying the opportunity of snuggling next to him. Sebastian is out like a light and he doesn't notice a thing. They both sleep soundly through the night.

Early the next morning, loud monkey calls awaken Sebastian. He opens his eyes and finds Mya nestled right next to him. He gently tugs away so not to disturb her, but it is too late. Mya is already awake.

"Well, good morning there, deep sleeper."

"I'm sorry?" Sebastian questions.

"I said good morning, deep sleeper. You sleep like a rock."

"And how would you know? Animals keep you up all night?"

"No. I slept just fine thank you," Mya answers sweetly.

The beautiful morning haze looks majestic against the green of the trees, and the musical sounds of the forest animals feel like a symphony. Sebastian and Mya stand up and climb down from their homemade bed.

"Not bad, eh?" Sebastian says while admiring his handiwork.

"I suppose it wasn't that bad." Mya smiles.

Sebastian turns toward an exotic bird hidden amongst the trees. He admires its beauty and its magnificent ability to camouflage itself. As he watches the bird, he thinks of Aislinn. He imagines her beautiful, long, blond hair and her lovely golden eyes. He misses her scent and the way she jokes around with him. He just wants to be near her once again.

"We should try to find our way back to the village to find everyone," Sebastian states.

"Sounds good to me. Get me out of here."

Sebastian and Mya tread off toward Sir Mateo's village. Many of the trees and brush on the rainforest floor look the same. A few streams and bodies of water break up the consistency.

"Are you sure were headed in the right direction?" Mya asks.

"Not exactly."

"Well, that's great!" she snaps back.

Sebastian laughs at Mya's statement, causing her to become even more irritated.

"I'm glad you're enjoying this little escapade, because so far this trip has been a joke. A real joke."

"How can you even say that?" Sebastian scolds.

"We came here to learn how to control and understand our visions, and it seems to me that we've learned absolutely nothing."

"It seems like that, but it isn't. We have come a long way, but we're not finished yet and besides if you haven't of gone off in the first place then-," Sebastian pauses. "Never mind." Mya stays quiet.

Sebastian continues walking as Mya sighs to herself.

"Aha. I knew we were going the right way."

"And how can you tell?" Mya asks with disbelief.

"See that waterway and this huge tree," Sebastian proudly says, pointing, "I remember it."

"Well, that's great. So how much longer?"

"Maybe an hour. A little less."

"Let's speed up and make it in thirty minutes."

"Wait a minute," Sebastian says.

"Why? Let's go."

Sebastian puts his finger to his mouth signaling for Mya to be quiet. Mya crinkles her eyebrows and rolls her eyes.

"I heard something. Did you hear that?" Sebastian whispers.

"No. I don't hear anything. You must be hearing things."

"No. Something's out there."

Suddenly, Sebastian and Mya find themselves completely surrounded by a large group of native men coming out from the brush all around them. The men close in on them, leaving no opening for them to escape.

Bows and arrows are pointed directly at Sebastian and Mya. Some of the men wear multi-colored bandanas around their faces and camouflaged clothing. Unwelcoming faces and mean-spirited eyes shine down on Sebastian and Mya as the two inch closer to one another, fearful of what might happen next. Mya gasps as Sebastian visually scans their surroundings.

"Don't speak a word," Sebastian whispers. "Not a word."

∞ CHAPTER 18 ∞

Aislinn & Caleb

Caleb and I stand there frozen. We watch the jaguar slowly approach us and I stare directly into its eyes. The animal's eyes are completely mesmerizing. It's as if this creature can see through my very soul. I let down my guard and begin to feel relaxed.

"Aislinn, move back! I got this," Caleb warns while trying to push me aside.

But I firmly plant my feet into the ground. I get the sense that the jaguar doesn't want to hurt us. It wants to befriend us.

"No. It's okay," I murmur. The jaguar is no more than three feet away when it stops walking, lies down, and rolls over like a dog.

"What? I don't get it. Is it sick?" Caleb questions with wide eyes.

"No. It's showing submissiveness. Look, it's trying to communicate with us."

Cautiously, I approach the wild cat, feeling semi-confident in my assumptions.

I hold out my hand to the jaguar. Caleb nervously shouts, "Aislinn, no!"

The jaguar turns back on its stomach and gently grazes the palm of my hand with its soft head. I can't believe this is happening. This is the most amazing wild animal encounter I've ever had. It's actually the only amazing wild animal encounter I've ever had.

"I guess it's friendly," Caleb suggests, only after I've made contact with the animal.

Since the jaguar hasn't attacked me so far, I decide to go ahead and pet its head. It softly nuzzles my hand again and rolls over once more. I squat down next to it and slowly rub its belly. Black and tan rosettes lace its powerful body. This wild animal is one of the strongest predators in the rainforest and I'm petting it.

"Would you look at that?" Caleb says with astonishment as he kneels down next to me to touch the wild cat. "What do you think it wants?"

"I don't know. But, it doesn't want to hurt us. Maybe it's here to help us." I continue rubbing the animal as if it were my pet. Soft purrs escape from its body.

"You want to help us? Don't you, Beauty?"

"Beauty? Oh no. You can't name it," Caleb declares.

"And why not? It's beautiful, isn't it?"

"Yeah, but once you give something a name, it's hard to get rid of. Like looking at puppies through a window. Once you go in and give it a name, you're done. Finite."

"Well, I like it. Don't you, Beauty?" Beauty's purrs are completely heartwarming.

"I thought only domestic cats purr?" Caleb questions.

"I don't know, but Beauty does."

"I don't mean to interrupt your jaguar-girl bonding session, but we should really get going if you want to find Sebastian."

"You're right. Maybe Beauty can help us?"

"Well, if anything, he sure is good protection."

Caleb and I continue on our quest and amazingly, Beauty follows. Beauty walks near me and I start to feel a sense of ownership over him. It's like he's my own personal bodyguard, only he's a cat. A large cat. After walking through many of the large cylindrical trunks that periodically pop up on the forest floor, I realize that one in particular looks familiar. It has an etched look on the side of the bark.

"Look," I cry. "We've been here before. I think we're near the village!"

Caleb looks all around and down at the ground. He suddenly squats down and traces something in the muck.

"What are you doing?" I ask.

"Look. Footprints. Lots of footprints."

"Could it be from the Rebel Leaders or whoever those men were back at the ancient ruins?"

"Possibly. But, it's too hard to tell for sure. Let's move on. If we find the village, hopefully we can get some answers."

Another day in the rainforest and I don't feel a single step closer to finding Sebastian. I shake my head to clear my worries and tiny wet drops begin to trickle on my face. It's starting to rain, again. This time it doesn't feel like a storm, but more like a typical rainfall in the rainforest. I catch raindrops on my tongue and savor the wetness.

I notice that I have become much better at trekking through the rainforest. I barely trip over tree trunks or brush. I still notice the beautiful scenery, numerous insects, and magical wildlife, but it's all starting to become more natural to me.

The closer we get to the village, the more I start to smell a burning fire. Its pungent odor suffocates the forest. Beauty stays by my side as we journey toward the village and my fingers gently stroke his silky back while we walk. Something about him brings me great peace. Can this be real? Is this actually happening to me?

As we approach the village, under the brush and into the clearing, shock and sorrow instantly overcome me. The village has been burnt down and nothing is left. Small clouds of smoke hover over the air.

"Oh my God!" I shriek while running into the village. Caleb and I scan the area for any sign of life. Either the people of this village have been taken hostage or they've fled.

"This was it," I say with absolute shock.

"This was what?" Caleb asks.

"This was the vision I had back in the hut the other night and the one I had in the ruins. It looks exactly like it."

Caleb looks displeased, as if I could have warned the others. His eyes fall to the ground and I feel guilty. Guilty for not being able to warn the village people.

Guilty for not being able to do a better job interpreting my visions. Guilty for the loss.

"It wasn't a complete vision you know," I say breathlessly. "It was me running in the rain and smoke everywhere. It was so brief that it didn't make any sense then," I answer solemnly. "If only I knew, I could have done something." I want to cry.

"It's okay, Aislinn," Caleb says while putting his hand on my shoulder to console me. "You didn't know. There was nothing you could have done."

I agree with him, but I still feel terrible. This whole situation is completely abysmal!

"Come on. We can't stay here," Caleb affirms while leading the way back. This happy little village has been destroyed. Where will the villagers live now? Anger begins to take sorrow's place in my heart and revenge enters my mind. I need to do something to rectify the injustice.

"We should head toward the ruins," I say, determined. "I have a feeling that's where we'll find everyone."

"I was just thinking the same thing. See, great minds do think alike," Caleb agrees with a small, hopeful smile and a playful wink.

As we start to head away from the village, my stomach growls and reminds me that I need fuel. What feels like a lifetime of starvation has only been a couple of hours, but I'm famished. We have forgotten to eat since the whole jaguar encounter.

"Stop!" I say, making Caleb almost jump out of his skin.

"What is it? What's wrong?"

"Nothing's wrong. I'm just starving. Aren't you hungry?"

I know that it's bad timing, but if we don't regain our energy, then what use are we to anyone?

"I forgot about that. Yeah, I'm hungry. I'm always hungry."

We look at Beauty and he puts his head down.

"We don't want to eat you, Beauty. But maybe you can help us find some food," I say while petting him on his beautiful head. "Beauty, we need food. Can you help us?"

Caleb starts to laugh almost uncontrollably. "You're seriously asking a jaguar to help you find food? Have you gone mad?"

And as if Beauty could understand me perfectly, he lets out a soft growl and heads in a different direction. Caleb and I both look at one another, surprised to hear Beauty growl. The only sound we've witnessed him make was soft purrs. Beauty stops walking and turns to look back at us.

"I think that's our signal to follow him," I say, while trying to keep up with Beauty.

Caleb follows and mumbles something under his breath. I know he thinks this is a complete waste of time, but he is forgetting that although we don't have any access to our powers, we are still connected to the animals and to the earth! The connection that we've made with Beauty is proof that we have an innate connection with this sacred place. That very thought makes me think about our powers and suddenly an idea comes to mind.

"Caleb, remember when Sir Mateo told us that we are all connected?"

"Yeah."

"Remember how he was so confident that if we believe in ourselves and trust ourselves then we will know what we need to do?"

"Yeah, I suppose he said that in other words, but yeah."

"Well, I think that he meant for us to also connect with each other. When I was taken hostage by those men and Fred, I connected with my spirit animal through my mind. I tried to connect with Sebastian, but I was unable to for some reason. However, even though I didn't think we had connected, we actually did on some unexplainable level. I know this because he saw what was going to happen to me and came to my rescue."

"So, let me get this right. You didn't get a vision of Sebastian when you were being held captive, but somehow you connected with him and he was able to get the vision?"

"I guess. I don't how it works exactly. But, we have to believe in ourselves and trust ourselves," I say, taking a break from walking. "If we try to connect with Sebastian and Mya, then maybe they will be able to get a vision of what's happening."

What I'm saying to Caleb doesn't quite make sense, but I just have this inner voice telling me to trust my gut. And if there's one thing I've learned lately, it's to always trust your gut.

Beauty stops walking when he realizes we've stopped. He backtracks toward me and rests by my feet.

"So, what do you suggest we do?" Caleb asks.

"Hold my hands, close your eyes, and concentrate."

"Yes sir!" Caleb says.

Caleb comes closer and eagerly takes my hands. His hands are much larger than mine. They remind me of Sebastian's, only Sebastian's are much softer and they make me feel safe and secure. Caleb looks down at our hands and smiles.

"Okay, try to concentrate on visualizing Sebastian. Tell him, silently, what's happening and where we are."

"What about Mya?"

"Let's try focusing our energy on one person first. If we get through to him, then he can relate it to Mya."

The two of us stand face to face and close our eyes. I picture Sebastian and every detail of his body. I try to smell his scent and suddenly I get a feeling of his whole aura. I breathe him in, all of him. Then I tell him that I am okay. I tell him about the attack on Sir Mateo's men. I tell him about the village and I let him know that we're headed back to the ancient ruins of Sir Mateo's past. I also tell him about Beauty, the amazing jaguar that I have befriended. I close this energy by sending him my love, and I open my eyes. Although I didn't feel his presence, I felt something. I am hopeful that he got the message. A few tears fall from my eyes and run down my face. I look up at Caleb and notice him staring at me.

"Did you do it? Did you do what I told you?" I ask anxiously.

"Yup. I talked to him... silently," Caleb answers with very little embellishment.

When I try to drop our hands, Caleb continues to hold on a little longer. I'm not sure if it is accidental or if he is trying to be humorous; either way I break free, wipe my eyes, and reach for Beauty. Beauty's eyes are so intense, I feel like I could look into them forever.

"So, did you… get a hold of him?" Caleb asks.

"I don't know for sure. But I tried."

"You must have felt something?" Caleb asks digging for more information. He must have seen my tears otherwise he wouldn't be so persistent.

"Of course I felt something. I miss him," I say confidently.

I do miss Sebastian. This whole separation thing has made me crazy. It's like I forgot who I was and now I remember. I'm Aislinn and I am the red-tailed hawk and I will get out of this!

∞ CHAPTER 19 ∞

Sebastian & Mya

"We are not here to cause any harm. We come in peace," Sebastian says in English and then again in Spanish, hoping to relax the tribal onslaught.

The men stay positioned and look to a large, burly man with a large scar going down the side of his face. He gives them a command and they point their bows down.

"At least someone does," the man says in English, "because we don't." The rest of the men begin to laugh.

"Welcome to our land," the man says to Sebastian in a smug tone.

Sebastian carefully watches the man's demeanor and quickly realizes that he is trouble. Major trouble. Everything from the man's harsh body language to his stern facial expressions warn Sebastian as to this man's intentions.

Sebastian nods in response to the man's devious welcome.

"Now, if you don't mind, you'll be coming with us."

"Um, no thanks, Senor. We are going in another direction," Mya declares in a slowed speech as if they couldn't hear that well.

"I told you not to speak," Sebastian mumbles under his breath.

"Relax, I got this," Mya assures him.

Mya turns around and leads the way to exit the small circle they have been forced into while Sebastian stays absolutely still.

"Come on," Mya calls to Sebastian.

Sebastian shakes his head in disbelief as Mya tries to get through the men. The men stay firm, not allowing her to pass. She turns back to look at Sebastian for assistance.

"You'll be coming with us, Senorita," the burly man says. The men laugh as they proceed to tie Sebastian's and Mya's hands behind their backs.

"What's happening?" Mya asks Sebastian.

"I don't know, but don't fight them. There are too many of them and we don't have our powers," Sebastian whispers.

As the men finish binding their hands, the leader comes forward and looks over Sebastian and Mya as if sizing them up.

"You are a visionary, yes?" the leader asks Sebastian.

"A vision who?" Sebastian answers, trying to sound baffled.

"You are a visionary are you not?"

"We're not," Sebastian answers for the both of them.

"We'll see about that," the leader threatens, while signaling for the men to start moving. Sebastian and Mya have no choice but to walk beside the men. Sebastian quietly thinks about the situation and tries to figure out what is happening.

"Hurry up, we need to get the others!" the man shouts.

Sebastian realizes that the man is referring to Aislinn and Caleb. For some reason, this man is here to capture them. But why? Could they work for the secret agency? Maybe it is the Rebel Leaders that Sir Mateo had spoken about. That conclusion sounded more logical. Now if he could only figure out what they wanted.

During the fast and quiet walk through the rainforest, Sebastian worries that Aislinn could be in danger, but he knows that he must first save himself so that he can help her.

They continue walking while presumably searching for Aislinn and Caleb. Sebastian and Mya are careful not to trip over the large tree trunks that line the forest floors. Mya glances over at Sebastian, looking for answers, but he continues to keep his head forward, knowing that it would be in their best interest to remain silent. Mya already managed to get them into enough trouble.

While walking, Sebastian decides to use this time to try to contact his spirit animal. He speaks silently to himself, hoping to connect with his grizzly bear. He gets no response. *Come on, I know you're in there.* Sebastian grunts to himself feeling frustrated. One of the men by his side stares at him strangely.

"Who are you talking to?" Mya asks.

"Shhh, no talking," Sebastian reminds her.

"What are you? My teacher?"

"Were you born yesterday, Mya? Stop talking before you get us killed."

"Whatever." Mya sarcastically sighs and rolls her eyes.

As they trek through the woods, the men continue to push Sebastian and Mya and yell at them to hurry up. Mya is afraid and frustrated while Sebastian is angry and inquisitive. He can't stand the way the men degrade them, but at the same time, he is curious as to what their after.

After a grueling walk next to their captors, they finally reach the ancient ruins of Sir Mateo's past. Another group of men wearing the same attire wait near the clearing. They must have split up, hoping to cover more ground. When the men separate, Sebastian is able to see that some of Sir Mateo's men have been captured and held prisoner. But luckily, Aislinn is nowhere to be found. Sebastian mutters, *Thank God*, under his breath, feeling thankful that she hasn't been captured. Now he was wondering where she was.

"Where are they?" the leader of the group calls out angrily.

"They were not here, Andre. We look all over."

"You look all over, heh? Not good enough," Andre hollers.

Andre, the group leader, walks over to the guy who spoke and knees him in the stomach. The guy keels over and falls to the ground, wincing in pain.

Then Andre heads over to Sir Mateo's men who have been imprisoned. "Where are the rest of them? Where are you hiding them?"

The men look down at the ground and refuse to speak. They shrug their shoulders and stay silent.

"Useless," Andre says while he kicks dirt at them and walks away.

Andre tells his men to search the ruins for clues. The men quickly scatter around the premises looking for clues. Within seconds, one of the men yells for Andre. Andre hurries over, leaving Sebastian and Mya behind with his appointed wardens.

Sebastian waits for the captors to look away and then signals to Sir Mateo's men. He gestures with his body and shrugs his shoulders. He hopes to get some answers from them as to where the others are, but they shrug their shoulders back at him, looking confused.

"This is ridiculous. Where is Sir Mateo? I need to get out of here." Mya rants.

"You are going to stay quiet. You almost got us killed back there," Sebastian warns.

"Oh, please. You're only worried about your precious little Aislinn."

"So what if I am? Why should you care?"

Mya groans and purses her lips. Just then, Andre comes over and says, "Looks like your friends are missing. Do you know where they are?"

"Have you checked the village?" Mya hastily blurts out.

Sebastian shakes his head with disbelief.

"The village? Yes, we've checked the village," Andre interrupts Mya as she's about to answer him again and yells out, "The village is gone, so my question is where are they?"

Mya steps back appearing frightened by Andre's irate tone of voice. What did he mean by the village was gone? Feeling aggravated and confused, Sebastian felt like knocking Andre out, but he knew it would only start a riot, so he controlled his anger and continued to breathe deeply to help him relax.

Sebastian wisely hangs his head low, showing compliance and submissiveness, and Mya soon follows. Andre gives up and heads over to the rest of his gang. When Andre is out of sight, Sebastian turns to Mya and says, "What's a matter with you? Do you have a death wish?"

"Um, no. Can't you tell that he's looking for Aislinn and Caleb? I was helping to distract him from their whereabouts."

"You don't even know what you're saying. You don't go throwing the whole village under the bus like that. That's just stupid. Just do me a favor and stop talking before you get us all killed, okay?"

"Whatever. I was just trying to help."

"Well, don't. Don't do anything!"

Andre's men notice Sebastian and Mya whispering. They walk over and begin to encircle Sebastian and Mya. Mya nervously backs into Sebastian.

Suddenly, everything goes black!

∞ CHAPTER 20 ∞

Aislinn & Caleb

Beauty leads us to an area nearby that has the most beautiful fruit trees I've ever seen. Beauty jumps on a low-lying branch, knocks off fruit, and rolls it down to me.

"Amazing. Beauty understood us."

Caleb shakes his head in disbelief and then climbs onto the tree with Beauty to help take down more fruit.

"Thank you, Beauty! I've never seen fruit like this before," I say. They're perfectly yellow and red like a ripe mango.

"Me neither. And it looks good," Caleb pauses to take a sniff of the fruit, "and smells good too."

Caleb continues to yank more fruit from the tree and throws them down to me. "Look out below," he yells each time he throws a new fruit. I catch all of the fruit and put them in my shirt. My mouth is salivating.

I plop down on a large tree root to further inspect our catch of the day. I push my thumb into the soft flesh of the fruit and tear it open. There's no time to waste being etiquette. One lick of my fingers and I devour the sweet tasting fruit. I tear open another, and another, and another until my mouth can no longer chew.

"Delicious," Caleb admits while he slurps every last bit of juice from the fruit.

"It's heaven."

After devouring several of the fruits, I reach over to Beauty and caress his soft fur. He reminds me of Otie, the way he stays so close. A small noise in the forest brings Beauty to his feet, only to find that a pair of monkeys had climbed down to our level of the rainforest.

"Well, this was nice but I think we should be on our way," I share with Caleb.

"Yep. Let's go. I've had enough of this mystery fruit for now," Caleb says while stocking away some of the fruit into his pockets for later.

We travel quietly for a while and I can't help but enjoy the silence. It gives me time to think and breathe. I think about Beauty and how he came to us and didn't attack us. I think about how he showed us what to eat and how he stays by my side as if he's known me my entire life.

Caleb breaks the silence with a burp. I laugh a little and he throws a stick at me.

"Watch it," I squeal.

"What are you going to do? Sick Beauty on me?" Caleb jokes.

"Don't tempt me."

"I couldn't temp you. You're too independent for that."

I turn my head to look at Caleb. What is that awkward comment supposed to mean?

"There's nothing wrong with being independent. That's a compliment, so thank you," I say.

"I know. That's why I said it."

Not knowing where this conversation might lead, I decide to change topics.

"So, do you think Mya drank from the Agua Magia?" I don't know why I chose Mya as the topic changer. It just came to me.

"Mya?" Caleb repeats.

I raise my eyebrows.

"No. I don't think she drank from it. She talks a good game, but when it comes time to act on something, she usually backs out."

"Wow! How do you know that?" I'm surprised to hear his take on Mya's personality seeming on how he's only known her a few weeks.

"I can read people," Caleb says while looking at me.

"Really." I say. I know we can see things, but reading people is something entirely different.

"I can read you."

I pretend to concentrate on walking and look down at my feet. "You can't read me. I can't even read me."

"I can tell that you're a kind and caring person. You don't let people walk all over you and you enjoy things in life, simple things." I blush and continue walking. I don't want to look at him.

But, Caleb carries on, "I like that about you."

I was afraid this would happen. Whenever I try to force a conversation to go in a different direction, it comes back toward me full speed ahead.

"Thank you," I simply say.

As I continue walking, Caleb abruptly grabs my arm and pulls me close to him. Surprised by his forwardness, I stand there silently not knowing what to expect. Caleb grabs me with his other hand and pulls my body close to his. I back up as he leans in to kiss me.

"Caleb, no," I say softly, trying to be cordial but serious at the same time. Caleb stares at me.

"You're right. I'm sorry. I didn't mean to," he says solemnly while looking at the ground.

"It's just, well, I'm with Sebastian," I say. I pray that I don't hurt his feelings. He really is a good person, but I can't let him think this is okay.

"I know. It's my fault. I don't know what came over me. Guess I'm just drawn to you."

"It's okay. Let's just forget it." I smile hoping that he will smile back, but he doesn't.

"Yeah, sure," Caleb says.

He lets go of me and I start walking. Caleb takes a second and then catches up to me. Luckily, we reach a thick brush that seems to cover the way to an opening.

We pull it back and realize that we somehow ended up at the back entrance of the four stones where Sir Mateo had brought us.

"Beauty, did you lead us here?" I ask. "I thought we were headed toward the remains." Beauty snarls playfully at me and rubs his head against my leg. I stroke him gently and he purrs.

"Maybe we're supposed to be here," Caleb interjects.

"What do you mean?"

"Well, we tried to contact Sebastian, right? Maybe this is supposed to help us somehow. Come on, let's go back to the stones and see what happens."

Hesitantly, I follow Caleb, and Beauty trails behind me. I still can't believe that were back at the stones. Caleb walks around the stones and analyzes them. "Everything looks okay. Ladies first."

"Um, I'm not doing this again. The last time I did this, it didn't make any sense. You go first, I insist."

"Okay, I'll go. Can't hurt right?" Caleb walks over to the same stone he touched before with Sir Mateo. He gently places his right hand on the stone and closes his eyes. He takes a deep breath. This time his body stands still and his eyes do not flutter. I watch him closely, curious about what he sees.

Caleb finally opens his eyes and says, "Even more incredible than the first time. It's like looking into a crystal ball," he gasps. "Man! I still can't believe this is real."

"What did you see?"

"I saw the two of us," I cringe inside fearing what he might say next, "fighting the Rebel Leaders. The fight looked fierce and brutal. I also saw our spirit animals and they saw me. It's weird I know, but it was so real, it's just unbelievable." Caleb continues to look deeply into my eyes while I quickly glance away. "Go next, maybe you'll get more."

"I'm afraid."

"I don't believe you. You're one of the bravest girls I know, hell, you're one of the bravest people I know."

I sigh, "You're just being nice."

"I only speak the truth."

"Thank you."

Knowing that Sebastian could be in danger, I swallow my fear, walk up to the fourth stone, and take a long, deep breath. Procrastination seems like a safe option right now. I glance back at Caleb and he nudges for me to get on with it. I gently place my hand on the stone and slowly close my eyes. *Go on, Aislinn, just do it already.*

"Here goes nothing," I say.

My body shakes internally, but not on the outside. My heart rate is elevated and I start to see a cloudy haze. Suddenly, as if I have been transported into another world, I see my life through hundreds of images flashing by. It's like a picture book. It is truly incredible. The details of the images are so impeccable that I feel like I am really there. As soon as it's over, I quickly open my eyes and look to Caleb for comfort. My body is still shaking. I sigh as I lean on his shoulder to regain my composure.

"Well, what did you see?"

"It's as if I left earth for a while. It was so surreal." I pause a minute to gather my thoughts while Caleb waits there anxiously.

"You were right about the fighting. Late tonight we'll be in a full-blown war with the Rebel Leaders and lives will be lost. Our spirit animals have been with us from the beginning, we're just not accessing them correctly. And remember that thing that Sir Mateo said before about there being no accidents, only purpose?" Caleb nods and I take a deep breath before continuing. "Well, my purpose is to provide protection to visionaries and humans – to fight till the end – to stop something from destroying us."

"To stop what exactly?" Caleb asks.

"It didn't show. I don't know. But, I need to stop something before it's too late."

Caleb looks at me with fearful eyes. "So this is all going down tonight?"

"I guess so," I say solemnly. "And that's not even the craziest part. I came back here from the afterlife to complete this mission. I sent myself back here."

Caleb looks at me dumfounded. "Wow, and I thought my visions were wild. Yours are beyond wild. They're downright crazy!"

"Thanks." I sneer.

"Sorry. That was meant to come out much differently."

"It's so clear when you touch the stone, but in reality I don't remember any of those things. If I really came back here from the other side, then why can't I remember anything? Why can't I just know what my mission is and be done with it? Why all the mystery?"

Beauty comes over to us and lies by my feet, and I sit down next to him. Caleb takes a seat on the other side of Beauty.

"Funny, I didn't see you in my stone visualization," I say to Beauty as he rolls over, expecting a tummy rub. "And, I thought we were only able to see our past."

"I don't know," Caleb says while sitting down next to Beauty and me. "Maybe it shows us what we need to see."

"Maybe. But why does everything have to be so confusing? I mean, it would just be so much easier if we knew what to do." I complain.

"Then it would be too easy. Nothing in life is that simple," Caleb says.

"True. I just wished it were."

I look into Beauty's eyes and he looks into mine. He's telling me to let go of my fears. I ask him telepathically how to do it. He says that I need to just do it and the rest will fall into place. Did I just communicate with a jaguar? I smile at him and he smiles back.

Caleb stands up and asks, "So, what do we do now?"

I look at him and smile. "We go kick some Rebel ass baby!"

∞ CHAPTER 21 ∞

Sebastian & Mya

"Sebastian! Are you there? Can you hear me?"

Sebastian hears a low voice but can't seem to find where it's coming from. He looks all around and sees nothing but darkness. He tries to acclimate himself with his new surroundings. The soreness of his arm suddenly helps him remember his last memories. He was struck by an arrow. An arrow that must have had some sort of drug on it that caused him to become unconscious.

As Sebastian looks around, he realizes that the Rebel Leaders must have brought him to an undisclosed location. This unfamiliar place has the appearance of a large cave with very little light.

"Who's there?" Sebastian questions in response to the voice.

"What? Oh my God! Sebastian, is that you?" Mya cries. She begins to whimper.

"Mya? What's wrong? Why are you crying? Are you hurt?"

"No. I'm fine. I'm just scared. How did we get here?"

"I'm not sure exactly. I was hoping you knew," Sebastian retorts.

"Are we alone? Where is everyone?" Mya asks a little louder.

"Shhh. Let's not draw any attention to ourselves. Maybe the Rebel Leaders left us alone."

"They didn't do that. They never do that in the movies. It just looks like they did so that we try to escape and then Bam - they show up again."

"Hey you. Can you hear me?"

"Did you say just that?" Sebastian asks Mya.

"Say what? What are you talking about?"

"Did you say *hey you? Can you hear me*?"

"Um, no. I was talking about what they do in the movies. Are you okay?"

Sebastian follows his instincts and closes his eyes to concentrate. He wants to know who is talking to him. Then he hears the voice again, "It's me, Sir Mateo. They have me in a cage outside. They are going to sacrifice me soon."

"Oh shit! I'll be right there if I can just get out of this cage-"

"Relax. Remember, I'm immortal. They don't know that though. Now listen to me carefully. You need to contact Aislinn. Simply believe in yourself. Believe in her. She can save us. You need to work together - all of you."

"But how?"

"Contact her. Feel it deep within. She will feel you. You will feel her. You two have a connection that goes deeper than the physical earth."

He's right. Sebastian has never felt a connection like that with anyone else. He's seen Aislinn before he'd even met her. It's difficult to understand but he knows there's something special about their relationship.

"Okay. I will try. Is there anything else I should know?"

"You already know."

"Um, Sebastian. What are you doing?" Mya asks, sounding alarmed. "You're freaking me out dude."

"I was talking."

"To who? Yourself?"

"No. Sir Mateo. Never mind. Listen. You need to close your eyes and try with all of your might to contact us."

"Contact who?"

"Me. Aislinn and Caleb."

"Okay, but it's not going to work."

"Mya. It will work. Trust me. Trust yourself. We have to work together for this to work."

Mya agrees and the two became silent. Sebastian calls out to Aislinn. He tries to contact his and Aislinn's spirit animals. He uses his subconscious and breathes deeply the entire time. His body is completely relaxed and his mind is in a meditative state.

Then Mya calls out to Caleb. She thinks of everything they had learned of so far. Then she calls out to Aislinn, grudgingly.

As Sebastian concentrates on Aislinn, his body shakes uncontrollably against the cage. The metal rattles against the ground. Sebastian opens his eyes and continues to see visions of Aislinn. He sees her long, blonde hair and her golden eyes. He sees her as human and as hawk. He can see her soul and then the vision suddenly vanishes. Feeling more confident that

Aislinn is safe and that they can get out of this, he decides to step into action.

"Mya," Sebastian calls.

"What?" Mya answers with an aggravated undertone.

"Did you do it?"

"Yes, I did it."

"Well? What did you see?"

"I saw Caleb and Aislinn and I saw their spirit animals a little bit."

"Good. That's good," Sebastian says, feeling relieved that Mya actually followed his directions.

"Shut up," one of the Rebel Leader's members yells at Sebastian and Mya as he runs in. He must have heard the noise from outside. The gang member slams Sebastian's cage with a large stick causing the metal to pulsate in his ears. Mya gasps in fear and Sebastian lowers his head, showing submissiveness. He reminds himself that this is only temporary and that he will soon be out of this cage.

The man leaves and Sebastian decides to work on freeing himself from the cage.

"Mya. Start messing around with your cage and try to get it open. We need to get of here. Now!"

∞ CHAPTER 22 ∞

Aislinn & Caleb

Caleb and I begin to travel back into the forest. The ancient remains of Sir Mateo's past are our next destination. Hopefully that will guide us in the right direction. Beauty leads the way and the two of us continue with a fast pace to keep up with him.

"This doesn't seem right," Caleb shouts.

"What? What are you talking about?"

Caleb stops walking and looks around. Beauty stops and backtracks toward us when he realizes we have stopped. I scan the area. All around us lay brightly colored green trees and brush. The scenery is absolutely breathtaking.

"You don't feel it?" Caleb asks.

"Feel what?"

"We aren't headed in the right direction." I watch Caleb as he circles aimlessly trying to make sense of his loss of direction.

"How can you tell?"

"I don't know. I just can. My senses are starting to come around and this just doesn't feel right," he says. He sounds concerned.

I glance over at Beauty who's sitting so patiently. He reminds me of a child waiting for his parents to stop fighting over the map in a long car drive. I walk over to him and caress his face. I don't think I'll ever get over the fact that I'm petting a live jaguar. A wild one at that.

"Beauty is bringing us the wrong way. We need to head back," Caleb says.

"What if he's bringing us the right way? What if we weren't meant to go back to the ancient remains? What if he's bringing us toward Sebastian and Mya?"

Caleb walks over to Beauty and touches his face. "You're not trying to lead us into harm's way? Are you, Beauty?" Beauty walks away from Caleb and over to me. He lies down and places his head on my shoes.

"He would never do that. Now apologize," I say.

"I'm not apologizing to an animal. He doesn't even know what I'm saying."

"He does too! You're offending him. Now apologize to him or I'm leaving!"

"You're leaving. Where are you going to go?"

I ignore Caleb and continue rubbing Beauty.

Caleb grunts and resentfully says, "I'm sorry."

I look at Caleb and nod down toward Beauty. He then rolls his eyes and looks down at Beauty and says, "Sorry if I have offended you in any way."

"How was that?" he asks me mockingly.

"Better," I reply with a smirk. "Now, are you finished causing trouble? Because I'm not sleeping another night out here."

Caleb smiles. "Yes. I'm finished."

"Um, Caleb," I murmur. My mouth becomes dry and my eyes have popped out of my head. I can barely speak.

"I told you I'm done."

"No, look down by your feet."

Caleb makes a quizzical expression and then looks down. He gasps when he sees a snake slithering around his feet.

"More snakes. Man, we can't catch a break," he says. "And that bad boy is definitely a coral snake."

"How do you know?" It's not like he's Simon Wells, our school snake specialist.

"Red touches yellow, you're a dead fellow. Red touches black, you're okay Jack," Caleb mumbles.

We both stand still looking at one another. I don't know how to help him. I glance at Beauty and then he abruptly gets up and leaps onto the venomous snake. He bites it with his razor sharp teeth. Beauty pierces the snake with such might that it instantly dies.

"That was impressive," Caleb exhales.

"I'll say." It's like Beauty read our minds. "You still think Beauty's leading us in harm's way?" Caleb shakes his head no.

The two of us follow Beauty, again. After a while, I spot a small stream of running water.

"Hey, I see water!" I shout feeling excited.

"Water break," says Caleb. He runs over to the stream nearly tripping over his own feet. I hurriedly follow him. Beauty trails behind us and walks right into the stream. Apparently he loves the water. He's running around splashing.

I bend down, cupping my hands to drink some water, but my foot slides on the green, mossy ground and I fall into the stream.

"Great!" I fret. Now my clothes are soaked again.

Caleb pops his head up from drinking and sees me in the stream. He hurries over and reaches his hand out for me.

"Go on, grab it," he says. Part of me would love to pull him in the water so that he can be as wet as I am, but I don't dare.

I grab his hand tightly and he pulls me up out of the water.

"Thank you," I say.

"Of course." Caleb looks at me and I turn away.

I try to wring out my clothes the best I can, but that doesn't help much. They will just have to dry on their own. Feeling upset with myself for falling in, I let out a big sigh.

"Hey. It's not so bad," Caleb chuckles.

"Easy for you to say. You're not the one who's soaked."

"Could be worse. Could be freezing outside." He's got a point.

It is relatively warm and slightly humid out. I suppose it could be worse.

"I guess."

As we continue on with our venture, I think about what I saw at the stones. I think about my purpose and what I have been called to do. To the average person, this might sound borderline psychotic, but to us visionaries, it sounds like we're getting closer to the truth.

As I continue to ponder my predicament, Caleb throws his arm out and stops me from walking any further. Beauty stops fast and my heart skips a beat. We can hear voices. Unfamiliar voices.

∞ CHAPTER 23 ∞

Sebastian & Mya

"It's no use," Mya wails, "I can't get out of this torture chamber!"

"Don't give up now. Keep trying."

Sebastian and Mya continue to try to break free from the cages before the gang members return. Feeling frustrated, Sebastian violently shakes the cage.

"Are you trying to notify the gang members that we're attempting to break free?" Mya asks.

"Argh! If it wasn't for you we wouldn't be in this mess," Sebastian grunts.

Sebastian knows he is taking his anger out on Mya, but it is difficult for him to keep his cool given the current circumstances. He feels frustrated and hopeless.

Mya chooses to ignore Sebastian and works away at the cage.

Just then, a loud roar grabs their attention and Mya and Sebastian stop working on their cages.

"What was that?" Mya whispers.

"I'm not sure."

A large crowd begins to chant in unison. Then someone, presumably the leader Andre, yells out an announcement: "Silence! We honor this day with a sacrifice to the Gods! We give them this leader, Sir Mateo, in return for their power!"

The other gang members cheer and yell during this morbid speech.

"Now, bring me my sacrifice!" yells the leader.

"Oh my God! They're going to kill Sir Mateo," Mya calls out.

"It's okay. He told me this was going to happen. He's immortal, remember?"

"Did I miss something?"

"He contacted me through my mind. We'll talk about that later. Keep trying to get out of that cage."

"So, you're not worried about Sir Mateo?" Mya asks.

"Yes, but he'll be all right."

"What about us?" Mya questions.

"What about us?"

"We're not immortal. What if they come for us next?"

"Good point. Keep working."

Mya works feverishly at a metal bar in the front of her cage. Her fingers keep slipping from her sweat. She pulls the metal bar and rubs it against a vertical bar, hoping to unhinge it. She keeps doing this in the same motion, hoping to eventually open the lock, but it is no use.

"Ow!" Mya squeals in pain.

Sebastian stops working on the cage. "What happened?"

"I cut myself."

"Is it bad?"

"It won't stop bleeding."

Mya acquired a small laceration to the palm of her hand. Sebastian quickly thinks of a remedy to help control the bleeding. "Rip off a piece of your shirt and tie it around your cut."

Mya tries to rip off a piece of fabric from her shirt, but it won't tear.

"I can't do it," Mya grumbles with despair.

Sebastian grabs his shirt and tears off a piece from the bottom.

"Okay, how did you do that so fast?"

"Practice."

"You practice ripping off your own shirt? That's interesting."

"I was joking."

Sebastian then rolls it up into a ball and throws it toward Mya's cage. Luckily, Mya is able to reach the torn shirt and pull it through. She quickly unravels the material and ties it firmly around her cut.

"Thanks."

"No problem."

The rebel leader speaks again in another language to the crowd of listeners. The other gang members repeat sentences after the leader announces them. Then the leader makes a grunting sound as if lifting something extremely heavy-most likely Sir Mateo. The crowd falls silent and not a word is spoken.

The sudden sound of fire crackling and Sir Mateo screaming breaks the uncomfortable calm. Sir Mateo screams more. His loud screams sound terrifying and heart wrenching. The crowd starts to chant again, only this time they sound crueler.

"I thought you said he was going to be all right," Mya demands.

"I thought he was. He said he was," Sebastian answers, sounding doubtful. "Maybe he can still feel pain?"

Sir Mateo's screaming becomes unbearable to listen to, and Mya cups her hands around her ears firmly to block out the sounds of agony. Sebastian looks at Mya and begins to feel sorry for her. Then Mya begins to hum loudly to help block out Sir Mateo's cries of unimaginable pain as well as the loud, rambunctious cheers from the gang members.

Shaking his head in disbelief, Sebastian calls out to Mya, "Hey. Are you okay?"

"What do you think?"

Sebastian feels the same way Mya does, but he knows that they need to remain focused on their immediate goal, which is to get out of there.

"Listen, we can't help him by wasting away in here. We need to find a way out. Focus on your spirit animal."

Mya agrees with Sebastian. She realizes that she needs to do something, or they could be next. When Mya turned into the tarantula for the first time at the Agua Magia, she felt more alive than she had ever felt in her entire life. She wanted to feel that way again.

Mya wastes no time as she closes her eyes and envisions her spirit animal. She thinks about the hairy arachnid and how it felt to be inside its body. She becomes so in tune with her spirit animal that she starts to feel a sting of connection. Her body begins to feel warm and tingly inside.

Miraculously, each leg and arm begin to eerily separate into two hairy extensions. Her body starts to lengthen and her face slowly disappears. Finally, the transformation is complete!

After a continuous struggle to open the cage door, Sebastian stops and notices something different about Mya. Although he can barely see her due to the dimness of the cave, he knows something has changed.

"Mya. Is that you?"

Mya can't verbally communicate, but nods her head in such a way that means *yes*. Her body has become so unbelievably flexible that she is able to finagle herself right through the metal bars.

"Incredible," Sebastian says to himself, amazed as she makes her way toward him.

Mya attempts to pull the metal bars apart, but she is unable to make them move. She jumps away disgruntled as she searches for a tool or weapon to help loosen the metal bars.

"If you could access your spirit animal, then maybe I can too."

Sebastian closes his eyes and tries his best to access his spirit animal. However, he starts to think of Aislinn, and wonders if she is safe. He has difficulty focusing on his spirit animal as his mind continues to picture Aislinn as the beautiful hawk with flowing colors of red and brown hues. He finds himself in awe of this delectable creature. His heart aches to see her.

∞ CHAPTER 24 ∞

Aislinn & Caleb

Caleb and I stay extremely quiet. All you can hear is the sound of our heartbeats and the natural surroundings of the rainforest. We don't want to run the risk of our enemy finding us first. We duck down low and listen closely to the ongoing commotion. The sound of people chanting something over and over again makes me fear the worst. Caleb and I look at one another and know that something terrible is about to happen.

"What do you think is going on?" I ask Caleb.

"I don't know, but it doesn't sound good."

The chanting stops and someone begins to make an announcement. The person speaks about sacrifice and then we hear Sir Mateo's name.

"Oh my God! We have to help him," I plead.

"And how do you suppose we do that?"

"I don't know. We have to do something. They're going to kill him!" I rant. My leg keeps twitching like it sometimes does when I get nervous.

"Look, Aislinn. There are only two of us and all we have is some makeshift daggers. Who knows what they have?"

"You forget they we are visionaries. We have spirit animals to protect us."

"Yeah, have you seen yours lately? Because if you did, let it know that I've been looking for mine."

I look at Caleb's face. The worry in his eyes is hard to ignore.

"I know you're scared. But we have each other and don't forget," Beauty walks in between my legs as if he knew I was going to mention his name, "we have Beauty!"

Beauty snarls in agreement.

Caleb shakes his head. I glare at him, waiting for some sign of vengeance to shine through his frightened face.

"This is a death trap," Caleb sighs. "Come on, let's go around and get a better view."

I share a warm smile with him and he smiles back. I know he's thinking about survival, but what if Sebastian is there too? I have to save him. He would come for me no matter what.

As we creep around for a better view, we spot the source of all the commotion. Caleb and I look at one another and whisper in unison, "Sir Mateo!"

Sir Mateo stands before a large crowd. He is wearing painted symbols on his face and his head hangs low as two men hold him up toward the mob. Another man, tall and burly with a large scar on the side of his face, stands in front of him, encouraging pandemonium from the crowd while a raging fire roars beside them in a large pit. I can hear the rumble of the flames.

"They're going to throw him in the fire!" I cry hysterically.

"Shhh," Caleb warns as he grabs hold of me. I squirm free so I can see Sir Mateo.

The stout man standing in front suddenly turns around and picks up Sir Mateo. He holds him up in the air, as if he were as light as a feather, and the crowd goes crazy. The man yells something in another language to the crowd and they cheer louder. The man takes a step closer to the rampant fire and then forcefully throws Sir Mateo into it. Agonizing screams fill the air and I gasp in panic feeling horrified.

"Oh my God!" I cry.

I turn around and Caleb quickly pulls me into his arms. I bury my head into his chest as I try to forget what I just witnessed. I am in complete and utter shock. This is probably the worst thing I have ever seen or heard.

Sir Mateo finally stops screaming and the crowd becomes silent. I keep hoping to see Sir Mateo pop out of the fire, but that doesn't happen. The evil man who threw him into the fire slowly steps back and raises his hands up to the sky. He yells something to his people as he falls to his knees. The people around him begin to chant and scream with great joy and excitement. Some people also dance around and stamp their feet noisily. It seems barbaric and criminal.

"You okay?" Caleb asks.

"Yeah. I guess," I say as I back away from his tight hold.

"Still want to go in," Caleb whispers.

I nod my head yes in response. It's the right thing to do. Even though we have only known Sir Mateo a short time, I still feel a deep connection to him. Caleb gapes at me in disbelief.

"Aislinn, we can't go in there."

I turn back to view the scene. I don't see any signs of Sebastian or Mya. I feel so powerless. So useless.

"I'm so confused. How can Sir Mateo be dead? He's immortal, right?" I ask, remembering what he told us.

"I don't know," Caleb replies as Beauty brushes up against his legs.

Caleb turns his attention to Beauty. Beauty comes toward me and sits beside me. He stares directly into my eyes. I bend down and touch Beauty's soft head. Beauty stays still and continues to stare at me. I gaze into his eyes and begin to see human eyes take form. I stop petting him and back away slowly.

"Sir Mateo?" I call out.

Beauty jumps to his feet in response.

"Sir Mateo, is that you?" I say again, knowing fully well that it is, indeed, Sir Mateo.

Beauty growls and takes three small strides back. The fur on his body begins to shed and his skin starts to tighten. He stands on two legs as his paws start to stretch out and his fingers begin to emerge. Human legs start to develop and the rest of his jaguar body starts to slowly recede. The human figure stands tall and Caleb and I are completely speechless.

The jaguar went through its own metamorphosis into a human being. It's Sir Mateo. Sir Mateo opens his eyes and stretches his arms.

"Yes. It's me," Sir Mateo answers.

"But how did you? Where did you?" I am at a loss of words.

Sir Mateo walks over to me and places his hand on my shoulder, "It's all right, Aislinn. I'm okay. I'm back except for my ears, that is." He stops talking to touch his ears. "They seem to have been confused with the transformation. No worries. They'll change back eventually."

I glance at his ears and notice that the transformation left Sir Mateo with cute jaguar ears. Soft and fluffy. They are Beauty's. I will miss him.

"So that was you? This whole time?"

"No, not the whole time. The animals of the rainforest respect me as I respect them, and therefore we connect on many levels. Beauty, as you've named him, has guided me through my immortality. He'll remold again and soon he will walk these grounds."

I think about what Sir Mateo has told me. It is similar to my experience with the red-tailed hawk. However, now that Beauty is gone, I feel like I'm missing something. Something meaningful. He gave me the courage to believe in myself again. He gave me confidence. As I reminisce about his departure, I can feel my eyes begin to tear. They are holding back a flood that must not escape. I breathe deeply and regain my focus.

As I stare at Sir Mateo's jaguar ears, I notice that he is explaining to Caleb about Sebastian and Mya's whereabouts. Missing a third of the conversation, I eagerly jump in when I hear Sebastian's name. "So he's here?"

"Where have you been?" says Caleb. "Sir Mateo just told us that they're locked in cages."

"Sorry, I was distracted. Cages?"

"Thinking about Beauty were you?" Caleb asks, sounding empathetic.

"Yeah, I guess."

"The leader of the Rebel Leaders, Andre, has Sebastian and Mya locked in cages. We need to get them out before it is too late," Sir Mateo interrupts.

"Too late for what?" Caleb and I both question simultaneously.

"Before they are sacrificed."

The thought of Sebastian being sacrificed is purely unbearable.

"They must complete five sacrifices before the full moon tonight. This gives the Gods, the Gods they believe in, plenty of time to digest the blood before giving up their powers."

"What can we do?" Caleb enquires while I stare at Sir Mateo in disbelief. My legs keep shaking and I can't seem to stand still. I have anxiety written all over me.

"I will distract them, while you two get Sebastian and Mya."

Sir Mateo points in the direction of where Sebastian and Mya are located. "You will go that way. I will lead them in this direction."

"Okay. We got this. Right, Aislinn?" Caleb says sounding more self-assured than me.

"Yes. Of course we got this," I reply, knowing that I am not completely confident, but confident enough.

I turn to look at the clearing through the brush. It seems like a straight shoot down a small hill and into the cave-like structure. I notice that there are many Rebel Leader gang members hanging around. Too many to count. I turn to ask Sir Mateo a question, but I am too late. He is gone and all that is left is an odor that reminds me of Beauty. I breathe it in deeply so that I can soak up every last memory of him. Caleb watches me with a confused look on his face. I shrug my shoulders and spit out, "Okay. Let's do this."

∞ CHAPTER 25 ∞

"So are you excited?"

"I'm sorry?" I ask, not knowing how to answer Caleb's absurd question.

"Excited to see Sebastian."

"Of course I'm excited. But, right now I'm feeling a little bit more on the terrified side. What about you?" I ask. Caleb smirks. I only hope he doesn't speak like this in front of Sebastian. Having the two of them feud would only add more stress to our situation.

"I don't know what I'm feeling. I think I've been in the Amazon Rainforest too long." He can sure say that again. He wobbles a little almost falling over and then stands straight again. I think he's trying to be humorous or maybe he's just gone mad from being stranded out here in the middle of nowhere.

Suddenly, the Rebel Leader gang members begin running and screaming erratically. Something has either scared them or angered them. They are running in different directions, luckily nowhere near where we are.

"That must be our sign to go in. Come on," Caleb says while taking my hand.

I look at his hand holding mine and my concentration becomes boggled. I should be focusing on our mission and now my attention is focused on our hands. His large hands engulf mine. Within three steps, I gently tug my hand from his and place it on various trees while we walk. I catch Caleb look back at me, but I pretend not to notice.

As we enter the clearing, we notice that it is filled with an array of different snakes.

"Wow!" I say, stunned.

Large snakes, small snakes, green snakes, brown snakes, and more. I feel amazed and fearful at the same time. I have never witnessed so many snakes loose at one time. They are all moving about in such a sinister manner. Not a good place to be if you have a fear of snakes.

"Here's something you don't see every day," Caleb says.

"Uh-huh. Let's keep moving," I remind him.

For one, I am not a big fan of snakes, and two, we have to save Sebastian from being sacrificed. And Mya too.

Caleb and I carefully maneuver around the snakes. One slithers by my foot and I cringe inside while continuing my pace.

"Sir Mateo is definitely creative," Caleb says.

"Yeah. That's one way to put it."

"It's not that bad," Caleb says.

"Watch out, that one's poisonous," I say while pointing to a beautiful coral snake. It moves so gracefully. As it approaches my feet I scurry faster.

"You're right. It looks like many of them are venomous."

We finally reach the cave-like structure, and we slowly venture in. Most of the rebel leader gang members have dispersed into the rainforest, leaving only a handful straggling behind.

"Do you think they're in here?" I ask.

"They should be. But we need to be quick. I don't know how long a couple of snakes are going to hold off these crazy human sacrificing psychos."

"A couple," I mutter under my breath. That was far more than a couple of snakes. It was more like all of the snakes in the world gathered in one small place.

I let Caleb enter the cave before me. I would have gone in first, but he inched his way ahead of me taking the lead. Caleb looks at me and I put my fingers to my lips, gesturing for him to be quiet. There is a strong possibility that gang members could be in here with them. We slowly enter through the dark cave.

"Oh my God!" I whisper, startled.

"What? What it is?"

"I bumped into something and it scared the daylights out of me."

The two of us look at the object I bumped into and realize it is a cage. A medium-sized, empty cage. If we had flashlights, it would make this a whole lot easier.

"Look around for another cage," I tell Caleb.

I figure where there is one cage, there are probably a few more. Hopefully Sebastian and Mya are not stuck in the same cage. That would just be unfair.

Then I bump into something else and Caleb and I both scream. Another voice sounds and causes my scream to immediately come to a halt while my brain tries to register the source of the voice.

"Aislinn?"

"Sebastian?" I cry. "Oh my God! It's you."

"Aislinn!"

I jump into Sebastian's arms and he holds me tight. I kiss him a thousand times all over his face. Small streams of tears flow down my face, but luckily no one can see them since it's so dark in here.

"Wait a minute. If that's Sebastian, then what the hell did I just bump into?" Caleb says, sounding disturbed.

Sebastian carries me over toward Caleb and places me gently on the ground.

"Ahhhhh!" Caleb screams.

"Relax, buddy. It's okay. She won't bite."

Caleb pants, out of breath from his small but legitimate panic attack.

"It's just Mya," Sebastian tells him.

"Mya?" Caleb questions. "No, this isn't Mya. This is an arachnid. A very large arachnid," Caleb says while taking a closer look.

He walks up to Mya. "It is Mya! Sorry. I'm not used to your spirit animal yet."

We all laugh for a moment. Mya backs away as if irritated by the fact that she can't speak. I kind of like her this way.

"But how did she?" I ask, confused.

"Transform?" Sebastian finishes my sentence.

"Yeah."

"I don't know. My guess is the Agua Magia had something to do with it."

"That's what got us into this mess to begin with. If it wasn't for you-" Caleb stops ranting and raving when he notices Sebastian motioning for him to stop. It's as if Sebastian was worried about Mya's feelings. I think she should be reprimanded. Caleb's right. If it hadn't been for her selfishness, then we wouldn't have gotten separated.

"So how did you break free?" Caleb asks Sebastian, noticing the broken cage.

"Mya got me out. At first it didn't work. But she did some weird maneuver with her legs and bent the metal."

"How did you guys find us?" Sebastian asks.

"Beauty did. He's gone now, but he got us to Sir Mateo-" Sebastian excitedly interrupts me.

"Sir Mateo. He's alive?"

"Yes, alive and well and-" I begin to say as Caleb rudely interrupts me mid-sentence.

"I hate to break up your little reunion. But, the Rebel Leaders could be back any minute. Do you think we can discuss all of this later?"

"He's right. Come on, we were going to leave this way." Sebastian points to the opposite way of the entrance.

"What if there isn't an exit that way?" I ask.

"Well, it's worth a shot. Otherwise we're going to run straight into a ton of angry Rebel Leaders," Sebastian replies.

"Who want to sacrifice you," I say adding to his sentence.

"Come on guys, we don't have much time," Caleb remarks.

Sebastian, Caleb, and I follow Mya as she creepily leads the way. We figure that since she is in her animal spirit form, her senses and abilities are better than ours.

Watching Mya's eight legs intricately move is completely mind-boggling. How does she move all eight legs in such an alternating pattern? One, two, three, four, five, six, seven, eight large, hairy legs march one by one.

Looking at Sebastian, my heart is in a state of bliss. Pure bliss. I feel like I haven't seen him in ages. It's as if we were in two different worlds. I squeeze his hand

and it feels so warm and safe. What should I say about all that has happened? It's not like anything happened. It was just kind of awkward. And what is Caleb going to do? Will he continue to make friendly passes at me or is that part of our lives completely over now?

While Caleb was borderline inappropriate, I did enjoy his company. He was a good friend to me while we were stranded in the rainforest. He was kind, funny, and compassionate, but he wasn't Sebastian. No one could ever replace my Sebastian.

Sebastian looks down at me. "I feel like I haven't seen you in forever."

"Likewise. It's been crazy. This whole thing," I mutter.

"Tell me about it," he says while squeezing my hand. "So, who's Beauty?"

"Beauty? Beauty was a jaguar that I, we, befriended. He led me to you."

"A jaguar? Wow! That is crazy. Where is he now?"

"He's gone," I sadly admit. "Sir Mateo used him as a spirit animal to come back to life. He said that he will reform again though." I sigh. "But, he probably won't even remember me," I solemnly say.

"How could anyone, even an animal, ever forget you? It would be impossible."

That's my Sebastian. Always saying the right thing at exactly the right time. I look ahead and spot Caleb glancing back at us. He must have heard our conversation. His face seems disappointed. I frown.

"Thanks, Caleb," Sebastian calls out.

Caleb turns back around surprised. "For what?"

"For looking out for Aislinn."

"Oh right," says Caleb.

"Um, I can look out for myself-thank you. I don't need a babysitter," I hastily spit out.

"You know what I mean," Sebastian chuckles.

Caleb stares at me for a second too long.

"I know. Yes, Caleb. Thank you for-," I pause a moment, remembering that day in the water. "For being a good friend."

"That's what friends do," Caleb remarks, smiling at me- his voice sounding smug.

This awkward conversation makes walking in this creepy cave seem less eerie somehow. The cave is dark, but there are small pockets of light here and there, making it moderately easy for us to travel through. At times, the cave ceiling appears to be shrinking and at others it seems to rise.

"So how exactly did you guys end up here?" I ask Sebastian.

"We were caught by the Rebel Leaders. Sir Mateo told us about them. Funny thing is, the leader asked us if we were visionaries."

"That's strange. What did you tell him?"

"I didn't say a word. I acted as if I had no idea what he was talking about."

"So, do you think they wanted us or just Sir Mateo?" Caleb asks.

"It would appear that they were looking for all of us. They were made aware of our presence somehow. When they took us back to the remains, the leader was looking for you and Aislinn."

"Something doesn't add up. Somebody must have told them about us. Maybe one of Sir Mateo's men?" Caleb questions.

"I don't think so, because he held them captive too. They were taken somewhere else," Sebastian says somberly. "We need to find Sir Mateo. He'll know what to do."

Suddenly, Mya stops dead in her tracks. I look ahead of her and spot two paths. We are at some sort of crossroads and it looks like we will need to select a path.

"Which one do you think, Mya?" asks Caleb. He clears his throat after saying her name. He still sounds freaked out by her spider presence. Mya inspects both pathways and turns back toward us. One of the paths looks extremely small and the cave ceiling is very low. We will have to literally crawl on our hands and knees just to get through.

"Maybe we should just go with the larger one," Caleb proposes while inspecting the two paths.

"True, but what if it's a trap. Maybe we should try the smaller one," Sebastian suggests. Mya turns around and heads for the smaller one. "The smaller one it is," Caleb says.

Mya swiftly turns back toward him and practically pushes him with two of her creepy spider legs.

"What? What did I say?" Caleb protests.

Mya quickly turns back around and Caleb follows. She turns around and pushes him again- only this time harder. Caleb stumbles and falls to the ground.

"What is your problem?" Caleb grunts.

"I think she's trying to tell you to wait here a minute. Maybe she's going check it out and let us know," I tell Caleb while trying not to laugh.

"Women," Caleb grumbles.

"Spiders," Sebastian whispers. I giggle. Mya continues forward and goes through the smaller path. The three of us stand there anxiously waiting. Unexpectedly, the thought of my parents enter my mind.

"Oh my God! What if my parents tried to call my cell phone?"

"Don't worry. I'm sure Jerry took care of everything. He probably called her himself or had his assistant Mr. Schooner do the honors," Sebastian reassures. I smile forgetting how well Jerry can come up with a plan. He is brilliant.

"You're probably right. I was just thinking about them."

I laugh thinking about Schooner calling my home. I actually miss them. I miss my parents too. I miss Otie and I miss my bed. My comfortable, soft bed. I think I'm starting to get a little homesick.

"Oh shit!" Sebastian calls out.

"What is it?" I ask.

"Snakes. Venomous ones. Watch out!"

"Yeah. Those suckers just don't want to let up. Thanks Sir Mateo," Caleb says while inching away from a venomous green snake.

"What?" Sebastian asks.

"Sir Mateo. He made like a thousand different snakes bombard the area to scare away the gang members so we could come and rescue you. Man, you should have seen it. Gang members running everywhere, screaming and crying. It was quite the sight," Caleb says.

"Yeah, I think I've had my fill of snakes for a lifetime," I say. Then I feel a small amount of pressure on my foot. Grudgingly, I look down and find a snake slither right over my shoe. "Ahhh."

"I would say run, but we have to wait for Mya," Sebastian says. He comes over to me. "I'll just put you over here," Sebastian says as he moves me so that I'm behind him saving me from the slithering beasts.

"So, we should probably just stay put," Caleb advises reluctantly.

"Yeah, I wouldn't move around too much. Wouldn't want to provoke a venomous snake," Sebastian cautions.

Sebastian closes his eyes and stands perfectly still.

"What are you doing?" I ask.

"Trying to contact Sir Mateo." I look at him strangely, knowing fully well that he never closes his eyes.

He peeks at me with one eye and says, "My visions aren't working, so at this point I'll close my eyes, meditate, and even do cartwheels to get a connection."

I'm impressed. He's not trying to act all bravado. He's such a real person and I envy his modesty. A few seconds later, Sebastian's eyes pop back open.

"Any luck?" I ask.

"Nah. Not this time. Maybe he's busy freeing the rest of his tribe."

"Where do you think they are?" I ask, realizing that we haven't seen any of them.

"I don't know. One minute we're awake and the next we found ourselves in cages."

"Sounds familiar," I squeal, as two snakes slither around my feet. It reminds of my encounter with Fredrick's men when they drugged me. Not a good time.

Four snakes begin to encircle Caleb as he moves slyly away from them.

Finally, Mya resurfaces and notices all of the snakes that have managed to come our way. She backs away slowly.

"Guys, Mya's back. We should go," Caleb announces.

"Which path?" I ask.

"Apparently, the one she's crawling back through," Sebastian says. I thought for sure that we would be going through the larger tunnel. This one seems too small for all of us to fit comfortably.

Due to the lack of space in this extremely small tunnel, the four of us are forced to travel in single file. Mya leads the way, then Sebastian, then me, and last is Caleb. While we duck and practically crawl on our hands and knees through this tight space, I try not to be too self-conscious about the fact that Caleb is directly behind me and at times he is directly behind my lower backside.

We continue to scuttle through the small pathway. My knees start to hurt from the hard ground and my fingernails feel gritty and dirty.

"We have got to be almost out of this tunnel. We've been in here forever now," I groan.

"This is crazy. I don't even see a light up ahead," Sebastian complains. Luckily, the snakes neglected to follow us through this maze.

"What's touching me?" I say as I squirm. The feeling of creepy crawlies makes me shudder.

"It's not me," Caleb points out.

"I don't want to know. Just move faster please," I beg.

We get to a point where I can crouch while walking, and I notice that my feet are wet. I look down at the ground and see that it's starting to become wet and muddy. And as we continue further, the water appears to be getting deeper.

"Hey guys," I whimper. "The water. It's getting deeper."

"Hopefully, our passageway isn't blocked," Sebastian says. As we trudge further, the water soon reaches my waistline. An odd noise grabs my attention. A constant noise with no breaks or pauses. It reminds me of static on television.

Suddenly, I hear Sebastian scream. I look around for him, but he is nowhere to be found. Two seconds ago, he was right in front of me and now he's gone. I start to panic. I can't see much and that makes me very uneasy. I try to feel around for him, but it's no use.

"Caleb. Where did Sebastian and Mya go?" I ask. My voice is trembling.

Abruptly, I feel my feet elevate off the floor and my body drops down a long hole like Alice in Wonderland.

∞ CHAPTER 26 ∞

"Ahhhhhhhhhhhhhhhhhhhhhhhhhh," I scream as water engulfs my mouth and I fall down a long hole. I spit it out and desperately try to grab on to anything I can. It's no use. I claw at my surroundings as I continue to drop down. Everything is happening so fast. My whole life flashes before my eyes. Water is falling on both sides of me and I can see nothing but darkness.

Suddenly, my body stops falling and makes a loud splash. I have landed unharmed into a pool of fresh water.

"Sebastian! Sebastian!" I scream. I thrash around frantically trying to find him while spitting water out of my mouth.

"Aislinn! Aislinn! I'm right here," Sebastian calls out as he swims over to me.

"What happened? Where are we?" I cry.

Mya floats above the water behind Sebastian.

"We fell through a water hole. We're all here except for-" Sebastian is cut off by another loud splash. "Caleb!"

"That was awesome!" Caleb shouts.

Speak for yourself. As Caleb takes a dip under the water, flashbacks about our time together in the Amazon Rainforest pop into my head. Only this time I'm here with Sebastian. My brain tries to register what just happened. It was like being on a rollercoaster for the first time. The pit of my stomach felt like it was spinning and the thought of death crossed my mind more than once.

"Everybody accounted for?" a female voice sounds.

I look toward the voice and find Mya. Ugh. She's human again. First I fall about a hundred feet into the unknown and now Mya's back to normal. Can this nightmare get any worse? I think about what Caleb said about her having the hots for Sebastian and a small nauseated feeling takes the place of panic in my belly.

"Look who's back?" Caleb says jokingly. "And I thought we were going to have a furry pet for a little while longer."

"Um, I'm nobody's pet, thank you," Mya remarks snidely.

"Well, hi to you too," Caleb snaps back.

"Guys, if we stay here, we're sitting ducks. We need to get out of here. Come on," Sebastian directs. The three of us follow Sebastian as he leads the way.

The hole that we fell from lies near a straight, rocky wall with no way to get back up. It is quite a distance to land and it's been a long time since I swam laps. When I go the beach, I usually sit on my blanket and stare at the open water. This will definitely be a challenge for me.

As the four of us swim toward land, I notice Mya struggling. She's breathing hard, and she is lagging far behind. It seems as though her transformation left her a little breathless.

"Guys, we should slow down," I say, feeling sorry for Mya.

Caleb looks at me with surprise. Little does he know that I too am shocked by my concern about Mya. I suppose that just because I don't care for the girl doesn't mean that I would want to see her drown or become captured again.

"She's right," Sebastian says as he slowly treads water to stay afloat. Caleb swims back toward Mya.

"You should float on your back. It's easier," Caleb offers.

"I'm fine. Just because Aislinn says to slow down, doesn't mean you have to," Mya says. She sounds bitter. I try to ignore her comments and look the other way.

"I want to," Caleb replies.

Caleb has definitely shown some growth over the last couple of days. He seems more mature and caring. Sebastian and I continue treading water while we watch Mya and Caleb catch up.

"That was nice of you," Sebastian says to me.

"I didn't do anything."

"You know what I mean," Sebastian says while he swims closer to me.

"Hey," I say.

"Yeah."

"I missed you."

"I missed you more," Sebastian replies while he leans in for a kiss. His touch is warming and it reminds me of all the reasons why I love him. He looks at me with those eyes, which causes my heart to skip a beat.

"Do you think we'll get out of this alive?" I ask.

"Without a doubt."

While I know that his words are meant to be comforting, I can still sense the uncertainty in his voice. Caleb and Mya make their way toward us, and Sebastian and I begin swimming faster again. I push my body and give myself a silent pep talk to keep me going. My hands and feet have become slightly numb. And my chest is about ready to explode. Keeping the land in sight provides me with a visual goal. Sebastian slows down every now and then when he senses I'm lagging behind and Caleb does the same for Mya.

As I tread water slowly, trying to keep my head afloat, something shiny catches my eye. I stop swimming and stare out into the open water, hoping to spot it again. Finally, I see it. Two small, pink, shiny dolphins splash in the water. Sebastian stops swimming and looks at what I'm staring at. Caleb and Mya stop swimming as well.

"They're amazing, aren't they?" I say, feeling captivated by their beauty.

"I'll say," Caleb agrees.

"They're pink," Mya says with an edge of sarcasm.

"They are pink Amazon river dolphins," Caleb informs.

"Not these guys. There's something magical about them. Look at the way their skin sparkles in the sun.

And the way they seem so animated," Sebastian adds as the two dolphins jump into the air and then nuzzle one another.

"Look over there." Caleb points.

A large, pink, sparkly dolphin emerges from the water. It corrals the two smaller dolphins while making distinct calling sounds. The two smaller dolphins look our way and then turn to follow the larger dolphin. Within seconds they disappear into to the depths of the water.

"That must have been their mother," I squeal.

"Come on guys, we don't have much more to go," Sebastian reminds us as he begins to swim ahead.

Swimming slowly toward land, I picture myself as a dolphin. They are such docile and graceful creatures. Their movements are elegant and I am fascinated with their cleverness. I try to swim as gracefully as the magical dolphins, but I tire myself and must revert back to a slow and steady tread.

At last, we reach land and my fingers grasp at the soft sand. My knees buckle as I try to get up, so I roll over on my back instead. The four of us lie there catching our breath.

"Well, that was more than my usual workout," Caleb jokes.

"It wasn't that bad," Mya says.

Sebastian and I roll our eyes knowing that Mya is living in denial about this and many other things.

"What do we do next?" Caleb asks.

"We find Sir Mateo," Sebastian answers.

"Ladies, you heard the man. Up and at 'em," Caleb jokes.

"He's awfully energetic. You must have something to do with that?" Mya says while nodding her head toward me in a cunning manner.

"Excuse me?" I say, surprised.

"You heard me. It's not a secret, Aislinn."

"I don't know what you're talking about, Mya," I say as I stand up and wring out my wet hair. The blood through my veins begins to boil. Sebastian stands up as if to intervene and Caleb puts his head down as if ashamed or scared to become involved.

"You know damn well what I'm talking about."

"Mya, if you have something to say, then say it!" I yell back.

"Mya, I told you before. Stay out of my relationship with Aislinn!" Sebastian demands, looking as steamed as I feel. His face is red and his dark eyes are squinted.

"She got involved before?" I ask Sebastian, feeling even more enraged.

Somehow, I knew this was coming. I just didn't know when. The tension between Mya and me has been building for some time and it was bound to surface sooner or later.

Sebastian looks at me. "When we got separated she started rambling about stuff, and I told her I'd leave her in the Amazon, which sounds like a pretty damn good idea right about now."

"Don't look at me," Mya snaps as all of us stare at her angrily. "I'm not the one pretending to be a Miss Goody Two Shoes. We all know you hooked up with Caleb."

She must be referring to the Coffee Beanery. Caleb must have told her or she had a vision about it, which I highly doubt.

"Are you crazy? I didn't hook up with anyone," I answer.

Mya gives me wide eyes and a crude smirk.

"I don't have time for this. We've got a village to save. I'm done here," I say as I walk away into the forest. I'm so angry right now; I could have punched her square in the face. But I know that it's only my anger speaking. I would regret it later. And how could she even say that? She's trying to break Sebastian and me up. That little wench.

Suddenly, I hear Caleb speak.

"Mya. The next time you have something to say, check your facts first. Aislinn and I never hooked up. She wouldn't do that," Caleb says as he looks over to me standing at the brink of the forest. "She's a good person. You could learn something from her," he finishes. Caleb's words are kind and heartfelt. I feel thankful that he told the truth. I smile.

"Look. Aislinn's right. We don't have time for this. This is child's play. There are people possibly being sacrificed right now and you're causing trouble. Wake up! The world doesn't revolve around Mya!" Sebastian says, sounding angrier than I've ever heard him before.

Mya rolls her eyes and purses her lips.

"Now if you're done screwing around, we need to get moving. Let's go!" says Sebastian.

Sebastian walks over to me and grabs my hand. Caleb follows and Mya stands there motionless not muttering a word for once. She stares blankly at the sand.

Sebastian stops walking and turns around. "I said, let's go!"

Mya's face is full of disgust, but she unwillingly follows. She probably figures that she's dead without us. I suppose she didn't drink from the almighty Agua Magia. If she did, then she would have stayed there for sure.

The air begins to get cooler, considering that we're wet from swimming. Mya's outrageous comedy act took away from the fact that we just swam across the most surreal body of water I've ever seen. It's like we found this secret lake below the caves that no one knows about.

After a while, we stop for a drink from a small stream. Sebastian opens up the side pocket of his pants and pulls out something to cleanse the water. I laugh when I think about Caleb and I lighting a fire for nothing since we had nothing to contain the water.

"Where are we headed?" I ask Sebastian after a long bout of uncomfortable silence. Nobody spoke after that whole situation. It's like everyone was afraid to speak.

"We're headed back to the village," Sebastian answers, sounding a bit short. Caleb walks off to presumably use the forest bathroom and Mya stays clear from us, refusing to drink from Sebastian's container.

"It's been burnt down. There's nothing left."

"We heard about that from the Rebel Leader. But, I have a feeling Sir Mateo will be there."

Hearing Sebastian's voice and watching his eyes trail off lead me to believe that something is bothering him. He doesn't seem like himself.

Feeling guilty, I hesitantly ask, "Is something wrong?"

Even though I know that nothing happened between me and Caleb, I still feel a little remorseful. Caleb definitely has feelings for me, or at least he thinks he does. But that doesn't mean anything because I only have feelings for Sebastian.

"Why didn't you tell me about you and Caleb going to the Coffee Beanery?" Sebastian asks. Hearing him ask that question feels like a ton of heavy bricks falling down on my wounded heart one by one. I would never do anything to hurt him.

"I forgot. It was a while ago. It was nothing, Sebastian, really."

"If it was nothing, then why didn't you tell me?"

Feeling the need to explain myself, I decide to splurge and tell Sebastian every detail. I take a deep breath and just go for it.

"Look, I went to a yoga class and Caleb happened to be there. He asked me to go to the Coffee Beanery with him and I said no, but he insisted. I figured it was harmless. He wanted to know more about being a visionary. Then, a karaoke person came and I signed him up for a song without telling him. He was boasting about being a good singer, and I thought it would be funny. Then he signed me up for a song and I sang it. And it was amazing! Me. I mean when I sang that song by No Doubt, I just felt free. Free to be me, whoever that is." I sigh and look up into his eyes. "Sebastian, I'm sorry if I upset you. I care about you and I would never do anything to hurt you. Ever."

Sebastian smiles and looks deeply into my eyes. "I know. I just wanted to hear you say it." I blush.

"I trust you," he says.

"And I trust you."

Sebastian leans in to kiss me and my lips rush to his. Kissing him brings me to a place of complete serenity. Our kiss ends and I gaze into his beautiful eyes.

"Thank you," I tell him.

"For what?"

"For being you," I say.

Sebastian smiles.

"What's up, Caleb?" Sebastian suddenly says.

My eyes widen with confusion.

"How did you know Caleb was coming toward us?" I ask, bewildered, since Sebastian's back was to Caleb. There was no way he could have seen him coming in this direction. And I didn't hear anything either.

"I saw him standing there."

"Before he came?" I ask.

Sebastian turns around and looks at a surprised Caleb. "Yeah."

"Your visions. They're back!" I squeal with delight.

"If mine are back, then yours must be too," Sebastian says.

I close my eyes, knowing fully well that Sebastian and Caleb are both staring at me. But I don't care. I want to access my visions.

I pop open my eyes as fear begins to set in again. "Guys, we need to hurry. Sir Mateo needs our help."

"What did you see?" Caleb worriedly asks.

"I saw screaming and fighting. Lots of fighting. Women and children from Sir Mateo's village. It's horrific. It's probably that war we're supposed to fight in." I shudder while trying to digest the images I just saw.

"Fight?" Sebastian asks.

"I saw it when we went back to the stones. I can explain it as we go," I say.

"Let's go then," Sebastian yells.

Sebastian, Caleb, and I run as fast as we can through the thick rainforest. Mya runs, but deliberately stays back a few yards. The forest has become natural to us now. The way we jump and maneuver around the overgrown brush and tree roots. The way we constantly observe our surroundings looking out for wild animals or unsuspecting visitors show that we have adapted to the life of the rainforest. When I feel my internal abilities begin to kick in, I know that we are a force of one.

∞ CHAPTER 27 ∞

Within a short time, we arrive at the burnt village. It has only been a few hours since I've been here with Caleb and it still reeks of fire. We scan the area quietly.

A small rustling sound coming from behind a burnt hut grabs our attention and the three of us look at one another. Could it be a Rebel Leader? My heart begins to beat faster.

"I'll go, you guys stay here," Sebastian utters.

"No," I gasp. "You can't leave me again."

"Aislinn, I will never leave you again. Wait here," Sebastian says firmly. My heart pounds from fear. Sebastian soundlessly heads over to the suspected noise. I try to obtain a vision but am unable to do so. Caleb slowly heads toward Sebastian and I linger behind with Mya. I choose to look straight ahead and not in her direction. The sight of her makes me want to vomit, twice.

"It's okay, "Sebastian calls out. "It's Raul."

Raul? I don't remember meeting a Raul. I walk over to Sebastian behind the burnt hut and find a small boy looking miserable and disheveled. He can't be a day over five. His little brown eyes look in my direction and something about him feels oddly familiar.

"Hello, Raul, I'm Aislinn," I say while bending down on one knee.

He must be a nervous wreck. I'm practically an adult and I'm nervous; I can't imagine how he must be feeling, being so young.

Raul looks down at me and begins to say something. None of us know what he's saying, but we try our best to communicate with him.

"It's okay. We'll help you find your family. Okay?" I tell him.

Raul looks at my face and touches the side of it with the palm of his right hand. He smiles and I smile back. I reach my hand out for his and he accepts the invitation and grabs it. I catch Caleb looking at me. His eyes are wide with amazement and he's smiling. I blush, feeling uncomfortable. With all that has happened, I hope he just drops everything. I'd like to be able to remain friends.

Sebastian bends down and analyzes the ground nearby. Caleb decides to join in, as the both of them seem to be good at tracking. Different footprints lace the ground. They are unclear to me, but Sebastian and Caleb seem to be confident in their findings.

"Sir Mateo must be close. Come on, guys," Sebastian calls out.

Raul and I hold hands while we follow the crew. At times he looks up at me and smiles. I snicker. His presence is comforting, and I try to imagine what it must be like for him. He must feel so alone and frightened; although you couldn't tell.

Sebastian and Caleb suddenly stop walking. They both look around. I look at Raul's eyes and see a little boy who misses his family.

"Sir Mateo, how did you find us?" Sebastian unexpectedly calls out, scaring me half to death.

"Oh, it was not hard. I can hear you all for miles," he jokes.

It feels good to have finally run into Sir Mateo. Hopefully, we can get some answers and direction.

Sir Mateo bends down to Raul and says something to him in their language. The little boy laughs and looks at me.

"What did you tell him?" I ask.

"I told him that he was a very lucky boy."

Sebastian and Caleb both laugh. I suppose that comment was about me, but since I didn't get the joke, I don't feel like asking about it. I smile bashfully.

Sir Mateo walks over to Mya and puts his hand on her heart. "Ah. You did not drink from the Agua Magia. Your spirit animal must have guided you well. You are very lucky to have listened. To be living as long as I have, well, let's just say that it gets tiring after a while."

Mya says nothing and smirks. A shrug of her shoulders tells me that she wishes she did drink from the Agua Magia.

"The Rebel Leaders have taken some of my men captive, but the rest of the village is at our sister village."

"Is it far?" Caleb questions.

"It is not too far from here."

Remembering my vision, I quickly walk over to Sir Mateo. "Sir Mateo, there's going to be a war. A terrible war."

Sir Mateo nods his head and smiles. "I know. It is okay. You are all here now. You will know what to do."

Hearing him say this only adds to my frustration. Why does everything have to be so complicated? I wish that we could just get straightforward answers.

"But, Sir Mateo. We don't know what to do. There are only four of us and we haven't any weapons."

"You don't need weapons. It is your heart that you'll need. Come now. It's time to go."

Sebastian and I exchange looks. I know that we should trust him. It's just hard to feel confident going up against a ton of people who seem to be ready to fight to the death.

During the way, Sir Mateo periodically picks things off the trees and eats them. I watch him intently and he notices me. I quickly look away but it is too late. He hands me a piece of something that he peeled off of a tree. I politely refuse.

"This is growth. You need your energy. Eat," he demands. Sir Mateo holds the growth in front of my face.

I sigh and hesitantly take the offering of growth. I place it gently on my tongue and begin to chew it slowly, hoping that it doesn't taste repulsive. At first it tastes like a bland piece of meat. But as I chew on it, it begins to taste sweeter and sweeter like a fruit.

"Don't assume that this piece of earth will not taste good because it doesn't look good. One must be confident that it will taste good and so it shall," Sir Mateo preaches.

Sir Mateo gives some of the growth to Raul. Raul smiles widely. He seems to be more than delighted. He eats the growth within seconds.

Whatever did Sir Mateo's comment mean? I felt like I was back in grade school again. I suppose Sir Mateo meant that I shouldn't judge a book by its cover. But he could have just said that. Sir Mateo soon hands Sebastian, Caleb, and Mya a piece of the growth.

"This will give you energy and provide you with inner strength."

Sebastian and Caleb each take a piece and quickly devour it. They show no signs of uneasiness. Perhaps they are both trying to appear strong and confident. Mya reluctantly reaches out her hand and grabs a piece of growth from Sir Mateo's hand. She takes one look at it and pops it into her mouth.

"It's not the worst thing I've had on this trip," she says.

Caleb and I glance at each other, but quickly look away. I can tell he's uncomfortable around me. Now there's a sense of uncertainty, which I hate.

"Come now. We must get there before dark," Sir Mateo says as he leads the way. I look up into the huge spread of canopy trees and see hues of pink and orange. Breaks in the canopy reveal the hidden sunset. The trees provide a constant shade and hide the true colors of the sky so you can never quite tell what time of day it is.

Following Sir Mateo is much better than leading the way into the unknown. He knows this forest like the back of his hand. He knows what to eat and drink and everything else one should know about survival in this remarkable land. Since our fast-paced walk has been a rather quiet one, my mind starts to focus on the natural sounds of the rainforest. It's difficult not to find serenity when you hear animals, birds and insects. It's not noise at all, but rather organic sounds.

I can't help but notice that Sir Mateo sure is quick on his feet for being a couple of hundred years old. I watch him quickly glide over large tree roots and forest floor brush. He's fast and alert.

"Not quite the adventure you signed up for, huh?" Sebastian whispers into my ear while we keep up with the pace.

"No. Not quite."

"Well, if it means anything, I'm glad we came here together. I couldn't have done it without you," he tells me.

I smile, feeling warm all over. "There's no place else I'd rather be."

Sebastian reaches for my hand and we hold hands for a little while. To be honest, there really is nowhere else I'd rather be. Although we're in danger and our lives are at stake, I have this feeling of familiarity that's hard to comprehend. It's like I'm supposed to be here at this very minute.

"I think we should break for water," says Mya.

"Of course. Let's stop up ahead. I know a good place to drink," Sir Mateo answers.

Sir Mateo brings us a little further to another hidden paradise. It's an area that has beautiful scenery and a perfect body of crystal clear water. It's as if he created it especially for us. Raul happily skips ahead and frolics by the water.

"Is this place for real or am I seeing things?" Caleb questions.

"Oh it's very much real my friend. Go ahead and have a drink. It's safe," Sir Mateo reassures.

Caleb suddenly takes off his shirt, pants, and shoes and jumps in. An instant replay of that time we had the other day in the water.

"I don't think we have much time," Sebastian calls out.

"It's okay. We have some time. This may be the last time you get to take a water break," says Sir Mateo.

"Well in that case, I'm going in. It's been a while since I had a shower. Aislinn, will you join me?" Sebastian asks.

My mind is racing. I can't go in there. It would just be too weird.

"I'm okay. You go in. The water looks great."

"Come on. One quick swim?" Sebastian begs.

"No really. I'm finally dried from our last venture in the water and I really don't feel like getting wet again. You go in and enjoy yourself. I'll watch."

"Okay. But, I'll be watching you," Sebastian says jokingly.

How did I get so lucky? He's as gentle as baby kitten and as ferocious as a grizzly bear. I stand for a minute and watch Sebastian cool off in the uncontaminated cool water. The ripples in his six-pack are mesmerizing.

Feeling the need to rest my tired feet, I find a seat on a long log that seems to be clear of bugs. I'm sure to check all around as I know there are many creepy crawlies everywhere in the rainforest. Sir Mateo comes over and takes a seat next to me and Raul happily jumps in the water. Caleb and Sebastian quickly befriend him.

"You and Sebastian make a strong team."

"Me and Sebastian? Yeah, I think so," I say as I watch Sebastian romp in the water with Raul.

"You didn't forget what the stones showed you, did you?"

"How could I forget?" I say breathlessly. "I can't stop thinking about it."

Thinking about the fact that I am here from another world, or the afterlife, is completely mind- boggling. As if being a visionary wasn't enough.

"You are here for a reason. I can feel it. You will reveal your memories soon," Sir Mateo says in a low voice. I look at him.

"Why can't I just know everything now? Can you tell me? Please? It would make things so much easier."

"I don't know everything. I know what you know."

"But you're the visionary guru. You're supposed to know everything."

Sir Mateo laughs. "Thank you. Sometimes I think I do know everything and then nature reminds me otherwise. You see, life in itself is a mystery. And you," Sir Mateo pauses. "You are a warrior. Your memories are in between the living world and the afterlife. You'll recall everything with time. Trust yourself more."

I sigh with despair. "But I feel so alone."

"You are not alone. You see, Sebastian, he loves you."

"I know he does and I love him too."

"He has come back here with you. To protect you. To fight with you." Sir Mateo smiles at me as he places a comforting hand on my shoulder.

I look at Sir Mateo and stare into his eyes. His words give me chills and I feel it in the pit of my stomach. He's right. I'm just taking a while to adjust to everything. I smile softly back at him. After a moment of silence, Sir Mateo stands up, and Caleb and Sebastian take it as a sign to get out and get ready.

While Sebastian and Caleb dress, I glance around for Mya. I can't find her anywhere.

"Sir Mateo," he looks back at me, "have you seen Mya?"

"She seems to have taken off, again."

"Not again! Guys, Mya took off again," I whine.

"I'm not looking for her again. This is ridiculous," Sebastian rants.

"I'm not either," Caleb agrees.

"It is okay. We do not need to find her. She is headed in the right direction. We'll catch up with her soon," Sir Mateo informs.

We gather ourselves and follow Sir Mateo. Sebastian and Caleb share irritated thoughts about Mya.

"She had to do it again. It's like she wants to cause more trouble," I mumble to myself aloud.

"Well, she can cause all the trouble she wants. We have other things to worry about now," Sebastian says reassuringly.

Caleb stays silent and hurries ahead to walk with Sir Mateo. It seems as if he has something important to tell him by the way he rushes toward him. I hope he's not declaring his undying love for me. That would be stupid.

As we scurry through the forest like animals, rain begins to fall. There isn't any thunder, just soft rain. Since I didn't go into the water before, it feels good to be rained on. Not only is it washing away my sweat, but my guilt that I keep holding on to. Even though I know I didn't do anything inappropriate, I still feel shamefaced for not telling Sebastian sooner. If he really did follow me here to this earth to protect me, then he is the true warrior. Not me.

∞ CHAPTER 28 ∞

We finally complete our journey and feelings of relief and uncertainty mix in my brain, giving me a small headache. Before we stroll into the sister village, Sir Mateo gathers us around. He places a hand on Raul's shoulder, and Raul looks up at Sir Mateo with large, bright eyes.

"Now, some of my tribe will be here, and some are still with the Rebel Leaders. Remember that this original tribe is not exactly the same as what you are used to. They are a little...different," Sir Mateo says, sounding rather restrained. What is he not telling us about this village? "Remember to keep an open mind," he says while signaling for us to move ahead.

Feeling anxious, I look around for Sebastian and he quickly appears next to me. He takes me by the hand and escorts me into the village. With him by my side, I feel confident that we can get through anything. Caleb meanders behind us. I can feel his eyes on me, but I choose not to look his way.

Suddenly, we hear a rustling sound. We stop walking while Sir Mateo pulls away the brush, and we find a bent-over Mya, looking dazed and confused. She's visibly shaking and refusing to look our way.

"Mya," Caleb calls out.

She doesn't answer him.

Sir Mateo bends down. "Mya, it's okay. What you saw is nothing to be scared of. If you had stayed with us you would have known what to expect. I suggest that you don't leave your group again. You are vulnerable without them, and whether you know it or not they need you."

An uncomfortable silence lingers as he waits for a response from Mya.

"And you need them," Sir Mateo says as he looks my way. "Together you are stronger and more fierce than you can imagine. Work as a team and you will be strong. Work alone and you will be defeated." I look at Sebastian and he gives me a hopeful shrug of the shoulders.

Feeling inspired and slightly optimistic, I decide to reach a hand out to the pitiful Mya and try to make things work. If I don't do it, then who will? And if everything is true about my reason for being here, then I need to be the bigger person and make things right.

"Come on. Let's do this together," I offer. Mya looks up at me and stares into my eyes as if she is mesmerized. I watch her intently and she reaches out for my hand. I pull her up.

"Aislinn," Mya utters.

"Yeah."

"I'm sorry."

"Me too."

"Did I miss something?" Caleb says comically.

Sebastian laughs. I laugh too and soon we're all laughing. Sir Mateo stands back and watches with a smile. I look up at him and curiously ask, "What was it that she was so frightened of?"

"I was just going to ask the same thing," Caleb chimes in.

"There were things, terrible things, little things, big things all walking around. They looked...like aliens," Mya answers with a shaky voice.

"It is okay. They are not aliens. They are the truth to the myths that circle around them," Sir Mateo answers.

"What?" Caleb asks.

"I think what he means is that we are about to meet true mythical rumors, legends, creatures of South America. If that's right, then this is just, just going to be amazing," Sebastian adds, sounding more ecstatic than the rest of us.

Caleb, Mya, and I stare at Sebastian with wide eyes. What exactly are we about to walk into? Sir Mateo smiles and says, "What are you all waiting for? Shall we?"

I look for Sebastian's hand and tightly grip it again. We begin to enter the village and Sebastian whispers into my ear, "You continue to amaze me."

I blush and forget about what we're doing for just a second. His voice still gives me goose bumps.

I stop walking as my feet become stuck to the ground and my eyes become fixed on what lies ahead of me. I rub my eyes to make sure I'm seeing things correctly. Everyone else stops walking, except for Sir Mateo.

"This is where we get to see life's mysterious legends first hand," Sebastian says quietly.

"Guys, do you see what I see? Or did I just hit my head and become delirious?" Caleb asks.

"Welcome to the truth," Sir Mateo says as he makes his way toward a standing cat. Or maybe it's a human cat. It looks at us and smiles. I stand there motionless as it speaks to Sir Mateo. "Hey! Nice ears."

Sir Mateo laughs as he touches his jaguar ears. "Good to see you old pal."

"So good to see you too, Sir Mateo. It has been far too long."

"Did it just speak?" I whisper to Sebastian. The human cat speaks perfect English.

Sebastian nods without taking his eyes off the cat species. The human cat looks at me sharply and says, "So I'm an it? Not a scary cat human or man cat, just an it?"

"I'm…sorry," I say, stunned to hear this human cat speak.

"I'm just joking. It gets people every time. I'm Yakity Man. Nice to meet you," he says as he reaches out his paw which has elongated fingers and long fingernails.

I try to speak but the words won't come out. Sebastian lets go of my hand and reaches out to shake Yakity Man's hand.

"Nice to meet you. I'm Sebastian and this is Aislinn and Caleb and Mya."

Yakity Man smiles at each of us and says, "Well, if I shocked you guys, I can't wait to see your faces when you meet the others."

Okay, Aislinn. You need to snap out of it. Why is this shocking you? You turn into a red-tailed hawk every now and then; this is just another day in the life of a visionary. Get over it!

"He is a human cat for all intents and purposes. Earlier civilizations referred to him as the forest cat: one of four animals who brought sacrifices to the Gods, which helped them to create man. He's very friendly and has been around for centuries," Sir Mateo explains as Yakity Man runs off.

We continue walking further into the village and see interesting beings all around us going about their everyday business.

Sir Mateo points out another animal. "That is Utical. A coyote man, another one of the four that was believed to have brought sacrifices to the Gods. And over there are the other two, the Hohha and the Quelpa. Those two are not as friendly as Yakity Man and Utical. They view simple humans as sketchy and emotional beings. It's best not to engage in a conversation with them." Mya's eyebrows rise in response to Sir Mateo's explanation of Hohha and Quelpa.

I gawk at the creatures in awe. The Quelpa is half parrot and half man. He is tall and beautiful. He has long green feathers which cover his body and gleaming, large green eyes. The Hohha resembles a crow. His feathers are shiny black. He looks our way, and I turn my head quickly so that I don't look like I'm ogling at him. I turn back to see if he is still staring at me and to my surprise, he is. I share an uncomfortable smile and he shares bared teeth and an expression of pure disgust.

"Toto, we're not in Kansas anymore," Caleb says.

I roll my eyes at his humor. Mya stays silent and seems to be adjusting to her original fear. I wouldn't say that I'm necessarily scared, but more in a state of shock. The fact that these animals are so human-like or these humans are so animal-like is completely puzzling.

We continue to walk past more amazing creatures and finally come upon a large hut. Sir Mateo opens the entrance for us and eagerly we all barrel in. Even though we should be hesitant about encountering these new creatures, it seems as if most of us are more than intrigued, except for Mya. Our eyes are wide open and alert. This place is like a candy store for curiosity. I can't wait to see what's next.

Upon entering the hut, we find the rest of Sir Mateo's tribe bunched together inside. They seem more than happy that their leader, Sir Mateo, has arrived. Some or the people cheer and immediately bow down to him.

He quiets their excitement with a polite, "hush now," and speaks to them in their native language. The four of us stay quiet watching. Their faces stay glued on their leader. Then Sir Mateo turns the attention toward us and the tribe begins to make noise and shout. Their shouts sound happy as if they're cheering for us. They come up to us and touch us on the face and bow down to us too. I lean over to Sir Mateo and ask, "What did you tell them?"

"I reminded them why you're here."

"Which was what exactly?" Sebastian chimes in.

Sir Mateo puts a hand on Sebastian's shoulder. "I reminded them that you are here to fight for them. To protect them against the Rebel Leaders."

"Yeah, about that. How is this going to work if we can't even protect ourselves?" I ask.

"Don't worry, Aislinn. You will find a way."

"I had a feeling he was going to say that," I say to Sebastian.

"Sir Mateo. We came here to find you. We wanted to learn about being a visionary. We wanted to understand our gift better. Don't get me wrong. We will help you and your people the best that we can, but I don't want to disappoint them if we do not succeed," Sebastian says.

"Don't worry, my friend. You are learning about your gift. You will understand more soon. And you will succeed."

Sebastian smiles but says nothing in return. Feeling confused and overwhelmed, I look at the ground. Sir Mateo takes both my and Sebastian's hand into his hands.

"You will see," he says with an encouraging smile.

"Thank you," I say, not knowing what else to say. What I really want to say is, *What will I see? Can you provide me with a little more detail, like every detail?* But instead, I nod and remain silent.

Meanwhile, the tribe has started to surround Mya and Caleb. Mya has a solemn half smile painted on her face and Caleb is trying to shake everyone's hand, but the tribe doesn't seem to understand that form of gesture and they keep trying to hold on to his hand.

Just then an extremely large man who looks like a jaguar walks into the hut. His head is that of a jaguar and his body is that of an overly large furry animal with human hands and feet. He is intimidating the way he stands there broad shouldered and sour-faced.

"He looks just like a jaguar," Sebastian whispers sounding awestruck. The jaguar character licks his lips.

"Do you think he's hungry?" I ask.

"What are you whispering about?" the Jaguar human interrupts.

Sebastian and I stop talking and look up at him. He is staring down at us with a wide grin. I would normally smile back, but I am too enthralled to do anything.

"My name is Jawanga and I prefer tasty fruit over human flesh. Most of the time that is," he says. He chuckles and proceeds to give Sir Mateo a great big hug.

Sir Mateo speaks to him in a language that sounds far different than the one he uses with his tribe. Jawanga nods his head and looks back at the four us.

"So you are the legendary visionaries?"

"I wouldn't say legendary but yes, nice to meet you," Sebastian intercedes.

"We have heard all about you, but we have never seen an actual visionary before," Jawanga informs us.

"Likewise," Caleb jokes.

"Well, I want you to know that you have our full support. We will fight with you against the Rebel Leaders. We have stayed away from them for far too long and they must be stopped before they become too powerful," Jawanga announces. His voice serious.

"Thank you. With your help we will be much stronger," Sebastian replies.

"As long as you don't eat us," Mya says under her breath.

I always thought that Mya was strong, based on her rude behavior and sarcastic nature, but really she is a coward hiding behind a mask. I am not threatened by her. At first, I foolishly worried that she would try to conquer Sebastian, but I now know that he would never go for someone like her.

Jawanga looks at Mya. He looks back at the rest of us with large, squinted eyes. He reminds me of Beauty. Seeing Jawanga's rose-shaped spots hits me like a ton of bricks. I miss Beauty and the way he made me feel.

"Pay no attention to her, she's still adjusting to everything," Caleb offers in attempt to make an excuse for Mya's impolite remark.

Jawanga sneers and then finishes speaking to Sir Mateo in their secret language. They hug once more and Jawanga leaves the hut.

"Now, why don't you four get something to eat? Jawanga said that there is food being prepared in the hut next door. You will need your strength before we fight," Sir Mateo says, wearing a comforting smile.

The four of us agree and we quickly exit the hut. When I look around, I notice mystical creatures all over the place. It's hard not to stop and stare. They're so unique. They look like something you would read out of a storybook. I use to make fun of people who believed in Big Foot and all of those other ridiculous myths, but now I stand corrected. I continue to watch in awe at some of the most fascinating creatures I have ever seen. There are a variety of animal and bird-like humans everywhere. Some have bright, bold colors and others are dark and mysterious.

"Come on," Caleb calls, slightly brushing my hand as he walks by me toward the neighboring hut. I look down at my hand that still tingles from his touch.

"Yeah. We should eat," says Sebastian.

He grabs my hand and walks with me to the next hut. I look at my hand that has just been touched by two people. It tingles. It's not an ordinary tingle like anxiety or excitement, but more like a physical, unexplainable tingle. It is very odd. I move my hand a little in Sebastian's hold and then I instantly feel the tingle move up my arm and down through my chest. I touch my chest with my free hand and feel my heart pounding through my body. I begin to feel warm and lightheaded. I try to carry on like nothing is happening, but as we continue to walk, my legs become tingly and they can barely move. Suddenly, the intense feeling stops and my body jolts backward.

∞ CHAPTER 29 ∞

"Are you okay?" Sebastian asks while trying to pick me up off the ground.

My eyes can barely stay open. My vision has become blurry. I look straight into Sebastian's eyes and try to focus. "Yeah. I think so."

"Something's wrong. I can feel it," Sebastian says.

"What do you mean?"

"I don't know exactly. Here, lay down," Sebastian says. He guides me down gently. Caleb and Mya stop walking and watch.

"No, I'm fine, really. Let's go eat," I say, feeling uncomfortable with so many eyes on me. I attempt to get back up.

"I really think that you need to stay here a minute," Sebastian insists.

"I told you I'm fine," I say while standing straight up. I shake myself off as I break free from Sebastian's clutch.

"What's wrong with-" Caleb starts to say.

But all I can hear is a light humming noise. I see nothing but gray fuzz and my body feels even hotter and more tense. My knees start to buckle and I feel my body drop back to the ground.

My body lies still but my mind is freaking out. All I see is black now. Suddenly, my eyes begin to adjust and I start to recognize my surroundings once again. I begin to see people that I haven't seen in a long time. I feel like they are my family. A distant family of some sort. But I can't seem to remember who exactly. They float over to me and greet me. Have I died? I feel like I'm in a bubble. Words don't come out of my mouth or theirs, but I can understand what they're saying. They're happy I'm back. They keep saying how thankful they are that I decided to go on this trip. And they remind me that I'm loved. Where am I?

There are mystical creatures everywhere. They look like typical earth animals but more magical. Most have iridescent wings and a glowing hue to their skin. They are different than the mystical creatures that I have recently met. We are connected to them and they are connected to us. There are also vibrant green vines and beautiful flowers everywhere.

I turn my head and see Sebastian floating over to me. He smiles and tells me that he's happy I'm with him. He tells me that he'll always protect me. And then another voice sounds in my head. It's a beautiful, majestic voice. I look around and see bright colors, and whispers of pure, white mist hover all around me. The voice is coming from the most angelic woman I've ever seen. She wears all white and has long, silvery hair. When she nears me I feel euphoric. She brings an abundance of love and joy with her. I can feel it deep within my very soul.

I reach my hand out to her and she does the same. When our hands touch I immediately feel a deep connection. Suddenly, everything begins to feel familiar. I know this woman. She is an angel of the earth. She has asked me to return to earth as a visionary. Sebastian was also of this place and he agreed to be my watcher. My family is here supporting me every step of the way and they too are glorious. I have a new family on earth and they are wonderful too. I remember my mission. I must connect with fellow visionaries and protect our earth from its enemies. Many struggles lie ahead but many victories will also unfold. Protecting and teaching others the way of life is my stated mission. I remember when I agreed to this undertaking that my brain would function in the present time and that my stored memories of my real life will be stored away. That's why I'm having such a hard time fully accepting my gifts here on earth and embracing my transformation. On earth, I can't access all of my previous memories. It's almost virtually impossible to make my cells shift between worlds.

This place makes me feel so joyful and loved that I don't want to leave, but I know I must fulfill my obligations and return to earth with the others. The angel of the earth lets go of my hand and I stare at her with awe. She smiles again and drifts away. My family comes my way again and they too smile and drift away.

"Aislinn, Aislinn," I hear someone say. The words sound muffled.

I open my eyes and see Sebastian leaning over me. I look to my left and see Caleb staring at me. They both look scared. I sit up in a panic.

"Aislinn, are you okay?" Sebastian asks. His voice begins to sound clearer and I know I'm back in the present earth.

"Aislinn, wake up. Look at me," Caleb calls.

I look at him. "I'm okay. I'm better than okay."

They both look at me with creased eyebrows. Mya stands over them. Her face is blank and emotionless. I look down at my hands. The hands that touched the earth angel.

"I was just at home. My real home."

"Aislinn, you just passed out," Sebastian says.

"No, I didn't. I left earth and visited my home. It was heavenly. I saw familiar faces and I remembered why I was here," I swallow hard, thinking about my out-of-body journey. "It was just like what the rock told me, but this was so much clearer. And you," I look at Sebastian and his eyes widen. "You were there. Briefly. But you told me how you came here with me, to protect me, to watch over me." Caleb backs away a little as if disturbed to hear what I'm saying.

I try to stand up and Sebastian helps me to my feet.

"I believe you," Sebastian says.

"I don't know, Aislinn. People pass out all the time," Caleb says. His voice sounds doubtful as if I'm making this all up.

"No, I'm telling you the truth. This was real. Don't you believe me?"

"Look, if she says it's real, it's real," Sebastian says sticking up for me. I smile.

Silence falls upon everyone and we all just stand there looking at one another. I figure it's no use trying to convince everyone about what I saw. I know it sounds outlandish. If I were them I would not believe me either. Luckily, I believe myself.

"What are we waiting for?" I declare breaking the quiet. "Let's eat."

Caleb snickers and Mya proceeds ahead toward the hut. Sebastian reaches for my hand and we follow Mya and Caleb in.

"I'm glad you believe me," I whisper.

"I'll always believe you."

My heart melts. Sebastian is not only protecting me here on earth but he is also bringing me pure happiness. I sure hope that our relationship isn't just for earth but forever. I would be lost without him. He is my rock.

Thinking about what happened, I begin to ponder the details. To be able to step into another world without physically leaving this one is phenomenal.

We enter the hut and find a few more mythical legends standing around the food area. It's like one big melting pot. At first I was in a state of shock when I entered this secret village, but now I feel more fascinated.

Another large cat-like creature stands by a table that is adorned with food. The creature's face is gray and dark with white lines cascading down the face. Its eyes are bright yellow and its body is tall, slender, and hunched as that of a cat arching its back.

"Well, come in, come in. I don't scratch if that's what you're wondering," it snickers as the four us stand there star struck.

We walk toward the cat creature and I look down at its exposed razor-sharp claws. One swipe from those babies and you're kitty chow. Seeming on how no one has replied back to this cat creature, I step forward and introduce myself.

"Hi, I'm Aislinn and this is Sebastian." Sebastian politely waves his hand.

"I'm Caleb," Caleb chimes in. Then Caleb looks at Mya, giving her a friendly nudge reminding her to introduce herself. She stands there and gawks at the cat creature not muttering a word. Sebastian and I stare at her in disbelief. Is this the same Mya?

"And this is Mya. Say hi, Mya," Caleb says sarcastically.

"Hi," Mya says in a low, emotionless voice.

"We're here with Sir Mateo," I say, feeling the need to fill the uncomfortable silence.

"I know who you are. The question is do you know who I am?"

The four of us look at each other in hopes that one of us knows who this cat creature is. I'm pretty sure that none of us do. They don't exactly have a class in our school for South American mythical creatures.

Sebastian squints his eyes and looks away. I can tell he's pondering through his memories trying to figure out who this cat creature is.

"Not a clue," Sebastian says with an edge of humor.

"It's okay. No one ever knows who I am. They always say cat man or super cat. They never get it right," the cat snarls, his bright yellow eyes gleaming at us.

Caleb looks my way and mouths, "Cat man." He shrugs his shoulders. I smile.

"I'm Cocoa," the cat proudly boasts.

"Like the cocoa bean. I get it," says Caleb.

"No. Like Cocoa the great and powerful cat spirit who is in charge of wild storms and all of the world's natural and unnatural disasters."

"Really?" Sebastian replies. His eyes wide and curious.

"No. Not really. But that sure sounded good, didn't it?" The four of us stand there confused by Cocoa's odd sense of humor. He wiggles his long whiskers and makes a comforting purring sound.

"Some people who lived here a long time ago believed that about me. But, really I'm just a cat spirit who enjoys hiking and swimming as much as the next cat," Cocoa says as he scoops up some unidentifiable food onto plates for each of us.

As the four of us take our plates and thank Cocoa for his hospitality, my eyes are struck with amazement as I glance around the hut. This oversized hut holds four long, makeshift tables and many different types of seating. Some of the chairs are made from the various trees located in the rainforest. Some are short and wide and others are tall and thin. They are actually quite beautiful. I choose a tall and slender chair decorated with small carvings of intricate swirly designs. Sebastian chooses the same and Caleb and Mya are left with the short, wide chairs which are embellished with green vines. We silently eat while discreetly peering around to look at the different creatures that lurk around us. I feel as though I'm in a sci-fi movie or another planet for that matter. The creatures stare at us in return and we pretend not to notice.

"So, how about that ambiance?" Caleb jokes.

"It's definitely different, that's for sure," Sebastian replies.

"Well, I don't like it," Mya says curtly. She pushes her food around on her plate into the very middle making one large mound.

"What's not to like? Free food, freaky animals," Caleb responds.

"It's not that bad. They're just...misunderstood. Like us," I say as a small creature resembling a bright, green lizard strolls by. Its tail gently sweeps the floor from side to side as it exits the hut.

As I'm about to swallow a spoonful of green mushy stuff, a beautiful, snake-like woman sits next to us. She has a human head, human feet, and human arms and hands, but the rest of her body is all snake. Her long, green and brown tail with black spots whips from side to side behind her chair.

"Is this seat taken?" she asks.

The four of us shake our heads no.

"What's on the menu today?" she says as she licks the entire plate in one noisy gulp. "Rat brains, my favorite."

"Looks like you were hungry?" Caleb asks.

The snake-like woman smiles at Caleb and slithers closer to him. Caleb backs away a little. He seems nervous.

"I'm always hungry," she says in a matter of fact tone. "In fact I'm still hungry." She licks her lips.

Caleb looks up at me alarmed. The only thing I can think of that might work to diffuse the situation is to simple engage in conversation.

"Hi. I'm Aislinn," I introduce myself while imagining her eating us in one large bite.

The woman looks my way and says, "I'm Maladi the anaconda, who is known to kidnap women and their babies. I also rescue lost and lonely travelers." Maladi eyes Caleb and stares deeply into his eyes. He quickly looks away uncomfortably and gulps.

Mya raises her eyebrows.

"Male travelers that is," Maladi says with her deep, raspy voice.

"You didn't happen to see us when we first got here, did you?" Mya asks.

"No, why?"

"No reason," Mya answers. Sebastian and I look at each other. We smile and I shrug my shoulders as I have no idea what Mya is referring to.

"No, Mya. That anaconda was a real snake, if that's what you were thinking," Caleb answers.

"I'm a real snake," Maladi says while caressing Caleb's hair with her hand. "And half lizard." Her tail whips around to his feet and encircles him tightly. Caleb anxiously chuckles. His body seems tense. I've never seen him act this unsure before. It's sort of enjoyable in a warped kind of way. Then Maladi's tongue whips out and grazes Caleb's chin.

Just then an attractive hairless dog creature comes by our table. She has brown tight skin, beaming red eyes and the biggest fangs I have ever seen. Her face is human but her body resembles a dog. Her long tail wags back and forth like an excited puppy.

"Stop teasing the guests, Maladi."

"I was just introducing myself, Chupa."

"Chupa....cabra?" Sebastian remarks.

"Yeah, that's me."

"Wow. I would have thought you were a male or werewolf even," Caleb adds.

"Who says I'm not," she says slyly in a deeper tone of voice.

The four of us look at Chupa, who is grinning from ear to ear. Apparently, we're being toyed with. Someone in the distance yells, "dessert," and Maladi and Chupa take off faster than a NASCAR driver.

"That was interesting," I say.

"Creepy," Mya mumbles under her breath.

"Yup. Definitely interesting, let's eat, shall we?" Sebastian says.

"I'm good. I think I lost my appetite," Caleb mutters and he pushes his dish away from him.

After devouring a hearty meal of mystery food, we gather outside and wait for Sir Mateo. Caleb lets out a loud burp that goes unnoticed by the creatures nearby.

"Have you no manners?" I ask Caleb.

Mya rolls her eyes and turns the other way. Her recent loss of words has been a blessing.

"Excuse me. Guess my intake of animal guts and vegetation doesn't sit well with me," Caleb says as he belches once more. Caleb looks at me and smiles.

Moments later Sir Mateo walks out of the hut and heads straight toward us with Jawanga and Raul. Raul seems unfazed by these mystical creatures. It's as if he sees this sort of thing all the time.

Sir Mateo's face appears serious. His lips are pursed and his eyes stare straight. He stops walking as he reaches us and says, "It's time." I glance at Sebastian and the look on his face says it all. He's worried and so am I. We have no idea what were up against.

Sebastian breaks his attention away from me and looks back at Sir Mateo. "We're ready!"

∞ CHAPTER 30 ∞

I start to feel anxious as I walk through the forest with Sir Mateo, his tribe, and the mystical creatures. I'm amazed at how fast everyone in that tribe got ready. Sir Mateo's men have bows and arrows and the mystical creatures have other interesting looking weapons made out of the rainforest. Things that one would take for granted, like strong vines, wooden stakes, venomous flowers, venomous snakes (which are really elevating my anxiety), and other daily commodities of the rainforest are just a few of the items that the creatures have used creatively to construct weapons. Not to mention that these mystical creatures each have unique capabilities.

Everyone is so incredibly quiet. There must be a hundred of us all together and yet no one makes a single sound. From what I remember, the Rebel Leaders didn't have nearly as many people as we do.

Maybe seventy-five at the most. There's no way they can defeat us. We have larger numbers and more defense mechanisms, I think.

"So, what's the plan?" I ask Sir Mateo. He didn't quite go over a specific strategy back at the village. He pretty much just told everyone to gather every weapon they had and head toward where the Rebel Leaders were. He said that the Rebel Leaders were planning an uprising of their own to get what they wanted. They had planned to sacrifice more people of Sir Mateo's tribe to please their Gods.

"Plan? There is no plan, Aislinn. One can never assume that things will go as planned. We can only prepare for the unplanned."

"Which is?" I demand to know, since I am in this whole mess.

"To fight till they surrender their powers."

"What powers?"

"The power they gathered today."

"I wasn't told of any power."

"That's because you didn't ask," Sir Mateo answers with a smile. "It is okay, Aislinn. You are not alone."

Here he goes with this whole, "you are not alone" business. I smile and continue walking. I take one more look at him and spot his jaguar ears transform back into human ears. He looks back at me and smiles. I glance over at Sebastian for support and he slyly puts his hand into mine.

"It's okay, Ais. I spoke with Caleb earlier and we're going to all stick together, Mya too, until we can figure out what to do."

"That's the plan. That's the plan that we've got?"

"Do you have anything else in mind?"

"I don't know. Something more concrete."

"Concrete," he repeats. I sigh with disappointment. Why is it I'm the only one who seems to be on a different page?

"Never mind," I say.

Sebastian squeezes my hand. "Hey, it's going to be all right."

"How do you know?" I question.

"I just know."

His eyes meet mine and I can't help not to smile. I can't be mad at him no matter how hard I try. I love him.

Caleb whispers to Mya, and she nods her head as if agreeing to the plan. Whatever that may be.

After a long walk, our team of warriors stop for a break. We follow some of the tribal men to a running brook and drink pure water. Sebastian stops and talks with Caleb, and I take a seat and rest my sore feet. They need a pedicure and a deep foot massage. I lean back and stretch my torso. I feel like I've been working out at the gym for twenty-four hours straight. My muscles feel toned and my legs feel stronger from all of this walking. I'm tired and energized at the same time. I place my fingers gently down on the ground behind me and breathe. Suddenly, something glides over my hand and stays there. It feels moist and smooth. Without moving my hand, I quickly turn around to see what it is.

"Oh My God!" I scream. I fight the urge to move my hand. I don't know what I should do.

Everyone looks at me, including Sebastian, who runs to my side. I look down at my finger and spot what seems to be a golden-colored poison dart frog sitting on top of my hand. There's no mistaking the identity of this poisonous frog. I learned about these in school. Their brightly colored hues are meant to ward off potential predators like myself, only I didn't notice it until now. I wouldn't mind seeing one of these in a museum since in captivity they tend to lose their toxicity, but in the wild they are considered to be one of the most toxic species on earth. The poison is on the frog's skin and it must have been on my hand for a good minute or so. If I remember correctly, they are poisonous not venomous and only harmful if eaten.

But for some strange reason, I can't seem to feel my hand. My heart starts to race with fear as I begin to think about instant death. I'll never see my family again or my dog. I'll never get to go to college or drive my car again. And worst of all, I'll never see Sebastian again! *Calm down Aislinn. It's not like you ingested the frog.*

Sebastian looks down at my hand. "It looks like a typical golden-colored dart frog, but something is a little off."

Panic paints his face and I close my eyes afraid of what will happen next.

Unexpectedly, I feel someone else grab a hold of my hand. Is it Sir Mateo? I open my eyes to find Mya standing over me, holding my hand. Confusion comes over me and a million questions come to mind, but I'm unable to speak.

"This isn't a typical golden-colored dart frog," Mya says in an eerie tone.

"That's good, right? She should be fine. It's not like she was bitten by it or drank the poison?" Sebastian spits out hastily.

By now, many of the tribal members, mystical and human, have surrounded me. Mya continues to hold my hand as she observes it like a specimen. Her grip is strong. She doesn't seem at all like herself. She's different, as if she's caught in a daze or a spell. Her eyes move from side to side as she brushes a finger across the palm of my hand.

"Actually, this one's worse. It doesn't have a name, since it hasn't been found by a scientist yet, but this particular frog has a different type of poisonous coating. This coating, when touched, instantly penetrates through the skin and attacks all major organs," Mya says, not taking her eyes off my hand.

"What the-," Caleb says sounding stunned.

"It truly is a remarkable species," Mya says unnervingly. "Looks like we are the first ones to discover it." Mya's eyes are glossy and her lips are puckered as she examines the specimen.

Sebastian looks at Sir Mateo with uncertainty. Sir Mateo nods as if agreeing with Mya's hypothesis. Mya then pulls my wrists and drags me to a particular tree. "Come on. Come with me."

Feeling left with no other options, I oblige and follow her. Why isn't anyone else helping me? I look at Sebastian desperately, and he reaches out for my hand. I begin to feel dizzy and hot all over. My eyesight starts to become blurry and I can't make out anyone's faces. I can hear sounds, but I can't understand what people are saying. And then there's black. All black.

∞ CHAPTER 31 ∞

A potent smell awakens me at once and I am finally able to hear and see again. Sebastian is sitting beside me holding my hand and Caleb stands alongside him with Sir Mateo.

"Where am I? What happened?" I frantically ask.

"Mya...she saved your life," Sebastian says solemnly.

"What?"

Caleb chimes in, "It's true. She saved you."

"Aislinn, dear. You were touched by a mystical frog that only comes out during times of war. They carry one of the most fatal skin poisons on the earth. Mya reacted quickly and healed you," Sir Mateo says.

"The Agua Magia?" I ask, remembering what Sir Mateo had told us.

He nods and smiles as if to say, *See Aislinn, she's not so bad.*

"So I guess this means she has acquired healing powers," Sebastian says. My mind is racing. The same Mya who makes my skin crawl has made my skin pure. She saved my life. I'm shocked.

"Where is she? I have to thank her." I could have died. Who would have thought that I would ever have to thank Mya for saving my life? It's funny how things happen sometimes.

Sebastian and Caleb step aside so that I can see Mya standing down by the water. I jump to my feet and make my way toward her. As I approach her, I remember feeling dizzy and then everything going black and now here I am alive and well. All thanks to Mya. I owe her now. When someone saves your life you feel indebted to them. I may not particularly care for the girl, but I am truly thankful for what she has done.

Mya stands there looking at the water. She turns her head when she hears me near.

"Mya?"

She says nothing. Instead she turns away from me facing the water again.

"Mya, I just want to say…. thank you for saving my life." I pause, waiting for a response. And still she says nothing. "I want you to know that-"

"Save it," Mya says hastily, "you don't owe me anything. You would have done the same, right?"

"Of course," I say, feeling taken back by her sudden sharpness.

"Then we're good." Mya's eyes seem strange. They look distant and cold. Ever since she took off from us, the second time, and we found her stricken with fear from the mythical creatures, she's been different. I think it has something to do with the Agua Magia. It's as if she acts upon instinct when needed, but her personality still shines through from time to time.

"Okay," I agree as she nods her head and strolls back to the crew. I stay there a minute longer and gather my thoughts. What just happened? I stare off at the water and take everything into perspective.

Sebastian spots me and signals for me to come back. Sir Mateo's men are gathering their belongings. It's time for us to continue on our march.

"What happened down there?" Sebastian asks.

"I don't know. I tried to thank her and she told me that we're good."

"Well, that doesn't sound too bad."

"Yeah, but it's how she said it. I don't know, maybe it's just my imagination, but something's different about her."

"Something's always been a little different about her," Sebastian jokes as he nudges me.

I smile while catching a raindrop in my hand. It begins to come down faster and faster. The rain feels refreshing. It hasn't rained as much as I expected it to. After all, it is a rainforest. I always envisioned the rainforest to be sunny and raining constantly. It seems that the weather is dependent upon what season it is here.

We follow the crew into the night of the forest. The sun has definitely set, not that there's a ton of light during the day with this entire umbrella canopy hovering over us, but it's definitely darker. And the rain hasn't let up. I am completely soaked, but I don't mind.

The pace of our walk has increased to a steady canter. No room for slowpokes. As we walk, I try to recount all that has happened to me. The dreams or visions into the afterlife. The knowledge I've acquired of my true meaning of being a visionary. Beauty. Sebastian. Everything. Something about trudging through the vast rainforest in silence is enlightening. It's like I'm finally starting to connect the dots.

"So even though we're not supposed to fight or harm others, it's okay to participate in a sneak attack against the Rebel Leaders?" I ask Sebastian.

He bites his lip and hesitates for a moment.

"It's not like they don't know we're coming. They're holding Sir Mateo's men hostage. They've already sacrificed some of his men in order to increase their powers," he says with a slight edge of vengeance in his tone, "and don't forget, they're still looking for us."

"What do you mean by that?"

"Remember when I told you about the Rebel Leaders and how when they found Mya and me in the woods," I nod. "Well, the leader kept asking me if I was a visionary. Something's up with that. It's like someone is driving them to do this."

"Kind of like, they're the middleman and someone else is giving the orders?"

"Exactly!"

I think about that for a moment. Who could be powerful enough to drive the Rebel Leaders to such extremes such as abduction and human sacrifice?

"It has to be someone smart. Someone who knows a lot about us already," I say feeling out of breath from our continued, fast-paced hike.

"Yeah. Whoever it is, isn't playing around. They want us dead or alive," Sebastian adds.

Sir Mateo steps out of the lead and walks back around to speak with us.

"We will be at the village soon. Stay behind to be safe," Sir Mateo warns as he corrals and escorts us to the back of his men and the mystical creatures. Caleb catches my eyes as he walks with us to the back. I look away quickly, feeling slightly uncomfortable. I wish it could be like it was before. I hate having these awkward moments.

"So, this is it," Caleb says to Sebastian and me.

Mya stands close by but doesn't look our way. She looks as if her mind is in another place. Her eyes seem distant.

"I guess it's do or die," Sebastian responds as I continue to gape at Mya. She amuses me now. There's something she's not telling us or something she isn't aware of herself.

"Ais," Sebastian says.

"Oh, sorry, I was distracted. Yeah, I guess I'm ready." Sebastian smiles softly.

"We have a huge crew and some very creative creatures on our side. I think the odds are definitely in our favor," Caleb remarks, although he doesn't sound convinced himself. He sounds like he's trying to pump himself up. Whatever works. I just know that we are walking into a situation in which we have no idea what might unfold.

Sebastian politely whisks me near him.

"I'll be with you every minute. Don't leave my side," he says as he kisses my forehead. His words sound protective, but his tone is rather worrisome.

"I won't," I say as I look into his deep, dark eyes.

Before I can answer, our team of warriors in front of us suddenly stops walking and the three of us almost barrel into them. Sebastian grabs a hold of my hand and I squeeze it tight. I can feel the tension in the air. My mouth is dry and I shudder as my brain thinks about what will happen next.

Unexpectedly, ear-piercing monkey cries fill the air. The monkeys are far above us, but they sound like they are on top of us. They are literally going bananas. I have to cover my ears just to protect my eardrums. Sebastian and Caleb gasp as they cover their ears too. Mya just continues to stare straight ahead as if she doesn't hear a thing.

I know it's time to enter the fight, but I wish I had more time to figure things out. I feel completely inadequate knowing that I'm unable to access my spirit animal.

I take a deep breath, and then all I see is complete chaos. The men and creatures in front of us begin running into the Rebel Leaders' clearance. Screams surround the air and the four of us are left trailing behind. The thing about being in the back is that no one else is around to help us. The middle may have been a more suitable place, but it's too late now. Sebastian pulls me forward and Caleb runs along the side. Mya tries to keep up, but her energy seems low and she lags behind.

The Rebel Leaders are loaded with arrows and they seem to be positioned everywhere. They are prepared and unfazed by our presence as if they were expecting us. Sir Mateo's men attack the Rebel Leaders head on.

Some of the mystical creatures are beheaded right in front of us. It happens so quickly and I am left in shock. Blood begins to spill and I am splashed with droplets of random blood on both sides of my face.

"Come on!" Sebastian yells. A Rebel Leader spots us and begins yelling at one of his fellow members. The two of them charge at us. Sebastian continues running straight toward them and Caleb follows. They both knock out the two leaders simultaneously and we continue running.

The mystical creatures are using their mystical weapons. The Rebel Leaders are using their brute force, scalpels, and bows and arrows. The four of us have one knife, makeshift daggers and one bow and arrow set.

"Careful of the arrows," Caleb shouts while we're running.

"I know," I say while ducking to avoid getting hit.

"I mean, they're laced with poison from poison dart frogs."

The thought of that makes me sick. I almost died from a similar creature and these idiots lace their arrows so that they're even more deadly. Although, the more I think about it, I don't know why this shocks me. The mystical creatures do the same.

"Let's go!" Caleb yells behind me as he notices Mya's inability to keep up. She still continues to remain quiet while running just a little bit faster.

One of the mystical creatures falls right at our feet. The poisonous snake that he carried as a weapon proved inadequate as it slithers away. An arrow sticks in his arm. He tugs at the arrow and suddenly his eyes shut. He would have lived from such a wound if it weren't laced with poison.

"He's dead!" I cry. I bend down to see if he's all right and Sebastian quickly brings me back up.

"The poison. He's gone, Ais. We have to go," Sebastian yells.

All around us people are screaming, grunting, and running amuck. It's pandemonium in its highest form.

We pick up our pace, and I realize something doesn't quite feel right. We're missing someone. I look back and see Mya being attacked!

"Mya!" I scream.

We stop running. Sebastian and Caleb turn around and run to Mya's rescue. A Rebel Leader has gotten hold of her. He is a large man with black paintings on his face. He carries a bow and arrow over his right shoulder and a knife in his left hand. His right arm is huddled over Mya as she tries to wriggle free.

"Help!" Mya screams.

Sebastian attacks the rebel member while Caleb tries to release Mya from his grip. The Rebel Leader is much bigger than Sebastian and Caleb. As I stand there helpless, someone suddenly grabs me from behind. I kick and scream but the culprit has a strong grasp on me.

"Let go of me," I say struggling. "Sebastian. Sebastian!"

The rebel member drags me into the rainforest. I dig my feet into the ground, trying to stop him from pulling me in further. The Rebel Leader tightens his grip, leaving me at his mercy.

My feet begin to drag along against my will into the heart of the rainforest floor, leaving deep marks in the muck. Sebastian quickly looks up and our eyes meet. I have no strength compared to my capturer. He is big and strong. I struggle to free myself but it is no use. The Rebel Leader's arm is across my neck, cutting off my oxygen supply. I can't scream. I can't breathe. I manage to squirm a little and bite into his arm hard. The taste of human flesh and salty blood disgusts me. Screaming with rage and pain, the rebel member finally releases me from his grip.

I stand there, shocked, gasping to catch my breath. Sebastian finally comes out of nowhere and pummels the rebel member to the ground. The rebel member tries to stab Sebastian, but luckily Sebastian grabs the knife away from him and throws it aside. As the two battle it out, the rebel member overcomes Sebastian and throws him to the ground. Sebastian staggers to rise and the rebel member makes his way back toward me again.

"Get away from me. Caleb!" I yell, hoping that he can assist Sebastian and help me. But Caleb is still helping Mya.

Sebastian instantly jumps to his feet and grunts loudly like an animal. He runs to the rebel member and jumps on top of his back. The rebel member tries to shake him off, but Sebastian has a tight hold on him. The rebel member then reaches for his knife on the ground, but luckily Sebastian moves faster. He jumps off his back and rolls in a quick maneuver to obtain the knife. The rebel member lunges at Sebastian, but Sebastian stabs the knife deep into his chest. The rebel member falls to the ground, lifeless in a pool of blood.

I run over to Sebastian and he holds me in his arms.

"You okay?" Sebastian asks breathlessly.

"I'm okay," I reply.

"Good. Come on."

Sebastian grabs my hand and we scramble for a place to find shelter while Caleb and Mya follow. This place is complete mayhem. We've lost track of Sir Mateo and the others. There are people everywhere. It resembles some sort of a third world jungle war. We stagger past two mystical creatures using their spike studded tails to whip around three Rebel Leaders. Another creature is throwing its sticky web onto a pair of Rebel Leaders.

We find an area clear of the fighting and take cover.

"We can't fight like this! It's not working," Sebastian says.

"He's right," says Caleb.

"But, we have to help Sir Mateo and his men," I cry.

"You can barely take care of yourself," Caleb replies to me.

I roll my eyes at his snarky remark, but I know it's true. We have no powers. We're like sitting ducks.

"Look, we're missing something here," Sebastian says while looking at me. "Our spirit animals didn't leave us. We just can't get to them!"

"What if we split up? Two of us can go back to the rock and see if we can find some answers," Caleb suggests.

"No!" I shout.

"That's a terrible idea!" Mya says out of nowhere.

The three of us look at her out of shock to hear her finally speak. Her facial expression looks disgusted as she rubs a piece of sludge off her face.

"We can't split up. Sir Mateo told us that we need each other," Mya says in a grave voice. "Don't you remember?"

"I remember." I'm surprised to be agreeing with my arch-nemesis-turned-savior.

"What do you suggest then?" Sebastian asks.

"What do I suggest?" she repeats.

"Yeah," Sebastian answers.

"I suggest we start working together. I suggest we start believing in one another," she says. My eyes widen with disbelief. Is this the same Mya I thought I knew?

"Look, I swam in the Agua Magia. I know I've done some things that don't make sense, but somehow something has changed. I can figure things out without thinking about them," Mya goes on.

"Like healing me from the poisonous frog?" I interject.

She nods her head. "I don't have to think about what to do. It just comes naturally to me now. And right now, I know that more than ever we need to be together to make this work." She takes a deep breath. "Hold hands now!"

"What?" Caleb says.

"We need to hold hands now," Mya repeats sternly.

"This is crazy. I'm not doing this," Caleb shouts. "This is nuts. Are you guys really going to listen to her?"

Sebastian and I look at one another and without words I know that we both feel the same.

"Yes," Sebastian and I simultaneously say as he reaches out for my hand and Mya's. Mya humbly grins while Caleb shakes his head in disbelief.

"Whatever," Caleb says as he reluctantly reaches out for our hands. Caleb takes one of my hands and looks into my eyes. I look back only to quickly look away from him.

"For this to work, you must believe that it will," Mya declares, looking at all of us. "Now close your eyes. Feel your heart. Breathe! Find that inner strength that you all possess."

Then she begins to say something in another language. She continues with the same phrase over and over and over again. I can feel her words pulsate through my entire body. They are powerful. Her words become louder and louder. I feel like we're starting to spin in circles. Faster and faster we go as we tightly hold on to one another's hands with our eyes tightly shut. My feet suddenly begin to elevate off the ground and the air causes my hair to lift in the wind. We're moving so fast that I can barely catch my breath. Multiple images of myself and animals flash through my head as I concentrate deeply.

Mya continues chanting and then out of nowhere, I feel my body transform into my spirit animal, the red-tailed hawk. The beautiful, fierce red-tailed hawk.

I haven't felt its presence since that day near the Agua Magia with Sir Mateo. I open my eyes and let out a loud screech while spinning in the air. My arms and legs are no longer there. My body is no longer my body and I am no longer human. We have all transformed. Sebastian is the fierce grizzly bear, Caleb is the large

African elephant, and Mya is the complicated tarantula. It worked! It really worked!

∞ CHAPTER 32 ∞

We finally stop spinning and land gracefully on the ground. We can't exactly physically speak to one another in spirit animal form but we can communicate innately. We waste no time acknowledging our transformation as we quickly turn back toward the dark turmoil to help our friends.

I feel empowered! I feel free. I feel like me and it feels good. The four of thrash through the brush and head directly into combat. The war has gotten a lot messier. Wounded bodies from both sides dress the forest floor like fallen trees. I notice a mystical creature being stabbed by a Rebel Leader. I screech loudly and rise into the air so that I can pull him off with my strong talons. I feel comfortable. Too comfortable in my hawk body as if it fits better than my human body. I toss the Rebel Leader to the side as I puncture his skin with my razor-sharp talons.

Caleb barges in on another helpless victim being brutally attacked by two Rebel Leaders. He stomps his feet and the ground shakes. The two men stop and look up at this large African elephant stampeding their way. They look at one another and scream. As they try to flee, Caleb pounces on them with his giant feet and the Rebel Leaders melt into the ground like the Wicked Witch in *The Wizard of Oz*.

Mya's giant tarantula legs are even larger than before. They move around so creepily that I can't bear to look at her. After helping out a few of Sir Mateo's tribe and the mystical creatures, the four of us decide to look for Sir Mateo.

"Come on," I screech. I think I have picked up Sir Mateo's scent.

"No. This way," Sebastian says. "He's not too far from here."

We trust Sebastian's suggestion. His sense of smell is exceptional.

As we walk through the chaos, we engage in small inconveniences here and there. One Rebel Leader jumps out of a tree and Sebastian quickly stands on his hind legs. The Rebel Leader takes off screaming. Next, another Rebel Leader attempts to stab Mya with a sharp scalpel, but Mya picks up the Rebel Leader with one of her creepy legs and squeezes him so hard, he suffocates instantly.

As soon as it seems like we're alone, another Rebel Leader notices us and sends a poison arrow directly at Sebastian. Sebastian angrily catches the arrow with his large paw and throws it back at the Rebel Leader. The arrow lands in the Rebel Leader's rear. He looks back at us with his wide eyes, and then drops to the ground.

"Nice one," says Caleb.

Mya walks in an awkward manner with her eight legs moving in a zigzag pattern and then stops abruptly. She tells us that she can sense someone is following us through a distinctive vibration which only she can feel. We all possess a variety of gifts and each time we become our spirit animals, different gifts reveal themselves. Mya slyly turns around and notices a Rebel Leader hiding behind a tree, pointing an arrow in our direction. She hurriedly runs after the Rebel Leader as he takes off.

Guess they weren't expecting wild animals to be involved with this war. And I thought the mystical creatures were bizarre.

As we continue further into the clearing of the Rebel Leaders' territory, I feel something brush upon on one of my talons. I figure it's Sebastian, but when I look down, I notice a hand. It's Jawanga.

"Stop," I screech.

"Jawanga! Are you all right?" I ask. Jawanga lays there covered by the brush. His beautiful rose- colored markings around his chest have been splattered with blood and one of his tuft ears has been sliced in half.

He groans a little and says, "It's come for us."

Surprisingly, he understands our innate language, but I have no idea what he is referring to.

"What's coming for us?" Sebastian asks.

Jawanga points in the direction that we are headed.

"Death!" He sighs and whispers, "Save yourself."

"From what?" I ask, confused. He must mean the Rebel Leaders, but his reference to "it" makes me think otherwise.

Jawanga's eyes roll back as he takes his last breath.

"No! Jawanga! No!" I scream.

"Jawanga! Jawanga!" Sebastian yells.

It's no use. Jawanga is gone. I want to cry but there are no tears in my hawk eyes.

"What did he mean, it's come for us?" Caleb asks with wide eyes.

"I don't know. But, we can't stick around here to find out. Let's get out of here!" Sebastian advises.

Sadly, I close Jawanga's eyes so he can rest in peace. He lost his life to this senseless battle. While, I am saddened by his loss, I know that we must keep moving.

The four of us swiftly hurry past the fighting to an underground dugout while knocking out any lingering Rebel Leaders who dare confront us. Between Sebastian's huge claws and intimidating teeth, to Caleb's large incisors and bone-crushing legs, to Mya's frightening, exoskeleton body and oversized fangs and to my fierce talons and monster beak, we look like the gruesome four. It's no wonder that many of the Rebel Leaders choose to bolt rather than combat us.

The underground dugout looks to have been covered with leaves and debris, but the scent that Sebastian has picked up has led us to this point. Caleb uses his long proboscis to clear off the debris. He uncovers a deep hole, which looks to be about ten feet deep and three feet wide.

"I think it would be best if we switched back to human form for this," Mya suggests.

"I think so too. This hole looks a little too small for us," I agree.

"What if we can't change back when we need to?" Caleb asks.

"Do you believe now?" Mya questions Caleb.

Caleb looks at Mya and puts his head and tusk down. "Yes... I believe and I apologize for doubting you."

"Okay. So now you know. Let's change back now," Mya sharply says.

I close my eyes and picture my human form and within seconds, I feel my body being transformed back. The tightening stretch doesn't feel as uncomfortable as it once did. My hands and feet don't feel the same tingle it once did. It seems to get easier and easier each time I transform. I open my eyes and see everyone altered back to their human bodies.

"That was almost too easy," Sebastian admits.

"All you have to do is believe and think positive. The energy that the four of us possess is greater than you can imagine and you can't allow any negative thoughts or self-doubt; otherwise your powers will become less available," Mya says.

I'm starting to like the fact that Mya took a dip in the Agua Magia. It seemed to have changed her for the better. Goodbye sassy and Sebastian-obsessed Mya and hello to the new and improved, practical and mysterious Mya.

"Makes sense to me," I agree.

"We don't have too much time. People are dying out here," Sebastian says while analyzing the dim hole.

"So, who's first?" Caleb questions.

None of answer as we gape at the dark hole in the ground.

"No takers, huh? I'll go then," Caleb says.

"No, I'll go," Sebastian offers. I tug at his arm and Caleb notices. He makes a smirk and strides by us to the top of the hole and looks down.

"No. Really, I want to go first. Help me down," Caleb says as he glances my way. Feeling embarrassed, I immediately look away. I didn't mean that I don't care about him; I just didn't want to be separated from Sebastian again.

Sebastian steps away and looks around the area for something to use to help lower Caleb down into the deep, dark hole.

"Here, try this," Sebastian says as he pulls a thick vine from a nearby tree. Sebastian and Caleb work together to tie the vine tightly around another tree. He gives it a hard tug to test its strength.

"Looks good to me," Caleb says all too excitedly. Caleb takes the other end of the vine and throws it into the hole.

"Well, here goes nothing," Caleb declares as he lowers himself down the vine. He glances my way as he climbs down, kicking off the mud wall. He looks like an everyday rock climber.

"You see anything yet?" Sebastian asks.

"Nothing but complete darkness," Caleb replies breathlessly.

"I don't know about this," I confide to Sebastian. "This feels wrong to me." He shares a warm smile and touches my chin.

"His scent hasn't become any stronger. It smells the same to me," I say.

"It's because you're in human form. Your senses don't work the same as they did when you were in spirit form," Mya says. My attention turns to the hole and I can hear Caleb let out a loud sigh.

"I've landed," Caleb shouts.

"See if you can find a door or something?" Sebastian shouts back. Caleb feels around in complete darkness. I can hear him hit his hands against the mud walls.

"Ahah...I found it," Caleb snickers to himself. "Guys, there's a wooden door down here. But it's stuck. I need help prying it open." Caleb's voice echoes.

Sebastian looks at Mya and me. "Guess I should go down."

"We should really stick together," Mya warns. "Maybe we should all go."

"Yeah, but what if the door doesn't open and we need help getting out of here? I think you two should wait here," Sebastian says.

"I'm starting to get that feeling in my stomach again. I don't know about this?" I say.

"I'm just going to help Caleb open the door and then you guys can come down if everything looks all right. Okay?" says Sebastian. I look around to ensure we are alone.

"Okay, but hurry up!" I tell him reluctantly. He pulls me close and kisses me deeply, but I feel too uneasy to enjoy his kiss.

"See you in a few seconds," he murmurs.

Sebastian climbs down the vine with quick and smooth motions like a professional.

"It really is dark down here," Sebastian shouts.

When Sebastian lands, I can hear them struggle with the door. They grunt and groan. Mya and I peer over the edge of the hole trying to get a better view.

"Maybe one of us should have gone down there," I remark. Mya says nothing back to me. I turn my attention back to the boys.

"It won't budge!" Sebastian grumbles. He sounds exasperated. "Dammit!"

"Argh," Caleb grunts.

Suddenly, I hear a rustling sound in the leaves nearby. Mya and I turn simultaneously and find three Rebel Leaders coming toward us. They seem angry and shout something to one another.

"Sebastian! They're here!" I scream. *Just my luck.*

"Stay calm and believe," Mya reminds me in a low, composed voice. What the hell is she talking about? I'm in human form with no weapons or means of protection. How am I supposed to stay calm?

"Get them!" one of the Rebel Leaders yells.

I back away and try to change into my spirit animal but it doesn't work. Mya begins changing into her spirit animal, and I immediately become jealous at her ability to transform so quickly. The moment that feeling enters my head, she changes back to human form and then back to animal spirit and then back again to human form.

"Aislinn, I told you to-"

Her words are instantly cut off by a Rebel Leader grabbing her and covering her mouth. I can hear Sebastian and Caleb trying to make their way up the vine. They aren't speaking but I can hear their footsteps kick off the mud wall and I can see the vine being pulled.

The second Rebel Leader lunges at me and I thrust back. He tries to tackle me to the ground and I kick and punch him with everything I've got. He whips out a long knife and tries to cut me. My hands are pressed up against him, keeping a healthy distance between me and the knife. He forces it to my face and then a voice sounds from behind, "Stop!"

Who is this unfamiliar voice coming to my rescue?

"We need them alive!" the stranger commands.

Startled, the Rebel Leader slices my cheek slightly before the other Rebel Leader removes the knife from his hands and I fall to ground. I stand back up and wipe the blood from my face but it doesn't stop bleeding.

The third man quickly walks toward the dugout. He takes the knife that he took from his fellow member and uses it to cut the vine that is supporting Sebastian and Caleb. Without warning, Sebastian and Caleb fall helplessly to the ground. I can hear their bodies make a loud thump when they hit the ground.

"No!" I cry.

∞ CHAPTER 33 ∞

The Rebel Leaders hastily tie our hands with rope and take us captive. We walk through the outskirts of the ongoing battle. I keep trying to look back and see if Sebastian and Caleb made it out of the dugout, but the men keep pushing and shoving us forward. I'm frustrated and disappointed in myself. One minute I have my spirit animal and the next I have nothing.

It's hard not to look at the destructive warpath. I watch as Sir Mateo's men and the mystical creatures battle with the Rebel Leaders. It's difficult to tell who's winning at this point since both sides seem wounded and many lay unresponsive on the forest floor, either too weak to fight or unable to move.

I look at Mya and try to speak to her, but the Rebel Leader hits my hands with some sort of whip.

"Ouch!" I wince.

They pull us hard by the ropes and bring us against our will to another clearing in the rainforest. A robust man with a large scar going down the side of his face stands before us. He looks a lot like the same guy who sacrificed Sir Mateo.

"Here they are, Andre," the Rebel Leader says while pulling us toward him.

"Good," Andre says as I trip over my feet in the hastiness and collide into him.

As opposed to helping me, he backs away looking disgusted, causing me to fall face first to the ground. I wipe my muddy hands on my pants as I attempt to stand back up, but Andre lifts his foot to my head and forcefully holds it there.

He then turns to our captives and angrily asks, "Where are the others?"

"Hole," utters the Rebel Leader.

"Very good!" Andre says, sounding pleased.

He casually lifts his foot off my head and I slowly begin to stand up. Andre eyes me and Mya as if we were pieces of meat. Dirty, old, rotten meat.

"Senorita," Andre says to Mya with a shrewd smile. Mya looks away as if embarrassed.

"You are visionary, yes?" he then asks me.

Flashbacks of a conversation I had with Sebastian in the woods suddenly play in my mind. He told me about a Rebel Leader asking them questions about being a visionary. This must be the same person. I need to answer him wisely.

"Visionary?" I ask, sounding dumfounded.

"You sound just like Sebastian," Mya scoffs.

"Shut up!" Andre yells.

"You and you - you are both visionaries!" he hollers.

"No. We're not," I say, trying to sound convincing.

Mya stands in silence with her head down.

Andre walks closer to me and looks into my eyes. He grunts and walks away, mumbling something about Amory will see to it. What is he referring to? Then he speaks to his men and they start to pull us in a different direction.

"What's happening?" I whisper to Mya.

Mya gives me a distant look and mutters, "Just believe."

I still can't believe that I'm asking Mya for advice. It's like she's morphed into another person. A person I actually look up to.

∞ CHAPTER 34 ∞

Sebastian & Caleb

Sebastian and Caleb struggle to escape from the deep hole. They attempt to climb with all of their might, but instead they continue to slide back down to the bottom numerous times. The mud walls are too wet and slippery.

"We have to get out of here!" Sebastian yells with frustration.

"It's too muddy. I can't get a good grip," Caleb groans as they continue to try and try to climb up, but it doesn't work.

"Come on. Let's get this door open. If we can't get to the top, maybe this is a way out," Sebastian offers.

Sebastian and Caleb struggle to open the makeshift door in the dugout. They pull and moan and pull and moan. Finally, the door gives way and they both go flying back. To their surprise, they find nothing but Sir Mateo's shirt tucked behind the door, snugly nestled in the mud wall.

"It's a trap!" Sebastian hollers.

"They did this," Caleb grumbles while throwing Sir Mateo's shirt to the ground. "Someone told them to do this. How could they know we would follow Sir Mateo's scent?"

"There's no way they could have known this on their own. They know we're visionaries. Someone is helping them," Sebastian utters.

"Yeah, well we're stuck in here now!" Caleb says.

"No, we're not!" Sebastian says, breathing hard. "Change back. Change back now!"

"What? How? Mya's not here."

"We don't need Mya to change. We just need to believe, Caleb."

Caleb gulps and nods his head. "You're right. Let's get the hell out of here."

Sebastian and Caleb close their eyes and simultaneously begin to believe in themselves. A sudden flash of light and harsh gusts of wind begin to blow by them. The bottom of the hole instantly elevates up to the forest floor, bringing Sebastian and Caleb with it. Smoke and dust encircle them in an enormous whirlwind.

And as if time stood still for a moment, Sebastian and Caleb are instantaneously transformed back into their spirit animals.

"We did it!" says Caleb.

"Now let's go!" Sebastian growls in the loudest voice imaginable.

His anger has elevated and he looks more vicious than ever. The thought of losing Aislinn is completely agonizing to him. It's not an option.

Caleb feels the same about Aislinn. He lets out an ear-pinching trumpet and takes off in a fit of furry alongside Sebastian. The two begin running, causing the ground to shake and trees to fall.

∞ CHAPTER 35 ∞

I get the feeling that Andre's men are taking us to be sacrificed. Something about the way they appear to be so cold and determined to reach their destination affirms my suspicions. Suddenly, my feet stop walking. The men dragging Mya and me turn around angrily as they pull at the rope, trying to force me to continue. But I stand firm, acknowledging the pulse running through my body. Tiny vibrations start to shoot up my legs and into my chest. My heart starts to beat faster and faster. My spirit animal is calling out to me.

I glance at Mya and give her a look. Hopefully, she will understand my gesture. She tilts her head and then closes her eyes. She got it! I close my eyes too. We both know what we need to do and we call out to our spirit animals innately.

A fast tug of the rope causes me to fall to the ground, breaking my concentration. The familiar taste of earth lingers in my mouth as I lick my lips. Gently, I touch my cheek and notice that my cut has started to clot.

I look up and see the men becoming more and more frustrated. They exchange irritated words with one another before yelling at us. Just then Mya goes flying to the ground. I turn around and find Andre deviously standing there with a smug look on his face. He kicked Mya with the same heavy boot that was previously on my head. I can tell Mya is in pain. She shudders timidly and holds her backside as she huddles into a ball.

Andre steps up to me and picks me up by my hair. I gasp as I feel all the hairs on my head being viciously pulled.

"Visionaries!" he says as he spits in my face. My eyes fixate on his and suddenly I am no longer fearful. I am angry beyond words. I feel flush all over. I want to hurt him.

"What did you say?" I demand.

While still holding my hair, Andre begins to swing his other arm toward my face and surprisingly I catch it with my right hand. Somehow my instincts have kicked in. My eyes start tingling and the vibrations that were in my chest seemed to have elevated to my head, and I can feel Sebastian and Caleb are nearby.

"Mya, now!" I scream with my hand firmly holding Andre's fist.

Without wasting any time, Mya and I instantaneously transform into our spirit animals. *What took you so long*? Andre lets go of my hair, as he is left with no choice, since I am more than double his size. He backs away slowly as I continue to grow. The other Rebel Leaders try to pull at Mya's ropes as she stands tall with her eight legs, but the ropes break apart.

Andre commands his men to seize her. They try to grab her legs, but Mya bends down and injects paralyzing venom into their bodies with her sharp, hollow fangs. She then begins to shoot hairs off of her body. The hairs stab the men's skin, causing great discomfort. They scream as they take cover.

Suddenly, I feel a sharp pain in my left wing. During the confusion, Andre has managed to cut my wing with his knife. I look down at my injured wing and Andre goes to stab me again, but he is tackled to the floor by the fiercest grizzly bear I have ever seen. Sebastian!

Sebastian looks infuriated beyond belief. He roars so loud that the hair on Andre's head stands up straight. Then, Caleb comes barreling into the clearing like an elephant on a mission. The ground rumbles and shakes. He slows down and walks over to me. His long trunk gently touches my wounded wing. He seems concerned, but I turn my attention to Sebastian, who is angrier than I have ever seen him.

"Come on, Visionary!" Andre yells from the ground while attempting to egg Sebastian on. "You are nothing. Nothing! Your time will come!"

Sebastian ignores Andre's words and turns his attention to me for a second. Andre takes this moment and makes a fast dash toward Sebastian. Sebastian then looks down at his leg and sees a large dagger sticking out of it. Andre stands there fearless, waiting for another chance to strike at Sebastian.

Sebastian lets out another ferocious roar that is so incredibly loud, I can feel the air escaping from his mouth. It moves past me with such speed that my wings flutter. Andre attempts to stab Sebastian again, but luckily Sebastian is quicker. He sends Andre a fatal blow to the head with his enormous bear claw. Andre goes flying into a tree and falls to the ground.

"Sebastian!" I yell. Sebastian stands on his hind legs waiting for Andre to get up, but Andre is unresponsive. He takes his last breath and then dies.

"Sebastian!" I yell again. Sebastian picks up Andre and slams him into the ground again. "Sebastian, stop! He's dead!" I yell. Sebastian roars again.

I cautiously walk over to Sebastian but Caleb tries to stop me. I push past him. As my wing grazes Caleb's body I feel an odd sensation. I ignore it and stride right up to Sebastian.

"It's okay. Sebastian. It's okay," I cry. He finally looks at me and notices my wound. "I'm okay, I'm fine," I tell him.

"You're hurt?" he asks as he turns back to Andre.

"Sebastian, I'm fine. I'm fine," I say softly while touching him with my other wing. "See, I'm okay."

I've never seen Sebastian this disturbed before. My eyes meet his and we stare at one another. Sebastian starts to calm down and begins to look like his normal bear self again. His angry bear eyes have turned soft again. I nuzzle in his caress and he holds me tight. If any other person were to have seen this, they would think they've gone mad. A large red-tailed hawk and an enormous grizzly bear hugging each other. Not something you see every day.

"Guys, we need to end this war. Now!" Mya says.

"It shouldn't be a problem now that their leader is dead," Caleb remarks.

Sebastian and I reluctantly break apart. We have business to take care of and our love for one another must wait.

Sebastian looks at me as we pull apart and intuitively says, "I would have died if something happened to you. You know that." I lower my hawk eyes and nod my head. There's nothing I can say at this moment because I would have done the same.

"How did you guys get out of the dugout?" I ask.

"We climbed out," Caleb remarks. Mya and I look at him with confusion. How did they climb out of such a deep hole?

"There was no door there. It was a trap. And no Sir Mateo. Just his shirt," Sebastian says.

"Yeah. They fooled us," says Caleb.

"That's strange," Mya remarks.

"Andre, the leader, wasn't even convinced we were visionaries until the end," I chime in.

Sebastian shakes his large bear head with disgust. "I don't know. Something's not right."

"There's no time to think about that now. We have to help the others before more blood is shed," I say.

We hurriedly run back to the ongoing war. We move at such high speeds that we're there within seconds. The battle is still going strong. Neither side wants to give up. The mystical creatures look to be somewhat in the lead now, but it's still too difficult to tell.

One Rebel Leader comes running at us, screaming and carrying a long spear. Caleb effortlessly lifts his front feet and stomps on him. I feel sad knowing that we have taken the lives of some of the Rebel Leaders, but they would have taken ours in a heartbeat. I think back to that time at the secret agency campsite with Sebastian. I was so sick to my stomach by the thought of someone dying, and now I have become almost numb to it. Funny how time changes everything.

Scanning the environment, I notice Raul huddled by the corner of an abandoned hut. He doesn't necessarily appear frightened as he does confounded. I run over to him and leave my crew behind. Raul backs away cautiously. I forgot that I am in the body of a large bird of prey. I crouch down low and tilt my head to the side. He looks at me and stares into my eyes. I sense his mind beginning to recognize me and suddenly, he throws his arms around me and gives me the most intense hug imaginable. I proudly wrap my uninjured wing around him.

As I embrace Raul, I begin to feel a stinging pain in my body. I turn around and find a group of Rebel Leaders shooting arrows at me.

"Poison arrows!" I scream to warn the others.

Sebastian and Caleb charge at the Rebel Leaders. I nudge Raul out of the way, letting him know to seek protection. I spot Mya engaged in a scuffle with a few of the Rebel Leaders. She's shooting the poisonous hairs from her body at them, but they seem to be avoiding them by moving around. I fly to her side, but I have some difficulty since my wing has been injured. I'm still able to fly but at a much slower speed.

Mya's been hit multiple times with poison darts. Some of the darts fall to the ground and some stay lodged in her body. She was able to heal me before; she should know what to do, if we can only get her away from them. I pick up multiple Rebel Leaders with my talons and slam them into one another one by one. A peculiar-looking mystical creature runs to my side and begins to combat the Rebel Leaders alongside of me. His green hair and black spots remind me of Beauty. The two of us successfully fight off the Rebel Leaders together.

Then, another small group of Rebel Leaders appear from the brush. I lunge at them with my beak causing several to fall to the ground. Another mystical creature that resembles a large, orange snake joins us. As I continue to fight with my allies against the Rebel Leaders, I notice that Mya's eight legs have given way and she crashes to the ground.

"No!" I scream.

The poison must be too much for her. I hurriedly squawk and screech to get the attention of Sebastian and Caleb. Sebastian calls back to me, but Caleb is silent. I look their way and notice that Caleb also has multiple arrows stuck in his elephant body. What's going on? There are so many of them. The Rebel Leaders must have waited until we came back here to attack us. They knew this was the only way they could defeat us. More and more appear from the brush. It's an ambush!

I scream to Sebastian, who is warding off Rebel Leaders from Caleb. The melee is becoming intolerable.

Sebastian yells, "We have to get out of here. Our bodies can't take the poison!"

No kidding. I use my beak to pull Mya off to the side, but more Rebel Leaders seem to come out of everywhere.

"We're surrounded!" I shriek. I remember to stay focused. *No panicking, Aislinn. That won't help me now.*

"Sebastian!" I call. But he doesn't answer me.

"Sebastian!" I scream again. I turn around and see Sebastian on his hind legs. He's battling it out with five Rebel Leaders. He stands tall and strong as a grizzly bear. He bites off a head of a Rebel Leader and throws it to the side. He possesses so much strength and heroism. And one by one the Rebel Leaders fall to the ground, but he's no match for the number of Rebel Leaders beginning to surround him and Caleb. Sebastian tries to protect the fallen Caleb the best he can. He roars and growls ferociously and uses his inner strength to keep the Rebel Leaders at bay, but it doesn't work for long.

"Fly, Aislinn. Fly out of here while you still can!" Sebastian yells.

"No! I won't leave you!"

"Aislinn, go. You must go!" Sebastian yells back while being attacked by numerous arrows.

"No!" I scream. "I can't leave you. I can't leave you." I cry.

Sebastian continues to fight off the Rebel Leaders, but his body becomes weaker and weaker and he suddenly falls to the ground.

"Sebastian! Sebastian!" I bellow.

My world is crashing all around me. Intolerable worry and fear take over my mind. What is happening? I shake it off and stare at Sebastian. My Sebastian. Then I see Caleb lying near him and his eyelids are closed. Their gone! Both of them, gone. I continue swiping away Rebel Leaders with my talons, but my sadness is strong. I want to fall too.

Then, out of nowhere, rage comes over me. I am madder than ever. My body is boiling hot and I am infuriated. My weak posture straightens itself and I stand tall.

"AHHHHHHHHHHH," I scream. I squawk and screech and squawk and screech again while shaking my body, causing the earth floor to rumble. I've had enough of this. I'm done.

I screech again, only this time my screech is so loud that the ground shakes hard and trees begin to fall and a swirling wind begins to pick up speed all around me. The Rebel Leaders stop what they're doing. The mystical creatures stop what they're doing and an eerie calm begins to take place. No one says a word as all eyes are on me.

I stop my erratic outburst and notice my body has elevated into the air. I am not flying. I am hovering. Thousands of tropical birds start to surround me. My hawk body begins to leave and I feel my human body begin to take form. I struggle in the air trying to hold on to my hawk body, but it won't listen. *I can't change back, no, not now.* My head pops through and yet I am still floating steadily in the air. I desperately struggle to remain in hawk form. It is my only chance for survival.

Suddenly, I black out while airborne. I travel telepathically to the place I visited before. I move so fast I can barely catch my breath. I try to grab the walls around me. I need to be back at the village to save Sebastian. I struggle to go back, but my body continues to glide forward.

"It's okay, Aislinn," a familiar, gentle voice says.

"What? Who are you? Where am I? Am I dead?" I ask.

"You need to tell them who you are and what you're there for. They will listen to you. Your power is in your voice," she says. I try to look for the person who belongs to this beautiful voice, but there is no one around.

"I need to go back. I have to help Sebastian. He's dying."

"Aislinn, remember who you are," she says to me.

"But, I can't."

"You can. Believe," the voice says more firmly.

I close my eyes and try to believe, but sadness takes over my heart and I begin to cry. Sebastian is dying and he needs me. Everyone keeps telling me to believe and remember. I remember what this voice has told me before, but I don't remember my past on my own.

In that very moment, my eyes reopen and a powerful electrical jolt shakes my entire body. My brain starts calculating my repressed memories and my eyes start fluttering. Every memory flashes through my brain one after another and then I feel it. I know who I am. I remember!

∞ CHAPTER 36 ∞

I gracefully land back on the ground with my two human feet. I feel a small, tightening feeling in my back, but I shake it off and focus on the situation. Everything is so clear now. And I know what I need to do. It is in my voice. Everyone gazes at me as I stand before them. Confidence has wiped away all lingering doubts. *Speak strong Aislinn. They will listen.*

"I am Aislinn, Protector of the World and Protector of all of you. What you are doing is wrong. And you must stop now. You are hurting your brothers and your sisters. You forget that you, we, are all connected in this mighty world. If you don't stop hating, then your children and your children's children will suffer the consequences of your actions. And the very world as we know it will collapse. There will be no more animals. No more humans and no more life. Is that what you want?"

I pause as I look at everyone, waiting for a response. I want them to not only understand what I'm saying, but to feel it as well. They will relearn what they already once knew.

The Rebel Leaders and mystical creatures slowly begin to shake their heads as they stand very still. A variety of rainforest animals surround the area. I spot a jaguar standing on a fallen tree. It looks my way and I immediately know that it's Beauty. My heart warms and I continue with my speech. The words are coming from within my soul. They are spoken with magic.

"From this day forward you must fight, not with each other, but the world's hatred. The world's evil. You must believe in the good and help those around you. You will be honored for your bravery and your reward will be a peaceful life."

I take a minute to scan everyone's faces. They seem to be intrigued. Then I stare into their eyes and raise my right arm. My arm is warm and tingly. It moves on its own in a hypnotic manner.

"You are free from the evil. Now go on and help your brothers and your sisters."

I stop my speech and let out a big sigh. I have managed to stop the fighting, but not because they lost their leader. But because they remembered the true meaning of life. I brought them back to reality through my words. My words touched something inside of them. It worked. And I felt every word of my speech. I felt the anguish and the hurt, but I also felt the empowerment of the good. The uprising of the connectedness.

I look around and find that the animals have dispersed back into the rainforest. Beauty is gone. The Rebel Leaders, Sir Mateo's tribe, and the mythical creatures have all stopped fighting. They stand their motionless as if hypnotized by me.

I smile and lift my arms signaling for them to carry on. One Rebel Leader begins by reaching a hand to one of the fallen mystical creatures. Everyone gapes with astonishment and soon everyone begins to help one another. I can feel the peace begin to radiate throughout the entire rainforest. A feeling I haven't felt before. I stand there overwhelmed with joy and amazement.

I scan the area looking for Sebastian and find that he is back in human form again. He is smiling at me with those loving eyes of his and I smile back. Simultaneously, we run to each other.

Sebastian runs quicker and beats me to the chase. He picks me up into his arms and holds me as I kiss him all over his face. He kisses me back. My soul mate. He's alive.

"You're okay?" I ask, surprised.

"I knew you could do it," he says.

"I couldn't have done it without you," I mumble.

"I love you," he says.

I look deeply into his eyes and tell him, "And I love you."

A tear rolls down Sebastian's cheek and I get the most intense feeling of complete bliss. Sebastian and I are soul mates. My memories have shown me. And I really do love him with all of my heart.

"Your eyes are very golden right now. They're beautiful," Sebastian remarks.

"Thank you," I chuckle as I wipe a tear from my face.

Mya and Caleb soon gather around us. They seem unharmed by the poisonous arrows. They have been healed.

"You guys are all right?" I ask, "But the poison?"

"It cleared the minute you landed back on the ground," Mya says, surprised.

I'm not exactly sure how they were cured, but I'm pretty sure it had something to do with the celestial voice that spoke to me when I left earth. Sometimes magical things happen when you believe.

"You saved us," Caleb says. He stares at me and smiles.

"I didn't save you. We saved each other," I say.

While the survivors of the war begin to work to help one another, the three of us stroll back toward Raul. We still need to find Sir Mateo. As I walk past the Rebel Leaders and mystical creatures, they stop one by one and stare at me. Why are they staring at me? Was it my speech?

I look at Sebastian for answers. He points at my back. I turn my head as far as I can without breaking it and glance down. What? I have wings. Like angel wings or very thin hawk wings. They have an iridescent effect when I move. I feel so animal-like, so untamed. They're absolutely divine.

"I have wings," I say exasperated.

"They're beautiful," Caleb says, sounding awestruck. Sebastian crinkles his eyebrow at Caleb's remark.

"Thank you," I say.

I call out for Raul and he comes out from hiding underneath some brush.

"Raul, are you okay?" I ask.

He nods his head and smiles.

Caleb rubs the top of his head in a playful manner. "How did you manage to stay safe during all of this, huh, buddy?"

Raul shrugs his shoulders.

"Do you know where Sir Mateo is?" Sebastian asks. Raul turns around and points.

"Let's go," I say as I take Raul's hand and begin trekking into the rainforest. He must have gotten the gist of what we're asking him. Either that or he's taking us for a nature hike.

The four of us follow Raul in hopes of finding Sir Mateo. Raul bends down and analyzes some tracks in the muck. Caleb looks down and examines the tracks. He quickly picks up a lead and we follow him.

I don't pick up a scent, but I can see something strange up ahead. We look at each other doubtfully and pray it's not another trap.

"Here, he's here this time! I know it," says Caleb.

"He's right. I can smell his scent. His real scent," Sebastian says.

We finally come to another small clearing and find a large dugout, but this time there are people in it. Lots of people, including the one and only Sir Mateo. He's been trying to free his people this whole time, shirtless, of course. That explains the shirt that Sebastian and Caleb found in the other dugout.

The four of us stand at the edge of the enormous dugout along with ten of Sir Mateo's people. They have been pulling each other out one by one. Silence sweeps over the crowd and all eyes look up at me. Self-consciously I touch my cheek, remembering the gash. But it's gone. There is no sign of an injury. I bashfully smile, knowing that they're staring at my wings.

"Ah, so you do believe," Sir Mateo says, sounding awe-inspired.

"You were right," I respond.

"I knew you would figure it out, and now look at you," he says while glancing at my wings. "All of you." I blush.

"Let us help you," Caleb says. He quickly changes into his elephant spirit animal and lowers his mighty trunk into the dugout. He didn't even have to think about it. It just happened naturally the way it should happen. The tribe begins to cheer and clap. Sir Mateo's people climb onto Caleb's trunk and he lifts a few out at a time as if he were a portable elevator. Sebastian and Mya transform into their spirit animals to help Caleb. Pulling a ton of people out of a hole could take a while.

As the last person is finally lifted out, Sir Mateo walks over to us and says, "Thank you. My people and I are very thankful you came for us."

"Thank you for showing us what we needed to do," says Sebastian sounding humble.

"Yeah. You were the one who helped us," I say. "If it weren't for you, than none of us would have believed in ourselves the way we should have."

"My friends, I knew you had it in you," Sir Mateo declares as he takes a step closer to me. "And you, the protector of the earth, you are a very brave young woman. The world will be a better place because of you. You will save us from the dark times. And you, Sebastian, you will be here to watch over her and defend her." Caleb looks away as if uncomfortable with Sir Mateo's words.

"Come now," Sir Mateo says.

We follow Sir Mateo out of the clearing and into the rainforest. Sir Mateo walks over to Caleb and places a hand on his left shoulder. "And Caleb, you are clever and intuitive. She will need you too." Caleb nods his head modestly and looks away.

"And Mya," Sir Mateo states while looking into her eyes. "You are now a healer. You have the ability to help others. Aislinn will also need you."

Sir Mateo pauses as he realizes the difference in Mya. "And don't worry, you will soon start to feel like yourself again. The Agua Magia has a way of altering our temperaments when needed."

Sir Mateo catches my eyes and notices my disappointed face. He shrugs his shoulders and smiles.

Great! Does that mean she'll be back to her old ways once this honeymoon period is over? If I could have my way, I'd see to it that she stays like this forever.

Sir Mateo then turns his attention to all of us. "And all of you need each other, as you now know, we are all connected."

Sir Mateo's words are more than meaningful. They are powerful. He has taught us so much during such a short period of time. We walk back to the Rebel Leaders' village with Sir Mateo and his men. They are still helping one another other. Sir Mateo smiles as he admires the peaceful resolution taking place. To see people, who have fought for centuries, helping one another is completely remarkable. This act of compromise and forgiveness shows promise that it's possible for others around the world to adapt to this philosophy.

"So, what do we do now?" I ask Sebastian.

"Sleep," he chuckles.

We are all so tired. It has been a long and trying trip. What I really want to do is go home and tell my parents all about my destiny. But I know that the secret agency is still out there. And it's only a matter of time before one of us gets trailed again. Maybe someday my parents can know the truth about me. Someday.

"You can sleep back at the other village, since ours has been burnt down," Sir Mateo suggests.

"Sounds like a plan to me," Caleb says, sounding relieved.

Thinking about their village being burnt to the ground makes me feel sad again. I forgot about that. They will have to reconstruct their homes. Hopefully, the Rebel Leaders and mystical creatures can help them.

"You guys should go ahead and get your rest. You leave tomorrow, yes?" Sir Mateo says.

"Yes," Sebastian replies.

"Our passports! They were in our bags at your village," I say gloomily to Sir Mateo.

"Don't worry about that, I'll take care of everything tomorrow," Sebastian says while putting an arm around me.

"But, what about your people? You could use our help," Caleb asks.

"You have already helped us. We will be fine now. The suffering has ended and now we will rebuild. The evil here has been shut down and goodness prevails once again."

Mya walks up to Sir Mateo and stares at him.

"We won't see you before we leave tomorrow, will we?" Mya asks as if she already knew the answer to her question. Sir Mateo sadly shakes his head no.

"It feels funny saying goodbye," utters Sebastian.

"You will be missed," I say to Sir Mateo.

"As will all of you," Sir Mateo says.

I give Sir Mateo a great big hug. I feel the need to squeeze him. I am so blessed to have met him. He has guided me in the right direction all along. I look up at him and stammer, "Thank you."

Sir Mateo wipes away tears from my eyes.

"Thank you," he simply says.

Then Sir Mateo gives Sebastian, Caleb, and Mya meaningful hugs as well. I can see tears in everyone's eyes. We take one last look at Sir Mateo and instantly transform into our spirit animals. The change was extremely quick. No thinking required.

Raul comes out of nowhere. He heads toward Sir Mateo as the four of us say goodbye in animal form. I walk over to him and put my wings around him.

As I turn to leave, I think about the fact that I have wings as a human. I become slightly alarmed and turn back to see Sir Mateo. He is waiting there staring at me with a huge grin on his face. He winks and simply says,

"It's okay, Aislinn. Only visionaries will be able to see them from now on."

I smile, knowing that he knew what I was going to ask him. I nod my head and smile inside.

∞ CHAPTER 37 ∞

The walk back to the village was much faster than I had anticipated. I couldn't fly because of my enormous size and the entanglement of the rainforest trees. The village of the mystical creatures is completely empty. I think back to my first impression of the creatures. I was shocked and slightly frightened, and now I miss seeing them.

The four of us settle into one of the smaller huts and begin to relax from our strenuous journey. We change back into human form and I collapse to the ground from pure exhaustion. Sebastian snuggles next to me and I welcome his warm embrace.

Caleb takes a seat nearby and Mya lies on the opposite side of us, nowhere near Caleb. They used to be closer; now they barely even speak to one another. It's funny how one trip can reveal so much about a person. I learned so much about by myself and Sebastian. I feel like I didn't know myself that well before. I didn't know my meaning or my ability to last in the rainforest. Our survival skills have been put to the test and I think I did a fairly decent job.

The four of us lie there quietly until we fall asleep. There were no words to be said to one another. So much has happened in such a short amount of time. I want to peek at Sebastian, but I am certain that Caleb is staring at me, so I pretend to be sleeping. As soon as I sense that he is out, I open my eyes and notice that Sebastian is sound asleep. I watch him sleep as I admire his gentle face. This man is here for me. To protect me. How did I become so lucky?

Finally, I drift off into a deep sleep. My body and mind are thankful to be lying in a safe hut next to my bodyguard, Sebastian. My dreams are exciting and positive. They are vivid and seemingly real. I dream of soaring in the sky at unimaginable heights. I am free. There are others with me, gliding by my side. We are on a quest. Below us, I can see the rich colors of the earth. The mountains are silver and the grass below is bright green. Purple trees line up the side of a mountain. And colorful animals roam the land below. Then, we approach an area unlike anything I have ever seen before. It is dark and colorless. The trees are dead and the ground is barren. There is no love on this side of the land. It is cold and empty and strange creatures circle above us. One creature reaches for me and I dive fast toward the ground below. When I near the ground, thousands of scorpion-like beings race toward me.

Suddenly I awake. I find myself sitting straight up with a cold sweat. My heart is pounding and my hands are tightly clenched to the bedding. Sebastian awakes and sits up.

"What's wrong?" he asks.

I take a few quick breaths while trying to put everything into perspective.

"I don't know. I was dreaming. I always dream," I say frantically. Sometimes I feel like I'm caught in between two worlds and my dreams become intermingled.

"What was it about?"

Before I answer, I look to see that Caleb and Mya are still sleeping. I wouldn't want to alarm them.

"It was about me. I was flying with others like me. The land below was beautiful, almost dreamlike. But then, we entered this other land. It was dark and disturbing. And there were these evil creatures that came out of nowhere. One tried to grab me, but I nosedived for the ground. And then a ton of scorpion creatures raced toward me." I look into Sebastian's eyes, still feeling terrified by this surreal dream. "It was awful."

Sebastian pulls me close for a tight hug.

"You're okay. I'm here with you," he says while giving my forehead a strong kiss. "I won't let anything happen to you. Dream or no dream."

"Thank you. What time is it anyways?"

"About time for us to get out of here."

"Sounds good to me," I agree.

"Do you want to wake the others or should I?" Sebastian asks with a devious grin.

"Be my guest," I answer.

Sebastian slyly walks over to the sleeping pair. Then he puts a hand on each of their shoulders and shakes them. "Come on, time to go, come on. Up and at'em."

"What? What did I miss?" Caleb says, half-awake with extreme bed head. Sebastian smiles and I giggle on the sidelines.

Mya sits up and says, "There better be a good reason why you're waking me up this early. I'm exhausted and I need my sleep."

Nuts. She sounds like she's back to her old self again.

"It's time to go home, kiddos," Sebastian replies.

"Oh. Well in that case, let's get the hell out of here," Mya says. Sebastian, Caleb, and I look at one another and burst out laughing.

"Did I miss something?" Mya snidely asks.

"Yeah, a whole lot. But, it's good to have you back," Caleb says jokingly.

Mya rolls her eyes. Apparently, she doesn't have a clue as to what we're referring to. I'm going to miss the old Mya. The quiet, distant, sensible Mya.

The four of hurriedly get ready and prepare for our journey back. I take a quick walk to a nearby hut in search of food and see that some of the mystical creatures have returned.

"Good morning," a seven-headed creature with gleaming turquois eyes says to me.

"Good morning," I reply. I can't stop staring at his seven heads as he limps to another hut.

"Aislinn. Aislinn," another voice calls out to me.

I look around trying to find who's calling me. I can't seem to locate the voice. All I hear now is a familiar purring sound. I walk ahead further and then I see him. It's Cocoa. The cat man we met at the mystical village with the odd sense of humor.

"Cocoa. I'm so glad you're okay," I say.

"Of course I'm okay. I'm a cat. We have nine lives in case you didn't know," he says with a chuckle.

"You do?"

"No, I wish. I have a few, but nine, well that's just crazy," Cocoa laughs.

Cocoa's humor is so sporadic that I can't tell if he's joking or not.

"Hey, um. Do you know if Jawanga made it?" I ask.

"Jawanga? No, he's gone now. He's been here too long. He's on to bigger and better things," Cocoa replies.

"Oh, I'm so sorry."

"It's okay. At least the war is over," Cocoa says as he wiggles his whiskers. I smile back at him and notice my crew waiting for me.

"Well, I have to be going now. It was nice talking with you again," I say to Cocoa. But Cocoa isn't there. He just vanished. I look around and all I see is a grey mist in the air.

"Who are you talking to?" Sebastian asks.

"Cocoa. He was right here. Didn't you see him?"

Sebastian shakes his head. Thinking about what Cocoa said about Jawanga's time being up makes me think that he was also referring to himself. I was talking to a ghost.

"I think it's time for us to leave," I say.

Sebastian takes my hand and we walk over to Caleb and Mya. The four of us transform into our spirit animals. Being in this form will help us get to where we need to in a flash. We hurry through the forest, wasting little time. The forest is no match for animals our size. We quickly arrive at the meeting point for Apumayta and Cayo and transform back into human form. It would be faster to continue this speedy journey in animal spirit form, but onlookers might find us rather odd. Plus, we don't want to risk of running into the secret agency or any other enemies for that matter.

"I am so happy to be getting out of here," Mya says sounding relieved.

"Me too," Caleb agrees. Mya smiles at him the way she did before. Caleb quickly smiles back at Mya, but not without looking my way. He stares at me longer than usual. I turn away feeling more than uncomfortable.

"Hey, I see them coming," Sebastian calls out.

Apumayta and Cayo dock the boat and the four of us happily board.

"You came," Sebastian says.

"Told you we'd be here," says Apumayta.

"You were right."

"Man, it's good to see you guys," Caleb says as he hugs Apumayta and Cayo. Apumayta and Cayo seem confused as they awkwardly accept the hug from Caleb.

As I board the boat, I can feel Apumayta and Cayo staring at me. I have a funny feeling that they can see my wings. I'm not sure how they can see them since they aren't visionaries, but somehow they just can. I self-consciously look toward my back to catch a glimpse of my new iridescent addition. Sebastian notices me and reaches out his hand. I take it.

As we continue our ride on the boat, Apumayta asks us, "So, how was your trip?" The four of us look at one another with wide eyes trying hard not to laugh.

"It was some trip," Caleb answers. I turn my face into Sebastian's body to keep from laughing out loud. I don't know if it's from lack of sleep, but everything seems to be striking me funny. Even Mya's rude facial expressions are making me snicker.

∞ CHAPTER 38 ∞

As soon as the plane takes off, my mind immediately feels at ease. Luckily, Jerry had arranged for everything to be waiting for us at a hotel in Iquitos. Four backpacks, clean clothes, passports, money, soap, toothpaste, brushes, and everything else a girl could want. The shower at the hotel felt like the best shower ever. And a note from Jerry, in code of course, provided important details of our return flight home. Sebastian was right again. We had everything we needed. And more importantly we had each other.

Feeling safe at last, I rest my head on Sebastian's shoulder. Sebastian gently kisses my forehead, and I know that I can relax peacefully with him by my side. Caleb and Mya sit behind us. I can hear him joke with her about how they drank on the way down here and how he thought she was crazy for jumping into the

Agua Magia. The familiar sounds of their harmless banter help lull me to sleep.

My eyes close and I let my mind drift off. But before I slip away into a boundless dream, I get a vision. A disturbing vision. Someone is watching us. I can't make out any other details except for the eyes. Evil eyes that almost glow in the dark. Then something happens, that hasn't happened during a vision before. I receive a message from the eyes in my vision.

"I'm coming for you!"

The Three Rare Spirit Animals

Red-Tailed Hawk:

This spirit animal is the most majestic and divine of all spirit animals. The red-tailed hawk only chooses one person at a time to fulfill its prophecy, which is to protect earth and all living things. This person holds a special innate power that allows them to be able to protect the earth and its inhabitants through many methods. They can also convey positive messages that help humans to understand their wrongdoings while giving them the strength and courage to amend them.

Traits: inner-strength, compassion, strong adaptability skills, incredible soaring ability, exceptional eyesight, and unique special powers, which emerge throughout their lifetime.

Scorpion:

This spirit animal is the most wicked of all spirit animals. The Scorpion only chooses one person at a time to fulfill its prophecy, which is to destroy the human race and to acquire complete control and power. They will stop at nothing to accomplish their undertaking. They are extremely skillful at deceiving their targets.

Traits: ability to transform into other forms, strong adaptability skills, can detect enemies through a variety of senses, extreme survival skills, and can inject toxic venom causing immobilization.

Gray Wolf:

This spirit animal serves as the balance between the two forces. The Gray Wolf only chooses one person at a time to fulfill its prophecy, which is to report back to the higher powers and to control any imbalances in the system. They Gray Wolf is a warrior and a mediator at the same time. This spirit animal is highly trained and well equipped to handle challenging circumstances. This person has been sent here without emotional capabilities.

Traits: can track and hunt enemies quickly, exceptional hearing and sense of smell, and possesses distinctive fighting skills.

A Note from N. Dunham

Thank you so much for reading Visionary Untamed, book two of the Visionary Trilogy. I hope you enjoyed reading about Aislinn as she uncovered more about her destiny.

In book three, nothing will be held back. All spirit animals will be released and Aislinn's strength will be put to the test. Will goodness prevail or will evil forces take control of the world?

For more information about the Visionary trilogy or their spirit animals, please visit:

http://www.ndunham.com

~N. Dunham